HURON PUBLIC LIBRARY
333 WILLIAMS STREET
HURON, OHIO 44839

# THE WHISTLING SHADOW

BY MABEL SEELEY

**MYSTERIES**

The Listening House (1938)

The Crying Sisters (1939)

The Whispering Cup (1940)

The Chuckling Fingers (1941)

Eleven Came Back (1943)

The Beckoning Door (1950)

The Whistling Shadow (1954)

**NOVELS**

Woman of Property (1947)

The Stranger Beside Me (1951)

# THE WHISTLING SHADOW

A MYSTERY

## MABEL SEELEY

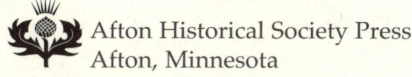
Afton Historical Society Press
Afton, Minnesota

Designed by Barbara J. Arney
Pre-press production by Mary Sue Englund

Copyright © 1954 by Mabel Seeley.
All Rights Reserved.
Published by arrangement with Doubleday, a division of
Bantam Doubleday Dell Publishing Group, Inc.

New material © 2000 Afton Historical Society Press

This first Afton Historical Society Press
reprint edition is limited to
two thousand copies.

Library of Congress Cataloging-in-Publication Data

Seeley, Mabel, 1903–1991
    The whistling shadow : a mystery / Mabel Seeley.
       p.    cm.
   ISBN 1-890434-16-7 (hc.)
    1. Minneapolis (Minn.) Fiction. 2. Minnesota Fiction. I. Title.
PS3537.E2826W48   2000                   99-30589
813'.54--dc21                                        CIP

Printed in Canada

The Afton Historical Society Press is a non-profit
organization that takes pride and pleasure in publishing
fine books on Minnesota subjects.

W. Duncan MacMillan        Patricia Condon Johnston
     president                            publisher

Afton Historical Society Press
P.O. Box 100
Afton, MN 55001
800-436-8443

## PUBLISHER'S NOTE

ON JUNE 9, 1991, Mabel Seeley Ross died at the age of eighty-eight in New Jersey. The *St. Paul Pioneer Press* carried a brief notice describing the former St. Paulite as a "well-known mystery writer in the '30s and '40s." Mabel Seeley had been largely forgotten, but not quite.

After hearing from several of Mabel's longtime fans, *Pioneer Press* book critic Mary Ann Grossman followed up with a feature article. She quoted reviewer Jeanne Fischer as saying, "Almost everybody of that era who read at all would recognize her name."

Jeanne had worked in the book departments at the old Golden Rule department store in St. Paul and at Powers in Minneapolis. "We had a lending library at the Golden Rule," she told Mary Ann, "and her books just came in and went right out. Several of them were national Crime Club selections. She was read by both men and women."

Mabel wrote seven mystery novels, and each one of them was greeted with glowing reviews. When *The Whistling Shadow* appeared in 1954, the *New York Times* called it "her best suspense story in fourteen years." The *New York Herald Tribune Book Review* commented, "In this new tale she is as adroit as ever in evoking and expressing terror, fed fat on intuitions."

Mabel Seeley wrote in the first person from a distinctly feminine point of view, but her stories are neither pratingly cozy nor hopelessly Gothic. Her characters are middle-class Midwesterners in commonplace settings. In *The Whistling Shadow* much of the intrigue takes place in the home of the heroine, a thirty-nine-year-old widow named Gail Kiskadden, in the Lake of the Isles neighborhood of Minneapolis.

Mabel Hodnefield Seeley Ross was born March 25, 1903, in the small town of Herman in west-central Minnesota. "No one ever mistakes me for anything but what I am, a Middle Westerner," she wrote in a biographical sketch for the book *Twentieth Century Authors* in 1955. She was also a born teller of tales who was already writing and telling stories in the first grade.

"In my family I early discovered the uses of story telling," she remembered. "As the eldest of six children it was soon my job to ride herd. My father is a librarian with a scholarly love for books and language, my mother a member of a clan whose delight is to gather in swarms for family meals and family yarning-sessions. What I learned at the family knee was that the most absorbing, the most amazing, the most amusing of all organisms are *people*.

Mabel's family moved to St. Paul in 1920 when her father, Jacob Hodnefield, landed a job as newspaper curator at the Minnesota Historical Society. Mabel's brother, Franklin Hodnefield, who is now in his nineties and lives in Roseville, Minnesota, remembers that they lived on Capitol Boulevard (where part of Bethesda Hospital now stands) and, later, at 1842 Laurel Avenue. Mabel attended Mechanic Arts High School and wrote creepy tales—one was titled "Fog"—for the school's magazine, *Cogwheel*.

She attributed her subsequent success as an author to the influence of two of her English teachers. At Mechanic Arts, Mary Copley "not only chuckled appreciatively—what note is more musical?—over my writing efforts, but got me a St. Paul College Club Scholarship, which took me to the University of Minnesota in 1922." At the university, "luck burst over me a second time: Mary Ellen Chase was then on the Minnesota English staff. Callow I may have been, but not so much so I didn't turn up in each course taught by Miss Chase; to this day she has a splendor in my mind that no one else touches."

Mabel wrote for the *Minnesota Quarterly* and after graduating summa cum laude in 1926 married fellow editor Kenneth Seeley. They moved to Chicago where Ken did graduate work at the University of

Chicago while Mabel wrote advertising copy. Two years later, after Ken contracted tuberculosis, the Seeleys moved back to the Twin Cities to obtain medical treatment. Mabel wrote department-store advertising for the next several years until 1936, when she "retired from a profession paced too fast for me, determined never to put pencil to yellow paper again." A year later she was at work on *The Listening House*, which was published in New York in 1938.

This first mystery novel was followed in quick order by *The Crying Sisters* (1939), *The Whispering Cup* (1940), *The Chuckling Fingers* (1941), and *Eleven Came Back* (1943). After the Seeleys' only child, their son Gregory, was born in 1943, Mabel spent less time at her typewriter. She would write only two additional mysteries, *The Beckoning Door* (1950) and *The Whistling Shadow*, as well as two non-mystery novels, *Woman of Property* (1947) and *The Stranger Beside Me* (1951).

Both non-mystery books are written in the third person and depict unhappy marriages, weak men who are less than successful, and sensitive women who strive for success in what is predominantly a man's world. They are very unlike her lively mystery novels, which usually portray a strong woman who not only solves crimes but manages to win a good man who encourages her in her work.

"Why did I choose mysteries for a major interest?" Mabel asked herself for *Twentieth Century Authors*. "Perhaps because I'd found them such a useful anodyne, perhaps because I have a natural relish for horror. If I had a premise, it was that terror would be more terrible, horror more horrible, when visited on people the reader would recognize as real."

Mabel and Ken Seeley eventually divorced, and Mabel and young Gregory were living in California when she wrote *The Whistling Shadow*. On a trip east to promote this final book, she was introduced to lawyer Henry Ross. "We met at a party given by a mutual friend," Ross told Mary Ann Grossman in a telephone conversation from his home in

Medford Lakes, New Jersey. "We spoke briefly, and a couple of our friends decided we ought to get married. I wrote an apologetic letter to Mabel, and that started our midlife romance. We were married in 1956."

Why did Mabel stop writing? Grossman asked Ross. "She married me," he replied. "Writing is hard work, and she felt she was burned out. Her books were well-received critically, and they were commercially successful, but she liked being married better. She was extremely intelligent, extremely generous, a devoted wife, mother, and grandmother."

Her son Gregory agrees. "She was a superwoman to me. Because she wrote at home, she was always there when I came home from school."

THE AFTON HISTORICAL SOCIETY PRESS is pleased and privileged to be able to bring Mabel Seeley back to print. We are especially grateful to a special friend for first mentioning her books to us, to Mary Ann Grossman and Jeanne Fischer for helping stir up renewed interest in them, to Franklin Hodnefield for sharing with us his first edition copies and the photograph of his sister that appears on the jacket of this book, to Gregory Seeley of Medford Lakes, New Jersey, for helping us obtain the rights to reprint his mother's books, and to Mabel Seeley fan Dennis Crow of Gresham, Oregon, for a wonderful packet of biographical material and reviews of her books.

Patricia Condon Johnston<br>
August 1999

# CHAPTER ONE

EVEN NOW, looking back, I can't see any least hint of menace in the way I found out my son Johnny was married. The only thing that seemed wrong, then, was that what I was hearing didn't go with Johnny. Any more than the rest of what had happened went with Johnny.

When the car stopped in front of my house, on the afternoon of what must have been Tuesday, November fourth, I was doing what I'd been doing since morning and for many days past—I was hunched over a lap table in a corner of the livingroom davenport, playing Canfield as steadily as I could play. Red on black, black on red, one-two-three—— Solitaire may not seem much of a refuge from grief, but it was one for me. When I'd played long enough, rhythmically enough, then the events of the weeks just past faded a little bit; I was able to sit in a comforting half fog, in which I felt little and thought less.

The car's halt struck a snag in the rhythm; my glance went to the windows across the room. If the car's occupants were neighbors or casual friends, then I could stay where I was, unmoving and unanswering; after a while they'd believe I was out somewhere, and go away. But it was no neighbor who emerged from the car, and no random friend. It was Phil Sawyer, accompanied by Bunky Knowles.

Ever since I was widowed, which is fifteen years past, Phil, who was my husband's closest friend, and Bunky, who was Johnny's, have been parts of my family. We've been together for all the events which bring out Minneapolis families—state fairs and museum visits, lakeshore picnics and tours of the Como Zoo, graduations and ball games. Now I might shrink from their coming as I shrank from everyone's coming, but I knew it was little use. Phil would know I wasn't out, and if I didn't answer the door chimes he'd have the house down. Before that could happen I started up, shoving aside the lap table, staggering as the foot I'd been sitting on found the floor.

Must I say what it's like to be mourning an only son? It can scarcely be necessary; in this story, as I realize, it's almost out of place. You'll recall from your own griefs that first stupefied dullness, and the dragging that hangs from your shoulders, a knapsack of stones. The anger, the wildness that shoot through its coma, the hunger to mutiny when there's nothing against which you can mutiny——

By the time the chimes sounded their second call, I'd reached the hall and, willy-nilly, the mirror there, over the phone table.

In the spring just behind me, for Mother's Day, what Johnny sent me from Fort Benning was a pin-up of Cleopatra on a barge; the two words he'd written beneath it were "Look Alikes." That was nothing but silly, yet I'd laughed and been warmed by it. No one would have sent me any such token now; Johnny'd never have written those words, seeing me now. I might dab at my hair, might try pressing color into my cheeks, but it didn't help; when I opened the door Phil's glance leaped to mine, and then another line bit itself in at the corner of his mouth. Johnny and I had added a fair number of lines there, these two months.

Accusing, reproving, but not actually expectant of anything better, Phil said, "Three o'clock, Gail, and you're still in your housecoat." He came stockily past me, overcoat collar up against a thin falling of snow outside, but hat pulled from his thick springing iron-gray hair. Rocklike and sorrowing and stern. Bunky, behind him, kept his light-lashed eyes downcast; he said awkwardly, "I guess we should've called you first," and then he too was in the hall, all twenty-year-old, familiar, one hundred and eighty-five pounds of him, brush-cut red head turtled into the shoulders of his dark leather battle jacket, right arm curled snailwise around the core of his textbooks. Maybe I should have noticed right then that the two of them struggled with a new evasiveness, the phrases they let fall were so stilted. "Snowing—can't last, though, not this early in November." "Just the same, I'll bet in two weeks I'm out on skis——"

But everyone near me, in these days, was ill at ease; it wasn't until Phil had laid his overcoat aside on a hall chair, and we were well into the living room, that I began sensing they had something special on their minds. Instead of settling, Phil stayed on his feet, wandering between fireplace and front windows in a kind of abeyance. Bunky dropped beside me on the davenport, jacket unzipped but not removed, books balanced on a solid young gabardine knee, yet his fingers too, stubby and amber-flecked, slid nervously up and down the cut edges lettered "Knowles, '54." Phil, according to pattern, should have continued reproof—"I ran into old Reverend Mr. Raeburn yesterday; he told me you'd turned down the Christmas pageant." Bunky should have added, "I saw Mother at breakfast; she said the kids at St. Adolph's still didn't have anyone else for their story hour——"

Instead, once their first words were out, they fell silent, letting me do the filling in. Neither one let his glance stray toward me.

It was this last, I think, which made a beginning alarm shoot up. Not fear; I'd have said I'd been given everything in fear's gift. More a driven unwillingness to meet a new eventuality of any kind. But tenterhooks haven't ever been very sufferable for me, either. So I asked, at once.

Phil was the one who began answering. Twisting about toward the fireplace but quickly turning back, brushing the heel of his palm up along his cheekbone and the thin long scar which was a memento of the one time Johnny and Bunky, then both eleven, had managed brief possession of a BB gun.

He said, "It begins to look—there's some evidence—I suppose you can just as well take it straight. We've got reason to believe Johnny was married, Gail."

I think what I first felt was that I must somehow pass it off. That I must manage, some way, to be humorous. But I wasn't able to make it. I sat on where I was beside Bunky, and what I went through was the second falling of a mallet blow. Bringing back all the initial concussion, the outraging of belief, the deep stunning plunge of the event eight weeks past. I rocked with it——

After a while I was speaking too, whispering, in unison with whatever Phil had gone on to add. "That's not ever true. Johnny was perfectly welcome to marry; I'd have liked it if he'd married. But he'd never do so, not telling me. You know me, you knew Johnny. He had no reason whatever to——"

No one should have looked at me; I covered my face. Feeling, after a while, pain recede and dull until it was like old thunder. And then, in the way he could come, I saw Johnny, all his grin and his mischief, the high clean look at his temples and the riffling of his tightly curled dark brown hair, his long boy's body and the turbulence of his unharnessed vitality. I heard him, teasing, "Remember me, Mother? When better scrapes are made——"

Straining, I tried to keep him, but no effort would hold him there. He faded away from me, dimming, losing sharpness, leaving little but sweat against my hands and a harsh coldness under my breasts. In that chill I grew aware of Phil once more——

"——may not prove true," he was saying. "I'd really have preferred not bringing this to you at all, but it was your right, we felt——"

My ears might be opening, but what they conveyed to me wasn't informative. I asked "Some girl came to you . . . ?"

He said, "No, not to me. She doesn't seem to have made contact with anyone. That's what's so——"

One of my shoulders, as I also grew aware, was being held in a firmly supportive grip; another more tentative touch lay under the opposite elbow. I looked up. "But then what——"

It was Bunky whose hand lay under my elbow; in youthful embarrassment he withdrew it as soon as I dropped my hands. Phil kept his grip of my shoulder an instant or two longer before he also fell back.

"I've been telling you. This letter from a lieutenant at Fort Benning. He replied to my——"

A flirt of hair, like a sparrow's tail, had been brushed up at the side of Phil's head by his brushing hand; he was meeting my eyes straightly enough, now, his glance understanding but driving through, the same one he'd worn pulling slivers out of small fingers and taping cut shins. Seeing that I'd lost half he said, he drew in a breath, starting over.

"Once Bunky'd come to me——"

Beyond where I now was, beyond the heard but unaccepted fact, lay circumstance and coming about. I tried facing up to it, but it seemed too much. I groped out, reaching, I suppose, for the escape of my lap table and the cards. Coming up, instead, against Bunky's leather jacket.

After the first stilted interchanges, Bunky hadn't put in much more, but now he turned to me the full troubled earnestness of his gold-freckled, still childish face. So much the same face from which, at four, he'd delivered an owl-eyed reflection: "You're not such a cross mother as my mother." Our relationships had shifted since that day; he now, not I, was the one who enfolded protectingly.

He said, "I can see how you hardly can believe it; I've a hard time believing it too. I don't want you to think I was in on it—Johnny didn't let on to me. It was just—well, one night last week I went out to the Palladium, in Hopkins." He'd been stumbling, but having reached that point began pouring out the rest more fluently. "I hadn't been going there—well, not since Johnny. But I was there in the bowling alley; I had a game with a couple of guys I know. I guess I sort of noticed this other guy standing around in the door to the bar; anyway it seemed that way afterward. Older fellow, maybe twenty-eight, thirty. He had a drink in his hand and was just there, that's all, about a minute or two, looking on. Then when I was going out to my car——"

The anxious fluency broke once more, returning to uncertainty. "Maybe this is the wrong way, Gail. Maybe you'd rather we just——"

"No," I said. "No, go on." A little vitality was waking again, and with it more puzzlement. Why should anything about Johnny come this way? I'd begun seeing a picture too—the long dimly lit bowling alley, Bunky and his friends throwing themselves forward after the balls, the man lurking.

"So—well, so I went out to my car and was going to get into it, when this same man I'd noticed came around from in back of another car. He said, 'Say, didn't I used to see you out here last year with Johnny Kiskadden?' I said yes, yes he did. Then—well, he——"

The earnest light eyes had looked at me through most of this, but now their gaze moved to the books he'd dropped on the coffee table. Still speaking, he picked up one of the heavier volumes, turning it in spread fingers.

"He'd been drinking—I'd guess he'd been drinking a lot. He wasn't too much of a customer to begin with, I guess. You get 'em like that, once in a while, out there at the Palladium. Kind of dark and tall and caved-in-looking. A piece of hair over his forehead and a big adam's apple jumping up and down. What he said was—well, he said, 'Anyway that so-and-so Kiskadden got what was coming to him.' I didn't know what to think. I didn't like what he'd called Johnny. I got mad. I said—well, I guess that's not important. I was going to light into him. He said something else about Johnny. And then just before I slapped him up against the car he said, 'I'm the one ought to know. He's the one sneaked my girl out away from me. He's the one married her.' It sort of knocked me for a loop. I'd already started in, hitting him, but my fist kind of glanced off. He'd pulled back along the car and then before I—well, I guess I didn't think very fast. Maybe I should have done something. Maybe I should have held onto him. But he kind of got himself together and went away and I let him go. I didn't know what to do. I didn't believe it, anyway. I went home, but I couldn't seem to forget it, either. So I went to Phil." A tight, sad laugh came in. "I guess that's where we all of us go when we don't know what to do."

"You may think we should have told you at once." Phil, still on his feet, continued pushing his stocky person back and forth. "I saw no use in bothering you, though, unless we had at least some confirmation. I wrote the Fort. That's the answer that came today."

"If you brought——" Once more I reached for what seemed sharpest.

"Here." From a breast pocket he produced an envelope, neatly, even in these circumstances, removing the inner sheet, handing it to me unfolded so that I could plunge immediately into the typed paragraphs.

"'—from our records, we are able to substantiate that Private John Kiskadden, 16438716399, filed with us on June 24th of this year a regularly attested notification of his marriage to Miss Sherry Lee Givens of Columbus, Georgia. Our address for Mrs. John Kiskadden, to which allotments were mailed, is——'"

The names, the dates, were so much more concrete than Phil's hesitance, than Bunky's stumbling; against them I felt the first crackings of the dam of denial.

"May not prove true," Phil said, but for him too, as for me, there must have been recollections to deepen those cracks. Johnny's frequent jumpiness, during the past winter and spring, a jumpiness entirely at variance with his usual high cheer. The sullenness he'd shown in March, when he'd come down one morning for breakfast, after a late night out, refusing explanation for a cut lip and black eye.

The day a month or so afterward when he'd thrown over the university courses in which he'd been doing so well, to enlist in the infantry. The distracted jerkiness and the changes of mood he'd again displayed while home on his September furlough.

Against the wash of those recollections, it wasn't possible to stand any way but weakly.

One of the hardest things for this story to do, it may be, is get you to understand about Johnny. His good solid core, but, outside that, his adventuring wildness. When he was little he had golden-brown curls, his skin was pale olive, his eyes were those of a Raphael angel, but few people said, even then, that he was one. The summer he was four I came home once from shopping to find his distracted sitter and a company of firemen maneuvering him down from a three-story roof. The year he was six he and Bunky—picked up from the neighborhood to be a man Friday—stowed away in a moving van, in which they weren't found for ten hours, when the van began unloading in Duluth. Since Horace and Pamela Knowles, Bunky's parents, are two of Minneapolis' most prominent attorneys-at-law, I was naturally being threatened with the works. Ten years later I found a note on the hall table the morning after school closed, a note saying, "Dear Mother, don't worry, I'll be home in the fall. Just thought I'd look around." He was home a month later, temporarily satisfied, having hitchhiked from coast to coast, for the most part in small private planes.

For any debit that could be charged against Johnny, though, a thousand items came in on the credit side. When he was nine he brought home a Mexican kindergartner whose mother was ill; we had that boy for six months, and Johnny cried terribly when he went home. No one ever said Johnny tattled, or side-stepped consequences, or was lazy or disloyal, or cold or self-seeking or cruel. Anyway, you don't love a son only if he's a good child; you don't build your life around him only if he's a standard insurance risk. Being submissive and decorous wasn't what I wanted of Johnny; I'd never had much use for tame men. I'd thought that what bounced him around was nothing but the bubbling of his youngness, and that after he'd finished his Army stint he'd come home to his love, which was engine engineering, and that as a man all his inventiveness and enthusiasm would help him do something outstanding and fine.

I'd thought a day might well come when I'd sit serene among the cavilers, thinking, even if I wouldn't say it, "I could have said so."

That wouldn't come about. Not with Johnny gone. Home on his September furlough, hurtled in his jalopy against a telephone pole off the Hopkins road. No more than twenty, like Bunky, but smelling of liquor, and with an empty whiskey bottle in the mangled car.

I hadn't accepted it. Death—there isn't much you can argue against death. But that Johnny should drive and drink—cars were the thing toward which he was almost more respectful than toward anything else. Like most twenty-year-olds, he must have tried his one drink, or two; he'd want to prove he was a man. But not more; I'd have expected his training and good sense to hold him. Only you don't argue with an empty bottle, either, or with witnesses who saw your son alone in his car, speeding, weaving long before he hit the pole.

Now it appeared this wasn't all, either. Somewhere there might be a girl to whom he'd been joined in a marriage kept secret and furtive, like something best under a rock.

Acceptance, in circumstances such as these, can't ever be happy acceptance, and beyond lies the question of what comes next. Johnny hadn't told me, the girl hadn't gotten in touch with me; I might try going on as I'd been before, pretending no knowledge had come to me. If that was the course I chose, then no word, I was certain, would leak from Phil's lips or from Bunky's.

If one set of instincts pulled that way, though, then another set jerked in contrary directions. I suppose it was pretty well set, even there at the first, just what course I'd be following.

Phil, sitting down, finally, launched into the advisings, the counselings, which he felt it his duty to make; I wasn't attending him. All I asked of his hovering, and of Bunky's, after a while, was that they get themselves farther off. At the door, when they were giving up, Phil did make one demand break through.

"Promise me just one thing. You know what you're like, Gail; it wasn't by accident Johnny jumped into things, and he didn't get it from Howard. Don't go off on this half cocked. See me before you make any start——"

I'd have agreed to anything. "Yes, I promise. I'll call you. I'll come in to your office. Just let me get used to it. Let me think——"

When the door was shut fast I returned my face to my hands. Then, dropping the hands, I walked back through the hall to the diningroom bay. There, on glass shelves set into the windows, sit the milky blue hobnail pitchers, the honey-brown sugar bowls, the flag-painted plates, the flower-decked cups and saucers which were my mother's and her mother's. From the center shelf I took an Irish Belleek cup so thin that even on this dim day a soft pallor showed through the wafer-crisp white when I held it up.

There's little strength, really, in loveliness, no matter what people say of it. Rather shortly I put the cup back. Went on to the living room, to the davenport and my lap table. Shuffled the cards, laid them evenly——

Shut it out. Convince myself that even if I did have to accept the rest of what had come to Johnny, I didn't have to accept this. Not his marrying behind my back, making it appear he'd picked a girl so wrong he wouldn't want me to know of her. Or else what was almost worse—that his life with me had never been open and free as I'd thought it was. But a matter of deceit, of unwholesome relationships hidden away from me——

Pinch that conjecture out, quench it, like two fingers squeezing a candle flame.

Yet all the while, there was only one way I saw myself. Alone in a car, heading toward Georgia and the girl as fast as I could go.

# CHAPTER TWO

BEFORE SETTING OUT I lived up to my promise about seeing Phil. Thursday, the sixth of November, that must have been. The second day after he and Bunky had come to me.

Through the weeks following Johnny's death I hadn't been going out. You know how it would be for me; everywhere I looked, Johnny's absence struck. He should have filled the empty seat beside Pat Evers when she waved from her convertible—faded sunshine had brought back a reprieved and pale Indian summer—before she quickly wheeled around a corner. His legs should have been visible under the Chrysler in the Knowles driveway, four doors down toward Lake of the Isles. I had to pass the Calhoun docks where his bright yellow canoe must still sit in the racks, past the Chevrolet garage where he used to work Saturdays, past the playing field at West.

Under the impetus that had now been applied to me, though, I was pushed ahead. Phil's office too is a place that holds memories, but these mostly go farther back. In the days when the sign said KISKADDEN AND SAWYER, and I was eighteen, I'd come there out of business school to type leases and check rent lists and hurry off by streetcar to register mortgages at the courthouse; that was where I'd met Howard, who'd been fifty and a widower and urbanely indulgent to my youth and impulsiveness. We'd had six mostly happy years of marriage before he died of a coronary when Johnny was five. Phil, ever since then, has been more than a substitute father for Johnny and a friend to me; he's also looked after the houses that Howard left. So I was familiar with the changes that had come to the long narrow building, the sign that had been SAWYER AND ALBIGUARD for several years past, Mrs. Minty at the nearest desk inside, and Phil's voice, instead of Howard's, saying "Come" when I knocked at the door of the one oak-paneled cubicle at the rear.

I wonder if it would have made any difference, if I'd listened harder to what Phil said that day.

"You can't take this on faith, Gail. I can guess what you're here to say, but don't say it. The last thing you should do is go there or ask the girl here, without probing first. What proof the Army demands on marriages I don't know; I suppose it's fairly thorough but we needn't take its word. I'll write to the local courthouse for a photostat of the marriage license. There would have to have been a judge or a justice of the peace or a minister. Witnesses. What you should do is hire a detective; he'll find out for you what's really what. We have an address now, too; if you like I'll write the girl direct, see what she says for herself."

He must have had it all in his mind well beforehand; certainly it came out non-stop, and not until he'd covered best courses of action did he pass on to surmise and conjecture.

"If we find there was any such marriage, then there's one fact I'm afraid you can just as well face. The girl won't be one you'll enjoy as a daughter-in-law."

Usually when I'm in his office he sits comfortably behind his desk, mobile, but only within the limits of a well-controlled responsiveness. The somberness into which he'd been thrown wasn't any more habitual to him than to me; much more normal, to Phil, was the relaxed enjoyment with which he taught the two boys to be fishermen, the dismay and exultance into which he exploded at high school games, the fairly devilish quirking of brows with which, a couple years earlier, he'd begun hinting that now Evie had left him, I might try for the place she'd vacated. On this day he stayed on his feet after greeting me, patrolling the room's narrow confines as he'd patrolled my living room.

"I suppose I'm getting to the place where I can understand about Johnny. We've got to remember he was twenty. Put a boy that age into the hands of a certain type of female—what I don't get, in that picture, is the girl. She'd have to have heard, long before this, that he's gone. She can't be getting an allotment any more; I don't know what pension she'd have coming, but it can't be much. He didn't make over his insurance to her, either. You got that, or at least you handed it to the kids at St. Adolph's. Why hasn't she gotten in touch with you? You may not rate as wealthy, but the income from two solid fourplexes and eight good rental houses is no item to make anyone sneeze. She may be afraid of you personally—I don't suppose any girl sees an unknown mother-in-law as anything except an ogre, even one weighing barely a hundred pounds. That wouldn't keep her from applying for support, not if she's——"

He might, so his manner said, have been a mastiff circling a stranger dog, nosing out the possibilities, reducing them to almost mathematical bareness. Inacceptable girl makes secret marriage with boy, boy dies, why doesn't girl push her claim?

I tried wedging a word in, "There might be——" but he was too preoccupied to listen.

"I've tried it every way. Johnny could very well have played an elaborate joke but not one involving deliberate theft—that's what it would amount to, with an allotment involved. One thing we must look into is whether some other boy from the Fort, a barracks mate, maybe, carried a marriage through, using Johnny's name——"

That time I got in my word. "What's the use of supposing, when we know so little and are so far away? You yourself know what I'm doing; I'm going there."

He flared at once. "What do you mean, going there? Haven't you heard one word I've said? Can't you see that the least——"

But he yielded, and not far along. Throwing up his hands.

"All right. I did know you'd go. Only—well, I wish I could be along. I might, too, if it weren't for—well. There's been a little something else—I haven't wanted to bring it up, the way things have been for you." He was twisting over this, as awkward as Bunky at Bunky's worst. "It looks as if I may be having Evie back on my doorstep. Any minute. She wrote me from Reno. She's been there, it seems, for some time. This other marriage of hers didn't work, either."

When you're sunk far enough in your own concerns, it can come almost with shock to remember that your friends have difficulties of their own. There've been times in the past when I've been thoroughly worked up over Phil's troubles; heaven knows, as Howard said of Evie the first time he looked at her, she was one for the books. From the day she paraded the drama of her white satin and her feverish fragility up the church aisle, she has managed to keep Phil well dunked in hot oil. Eyes shining and cheeks fiery, she told me at a bridal shower that all she asked of life, ever, was to keep Phil's house and bear his children—at least a dozen. Three weeks after the wedding she was back in her art classes, and instead of children there were flights to art jobs in San Francisco, New York, Philadelphia, jobs that were lofting her to undreamed-of heights. On the last job there'd been a man who was going to loft her to an undreamed-of height too.

Saying little that wasn't self-derisory, such as "Guess I can't hold a wife," Phil had let her divorce him, paying costs and far too much alimony. So far I hadn't gotten around to taking up his suggestions concerning the two of us, but that didn't mean there hadn't been times I'd considered it.

Rising at least part way from my own immersions, I charged: "She's expecting you to marry her again."

He admitted, "Not in so many words, but I gather it's the general idea. Anyway, we needn't settle that now."

He'd subsided, by then, far enough to rest against an edge of his desk. Years ago a fond amusement used to play around his mouth when he spoke of Evie; now he merely kept on looking tired. He continued, "What it mostly does is underline that I'd best stay here in case she turns up. You're the one woman she chooses to go into tantrums over, and Evie in tantrums——You'd do better to take someone else. Perhaps Dorothy Albiguard——"

My own swamp once more. "Dorothy's got Todd and Nancy, to say nothing of George. With Thanksgiving coming, and Christmas not far ahead."

"You mean you don't really want anyone. You mean you're not changing one spot on your adamant five feet of hide." There are things about me that touch Phil off the same way his infirmity about Evie touches me. He threw up his hands once more, returning to the warnings, the suggestions on checking. But then as I was breaking away he softened and quieted. Being fair, as he always was. Allowing every possibility. He said, "In spite of everything—in spite of the kind of man Bunky ran into there in the parking lot—in spite of the way things look— I suppose there's still a hope. The girl may be nothing but unworldly-wise and impulsive, as Johnny was. May really have loved him. Given him something we can be grateful to our dying days he had."

He'd no need to give it words. That was why, when I'd come, I was packed and all set to go. Of the things I must know, this one came perhaps first.

The trip wasn't eventful; its twelve hundred miles took me three days. Sitting in the car with my head in the shade of the visors and the sun in my lap, leaving familiar and haunted streets, emerging into the Minnesota countryside where snow had blown away but fields in early morning lay under a crumbling white frost-rime, taking 55 to Hastings and Red Wing and 61 to Winona and La Crosse. Moving on through the wood lots and hillsides of southern Wisconsin, where frost wasn't yet set and the trees and dank grass-sheathed earth gave out a chill ale-smell from retained and fermenting fall rains. Coming to Madison, Rockford, Joliet, Indianapolis, Louisville, Memphis, Tupelo, Birmingham, pausing only for gasoline, lunches, a grease job, keeping to the road until nine at night, waking in the pre-dawn gloom of squeezed barren motel rooms, crossing the Georgia state line at last.

From Louisville on I was in the South, feeling the sun in the afternoons take on an ardor which for me, at that time of year, seemed harassing and wrong, seeing meadows darken and foliage appear, seeing big white porticoed houses set deep at the end of tree-hemmed drives, and the other so much more numerous stilted shacks set haphazardly anywhere, seeing the station restrooms change from two to four, labeled *Ladies, Gents, Colored Men, Colored Women.* Seeing the contrasts of lush greenery and bare gullied earth.

It was a little past six on the evening of Sunday, the ninth, as I drew near Columbus, Phil's voice in my ear saying that, since the day had turned gray and a thick dusk was deepening, I'd best wait until morning to hunt up the girl's address. Short of the town I found another motel room, bathing there, eating at a roadside diner, returning to get into night things and settle with a portable radio, the lap table, and my cards. A single attempt at a game, though, was enough to teach me I'd never be resting; not that night; the cards dropped from my hands. No decision was necessary; after a few moments I merely found myself out on the floor getting into my clothes, hunting for garters and zippers with hands that shook a little from tension but also moved swiftly, pulling a comb through my bangs, snatching up a lipstick to color my mouth. Then the steering wheel in my grasp once more——

In Minneapolis it perhaps was snowing. Here, while I was inside, a thin rain had started up, spattering the windshield without cleaning it, leaving smeared semicircular streaks when I turned on the wipers, forcing me to drive lingeringly, eyes focused on the glisten of the lane marker, the winking of directional signal lights on other cars, the dart of pedestrians more intent on avoiding a wetting than on staying alive. In Minneapolis the AAA had given me maps, one of them including, on its back, small insets of downtown areas in the larger cities; I knew that the street I hunted was a midtown avenue at right angles to the highway by which I approached. After I'd come to thick traffic I peered out at all street corners, trying to read signs obscured by the dimming rain. Instead of the one I wanted I met a dead end at a river, and only after I'd U-turned did I find the right sign, two blocks back. There too I went astray, right when I should have gone left; I had to circle a block and then drag along, hugging cars parked at the curbs, before I looked up and across a small yard at a vaguely lit fanlight on which, in large black block numerals, appeared the number I sought.

Before leaving the car I did do an instant's reconnoitering. Taking in the house and the street in the rain-misty night, feeling the tremble that had begun in my hands spread until it was a pervading interior tremor. If Johnny's wife lived here, then hadn't Johnny been here too, in his uniform? Hastening here for his hours off, hitching rides, grabbing a bus or a streetcar or taxi? His anticipatory heels might have rung on this sidewalk, he'd have jumped these steps two at a time, scarcely able to wait——

Wide steps, visible even in this dimness as splintered and worn. A railed porch remaining from a day at least eighty years back. A dark-painted old turreted house from which, as well as from an even bigger and more dilapidated gray house on the right, an unkempt bush tangle on the left, rose that aura of forsakenness which clings to city streets after the original builders have fled, leaving their castoff domiciles prey to an alien invasion. Electricity might glow in the rooms, but only behind the concealments of the slitted window shade, the awry venetian slat; cars might stand bumper to bumper at the curb, but all were abandoned and dark; other still mobile cars might flash a brief radiance in the street center, but only with an effect of fleeting toward havens more wholesome. No pedestrian stamped past on proud confident feet; a single passing couple slunk close to the lot line, heads ducked into coat collars.

Dinginess of any kind wasn't native to Johnny. His allowance had padded his Army pay. "Our address to which allotments were mailed"—this wasn't a neighborhood to which the girl had fallen after Johnny's death, either. She might well—this was an eventuality I should expect—have moved on from here. It was, though, where Johnny had let her live.

Not understandable. My lips moved around a response whose very shape was coming to be familiar. There was a minute when, more sharply shaken, I thought back to my motel room—the waiting bed which at least was clean, the shaded lamp spreading visibility to every corner, the lap table, my cards. Behind that, winking faintly, was the capacious well-kept solidity of my house in Minneapolis, ready at no more than a finger's touch to bloom into softer and more habit-cushioned warmth and ease. But then the numerals over the fanlight seemed to stand out more blackly; somewhere beyond them, even if the girl were gone, must be a landlady who'd know something, who'd have seen not only the girl but Johnny——

A neighborhood may be dismal without being dangerous. On a rainy night people hunch their way along the best of streets. Besides, I couldn't live on in my present state, not even as long as the space of a night. I opened the car door and slid out.

It had been close in the halted car; outside a damp, fresher air swept at me, chilling my cheeks, changing the tremor inside me to a heavy thumping. By the time I'd mounted the steps and crossed the porch to a door with an old-fashioned turn-handle, though, the freshness had faded back, pushed back by the musty flat staleness seeping from the interstices around the heavy stained door. I twisted the turn-handle.

Deep inside the building a radio was on; faintly I caught the dusky, suggestive strains of a Pearl Bailey record so often repeated it has become unmistakable— "It Takes Two to Tango." Windows to left and right stayed covertly lit as they'd been. To my efforts with the bell there was no response whatsoever; likely it had long ago broken. I tried a second time, tried again, adding a sharp rap. Still no answer.

Among things apt to annoy me fast, one is being denied answer at a door where I know someone is home. The drumming in my breast slowing to a less threatened but more insistent beat, I put my hand on the knob. It turned, of course. People, in a house such as that one, wouldn't be optimistic about locks.

It was then, after I had the door open; in fact, it was after I was in the hall, directly under the single hanging light bulb, that a man began emerging from the darkness of the unknown deeps ahead, asking, long before he was clearly visible, "You looking for somebody?"

The voice had a low kind of hum, perfectly audible to me, yet pitched as if he didn't want others to hear. He continued coming into the light, willing, apparently, that I should see him, but gliding on such silent feet he might have been trying to keep his advance, also, as a secret for the two of us. I was startled, a little, but I can't say I was really perturbed by him then—he went so well with the house. An insinuating but otherwise mild little weasel, I'd have said, with an artificial, easily doffed dapperness about his narrow shoulders and an equally spurious and readily doffed smirk on his face. Dressed in bedroom slippers and a dark suit whose ministerial cut was a good deal at variance with its general state of bagginess, and also with a striped T-shirt visible between the lapels of the coat.

"Yes, I am," I told him. "I'm looking for Mrs. John Kiskadden."

Usually my voice comes out quietly. In that hall, and against the man's questioning purr, it clanked starkly, pushed by my nervousness, echoing back from the stair leading up on the right.

"Kiskadden? Say, you've hit on the right place then. Yes,

ma'am, you've sailed to home port. Go up along those stairs, third door back on the left. Ma'am, no trouble at all."

In the abrupt reversal, I knew how sure I had come to be that the girl wouldn't be here, that I'd go on to another address only to be told she'd left there too, that she'd dangle ahead of me, a will-o'-the-wisp forever somewhere, forever undiscoverable. Yet here, at my very first try, she was pinned no farther away than a few feet of staircase, a few feet of hall—quick panic fell on me, an icy sheet, chilling my shoulders and the hands I lifted to fend it off. I'd realized I had dreads to meet; should have, with Phil's briefing. Just the same, I had part way postponed them, and now they must loom as immediate. Yet less than ever could I continue in my necessity; without as much as noticing what became of the little man, or whether I said thank you, I turned to the stair and began rising. Reached a hall even more ill lit than the one below. Counted doors——

Three. The third door was the one behind which the radio played. Not "Two to Tango," any longer. Twin voices, light, playful and fluent, the tenor obviously that of Bing Crosby, were alternating in "You'll Never Get Away." Now that I was up here, other less definite activities were also audible over the rustling of my own person. Nearby an elderly woman was railing at someone or something in a querulous, unanswered monotone; farther on dishes clinked. I knocked.

The knock didn't silence the radio. Why should it? There isn't anything about a knock to halt a radio. Or for that matter anything else. Just the same I had a feeling as if the striking of my knuckles against the door emptied the house of most activity outside me. Certainly the old woman's thin railing died, the clinking of dishes stopped, even breathing might have stopped, so complete was the silence surrounding the radio's one stream of sound. But I had no more than an instant for feeling it; a girl's voice said, "Come in."

During the two days at home, the three on the road, I'd built up many shapes for her. She'd be dark and voluptuous, tanned, her umber skin plumped to bursting. More juvenile, of course, but not unlike Hedy Lamarr. Johnny liked girls like that. She'd be blonde, voluptuous, her eyes carrying an elusive invitation. Less groomed, of course, but not unlike a pin-up Hayworth. Johnny liked girls like that too.

She didn't open the door. There was that two-word invitation, then no more. I waited, and when it seemed certain there wasn't going to be anything more, placed the tips of my right fingers against the door, gathered such strength as my trembling left me, and pressed. The door moved inward, and I saw her, preconception sliding and changing in a moment's kaleidoscopic blur, settling to a reality.

She didn't look at all like Hedy Lamarr, not at all like Rita Hayworth. She looked like herself. She was sitting at a dressing table; she'd been brushing her hair. A cigarette, sending up a curling trail of smoke, lay balanced across the rim of a nearby ashtray. The brush, halted in mid-stroke, was still held at the height of her neck, the hair lay on her shoulders with the overhead light directly on it—hair champagne-colored, bubbled by gold, softly waved, sleek but thick, surrounding its owner with a nimbus so lovely that even I, on an errand such as mine and wound up as I was, had an almost irresistible impulse to reach forward to a substance that looked as if it would cling to the fingers like aerated floss silk. It was so eye-taking that time went by before I got to the rest of her—her slenderness, her lack of height. She couldn't have weighed much more or been much taller than I. Eyes—remarkably dark, quicksilver eyes—were of the kind that seem unable to open wide, and her lashes were of the kind that look sticky. A somewhat sharp little mouth in a pallid face. A girl who gave little impression of strength, more of a passive and responding weakness.

I'm thirty-nine years old. In course of time, without too much sadness, I've come to the compromises most people reach by that age. Trying to maintain some principles for myself and mine, accepting that a good many other people don't bother. If I'd seen this girl under other circumstances—on the street, as a stranger—I'd have said to myself fairly lightly, "Now, there's a chippy for sure," and gone my way. I don't know, exactly, what sparked such a judgment—something in her manner, it may have been. A faintly veiled defiance. Or a slipperiness about the eyes, or a weak hunger on her mouth. All I know is that conclusion came fast.

My hand, that had wanted to go to her hair, went back to the door panel it had so shortly left. From a spot directly under my voice box, where it seemed to have lain ready, a wide iron bar bell sank down through my chest. Had I really hoped? To what heights and what strengths, ridiculously, had I built up the possibility with which Phil had concluded? In the doorway, with nothing more accomplished than an initial view, I had at least one settled fact.

Eventually, I suppose, I'd have thought up some statement to get me on from there, though none seemed to lie on my tongue. I didn't have to make any such effort, though; she spoke. Without moving, without drawing the brush on through the rest of its stroke. In a voice soft, faintly slurred, faintly Southern, she said, "I'm Sherry Lee Kiskadden. You looking for me?"

Not especially hard, then, to reply. Even my shaking seemed to still a little as my voice automatically came out. "Yes, I am. I'm Mrs. Kiskadden too. Johnny's mother."

She said, "Oh." And what happened then wasn't in the pattern of conclusions I'd so far reached. She seemed to cringe. Not with any discernible action; just her slight person and her thin face appearing to narrow further, her shoulders ridging upward under the loose pale blue satin negligee that fell from them, her cheeks hollowing, the sticky dark lashes drooping lower.

My own trembling easing again under astonishment, I thought, "Why, she's afraid of me. Of me, or my coming here, or something connected with me——"

That, though, didn't have long to hold me, either. She began speaking again, rather flatly. "I guess you'd better come on in." While she was saying it she started rising. The brush at last lowering to the table, her body turning a little to come erect on feet in blue satin and eiderdown. The negligee fell in toward her figure, displaying what had been hidden while she sat.

She'd be having a child.

## CHAPTER THREE

AFTERWARD, WHEN I was leaving her, and later on too, in the motel, my impressions of what ensued from then on weren't clear. Emotion had collapsed over me like a fallen tent. You can't cry, not to any young woman, "This baby you're carrying, will that be my son's? Are you sure? Are you sure?" This too, this one wild hope more, hadn't entirely missed visiting me, but I'd cast it aside—nothing as heaven-sent as that could be possible. What I'd have done if I'd known the girl one whit more, if her name, even, had come familiarly to my lips, I don't know. I seem to remember a rocky second when I was about to throw myself at her feet.

What kept me from some such gesture, in fact, I don't know. Perhaps it was because, except for the shrinking, she stayed so matter-of-fact. When she'd risen she reached back to the dressing table, first to rub out the cigarette and then to turn off the radio. In the suddenly deepened silence she stood a little covertly taking me in—pretty well the same way, I suppose, that I continued taking her in. Terribly young—no more, I'd have guessed, than eighteen, at most nineteen. On her shoulders the curling of that exquisite hair, in her lowered dark eyes the slipperiness, over the sharp young mouth that shrewdness.

The radio she'd just switched off, the small blue plastic portable radio in a gray leather case, was a twin of the one I'd left at the motel. When Johnny went to camp I'd bought the two alike, one for him, one for me.

What caught me, in that welter of impressions, was chaos so great I couldn't turn toward anything—the hunger to draw her and her promise acceptingly in, or an equal resistant necessity to deny she and hers—proof or not, baby or not, Johnny's radio or not—could be any part of me. And once more, with a good deal more composure than any rags left to me, she piloted us both past an impasse, pointing to the bench she'd left, inviting, "You can sit here if you want; I just got the two chairs."

I managed some answer. "Thank you; no, don't move; this other is just as well." My feet must have taken me to the second chair, because through the rest of the hour that's how we were—she again before the dressing table on the backless stool, turned to face me, I in a lower overstuffed armchair beside a bridge lamp.

In a way, the ground we then covered was peculiarly, aridly factual. Peculiar, too, in the things it accepted and the things it left out. As usual, I hadn't prepared any statements or questions or attitudes; I stumbled along with what came to tongue. "You'll have to forgive me if I'm not—all the way sensible; you're so much a surprise for me. Johnny hadn't told me he'd married; it was only by accident——"

My trembling might continue, even if it had lessened, but her uneasiness, as far as appearances went, anyway, had vanished. Her eyes didn't open more widely, she didn't lose that air of sharp secretive defiance, but a fair measure of fullness had come back to her temples and her lower cheeks. Yes, she agreed almost smugly, she could imagine she had been a shock. Maybe she should have sent me a letter, especially after she'd found out about Johnny, but Johnny had said he was going to tell me first thing he got home, and she'd thought, well, if I knew and didn't want her around, she wasn't going to be a bother. She'd been getting along all right——

Candid, in her own way. Whenever I left space for an answer she put one in, hesitating sometimes just a trifle, as if she might be canvassing a reply before she embarked on one, but not being conspicuously wary. Willing, indeed, to proffer a picture of herself that couldn't be called self-flattering. No, she hadn't met Johnny here in Georgia; she'd met him up there, way up North. She'd been a cashier for one of the shows on the Midway at the Minnesota State Fair, fall before this one, and Johnny had come along. He'd asked for a date and they'd had one. She'd seen him quite often last winter and this spring. Then in April he'd gone off to the Army and she'd thought that was likely good-by. But then she'd found she'd be having a baby, so she'd followed him down. He hadn't wanted to marry, exactly; he'd thought I wouldn't like it much. But he had, in June; he could see how she couldn't work for a while. He kept on not being all the way happy, but they'd have made out all right——

No acceptance that it might have been normal, in a young wife, to rush North at his death, that a girl who'd loved him would have wanted her few last moments before he was laid away. No suggestion, indeed, that anything more had been involved than a boy's will-o'-the-wisp exploratory infatuation on Johnny's part and too easy compliance on hers. A picture that might have been sordid but that—perhaps because the boy in it was Johnny—was instead tearingly pitiful, not only for him but also, part way, for her; she might have been as much caught by not uncommon youthful circumstance as he. I struggled with perception, certain now I discerned the wariness, certain again I imagined it, and that a large part of what disheartened me might be her surroundings, in all conscience sad enough, consisting as they did of one highly varnished bed in a waterfall walnut, with a faded peach chenille spread over a mattress so flat it could never have known innersprings; the one perfume-blotted dressing table, the bench, the chair, the lamp, a scrofulous rug and a grape-pattern wallpaper so intrusively ugly it would have cast a pall over anything. While we were talking she took into her right hand, from the dressing table, a small porcelain dish or ashtray, an empty one; she sat fingering it, drawing her thumb back and forth over the raised violets on its surface, but except for that, and the radio, there was little you could call human in the room. Nothing but her brush, comb, and mirror on the vanity doily, the other dark metal ashtray filled with stubs, a lipstick overturned by the mirror. No magazines anywhere, no table, no books or newspapers, no pictures, no suitcases, no clothes, though these last must have been concealed by the closed closet door. My motel rooms, after I'd been in them for five minutes, looked more occupied. This girl had been here for months. Johnny had been here——

There was only once when hesitance might have been pinned as almost certainly there. It came when, having reached a point where I thought a first encounter might well end, I stood up, offering, "We haven't talked about plans, but of course we must. You'll have to tell me what you want to do. If you'll see me tomorrow—would you have dinner with me? You'll know restaurants here better than I——"

She agreed, very readily. "Sure, I'd like that fine. Could you come here to get me? I don't have any car."

By this time we were both near the door. I replied, "Yes, of course." Then again, as at the beginning, the need for some emotional overture struck at me; I reached a hand to her arm. "You mustn't think I'm not glad of this—that I'm not delighted about the baby. It's all——"

Partly what got me no farther, naturally, was a quick filling of my throat and a ridiculous stinging of my eyes; the rest was her response to this too. She didn't in any way shove me off; she just stood there tolerantly, as if she were saying, "Okay, paw me if you want." What she actually did say was "Oh sure. Sure, I know." But she too, in that minute, had a little something of her own to proffer. Something that came out more obviously halting than anything that had preceded it.

"You said—when you first came in—you said it was accident you found out. What kind of accident?"

Between getting myself together and switching back to a circumstance which right then had been far from my mind, I must have mangled my answer, but I managed some account. Bunky, and the incident at his car. This too she accepted with unbroken self-containment, standing quietly with the shining satin of the negligee straining a little over the watermelon bump at her abdomen but falling in graceful folds to her feet, her head slightly bent, slightly turned aside so the loosened fan of hair partly concealed her face.

She said, "Oh." I wasn't asking for explanations, but she supplied one. "I guess that would have been Roke that boy saw. Roke Bradsher. He's a man I used to know some. Before I met up with Johnny. He didn't like it too well, I guess, the way I took up with Johnny, and all."

It didn't astonish me that she'd known other men before Johnny. From that leave-taking, of which there was little more, I went on to the hallway below. A hallway in which, while I was abovestairs, someone had switched off the ceiling bulb, leaving only a faint, jagged rectangle of light lying along the floor and back sidewall. Light emanating, apparently, from a room under the stairs. In that rectangle, unmistakably, lay a shadow.

It's hard to describe what it did to me, seeing that shadow. Suspecting, immediately, that between shadow and light someone stood motionless—— My heart hopped like a frog from a lily pad, my hands, clutching my handbag, seemed to melt to an icy sweat. "You know who that is," I tried to assure myself. "It's that same man, the little young-old weasel, the one who came out before. You weren't afraid of him——"

But what my instincts perversely insisted on telling me, thrusting me fast for the door and the porch and the steps and the moist outside air and the haven of my car, was that I was escaping a lair. That the man under the stairs had been lying in wait. Yes, more than that. The girl upstairs, as well. The all too composed, too unmoved girl—against any contrary effects she'd managed, she'd been lying in wait too.

I got over it, naturally. There wasn't, so far, anything to keep me from getting over it. By the time I was back at the motel, common sense already was operating. By what had I been upset? The girl hadn't made one single effort to get me where I was. Nothing about her had frightened me. I'd seen reason for hope to be dampened, for dismay to deepen, but none for fright. As for the weaselly little man in the minister's suit, he, most likely, was no more than a busybody, compensating for a pitifully meager life of his own by curiosity about the lives of others. With a girl such as Sherry Lee, it wasn't impossible that even at his age he might have an interest. If I'd read her right, she wouldn't be fussy about who supplied her with commodities such as nylons and restaurant meals.

Oh, I'll admit they were grim, some of the thoughts I went through in my motel room that Sabbath night. I wonder how many other mothers, twisting awake in my bed, would have had softer thoughts. But morning neared, finally, and such tag ends of alarm as still clung to me died with the dawning light. I got as far, in fact, as having compunctions over my lack of free-flowing love and affection. Not, though, compunction so great that, when Monday's workaday hours began, I wasn't out doing what an image of Phil at my elbow said I should do. After seeing Johnny's radio I didn't really have any further expectation of finding the marriage invalid, but before ten o'clock I'd hunted out a porticoed courthouse and was waiting at a worn counter for a register to be laid before me with Johnny's unmistakable signature on the open page. I hunted again until I found a slightly vague, apologetic justice of the peace—— "When was that now, ma'am? Well, you know how it is. Younkers, so many of 'em, runnen in here—— Lessee. June, you say. Twenty-second. I'll have it in the book. Can't say I recollect much—say, wait. Soldier, wasn't it? Dark boy, real young. Blonde girl already—h'm. Not much, but I got 'em signed."

Johnny's signature a second time. And then, at Fort Benning, a lieutenant's desk and a lieutenant. At first smoothly condoling——

"—how extremely sorry we all are. It's nice you got down to see the Fort—you've been sent his things, haven't you? I'll detail somebody to——" Followed, once my errand was approached, by immediate stiffening.

"Our command doesn't extend to informing parents about marriages, ma'am, I'm afraid. We expect such matters to be taken care of by the parties themselves."

He was an extremely young lieutenant; he might barely have married himself. Before he knew who I was his eyes had lighted, apparently with the reflection that, for a woman my age, at least I'd kept my shape. Now a furious scarlet spread up from his shirt collar, suggesting he felt that his own manhood, his own years, were being impugned. While I was hastily disclaiming any intent to criticize, he was snapping, "If they're old enough to be in the service of their country, I figure, then they're old enough to be married without anyone's say-so." He had no doubts at all. He wasn't only the officer who had answered Phil's letter, he was also the one with whom Johnny in person had filed the necessary requests for an allotment and allocation of pay.

I must have dragged, leaving there, driving back to my motel, where I fell asleep. There was then, after all, little more than one immediate question left.

A place seen a second time, a person seen a second time, seldom carry as much impact as that place and that person when first seen. If I again trembled just slightly when I redescended before the girl's rooming house on the Monday evening, it was less with tension than with letdown. It was dusk again; in November it's dark by late afternoon, even down South. No rain fell on that day; the air and the porch steps were dry. While I was mounting those steps a woman somewhere called, "Lance-ee-ee! You come right on in here, now!" and the street was populous—men carrying newspapers, women bearing brown bags of groceries, a babbling and chattering clump of girls. That time I knew enough not to ring; no light was yet on in the hall; the vague rectangle again lay on the floor and the wall toward the rear, but no man emerged, lurking, and no shadow showed, either. Abovestairs there was the sizzle and scent of frying hamburger, the radio, muted, played "But, Remember When a Dream Appears," and when I knocked the girl opened the door wearing a navy-blue dress with a Peter Pan collar. A dress which, somewhat altered as to fit, might have passed muster at Miss Somebody's school for girls.

    I couldn't be free and relaxed with her. Couldn't, couldn't make it. She sat opposite me at the restaurant—she picked a nice place, too; quiet, unpretentious, food good and tablecloths clean—with an unassuming navy-blue hat partly concealing the blond fall of hair and adding to the subduing effect of the dress. The flags of her sticky lashes might have been a bit apt to dip in salute to covert glances from men at nearby tables, but quickly she jerked attention back to me. She called me ma'am, she smoked sparingly and neatly, she ate in honest hunger with entirely passable manners, she made obvious efforts to be chatty, avoiding much mention of Johnny but advancing the idea that Columbus had places I must see and she was the one to be listing them for me.

    I couldn't well burst at her, "You know I have only one interest in Columbus; you very well know what I'm here to decide. Should I ask you home? Or should I play this the other way, as Phil would advise me to play it, offering you an allowance, taking it for granted you stay here, keeping our relationship as it is now, impersonal? Accepting that, with the baby too, I'll be nothing but a faraway, indulgent but not well-known grandparent?"

    No word of hers claimed any least lien on me. After the dinner her only hint was a respectfully tentative "I don't suppose you'd be interested in a movie?" And after the movie she said good night at her door with nothing more than a pretty appreciation.

"That was nice, all this evening. I hope you can see me some more."

That second night at the motel was the one when I got down to it. Somehow from my last sight of her, which was of her back as she slipped inside her front door, my mind insisted on continuing. I knew it was unreasonable, impossible, and that under too much emotion I was slipping my tether, but I kept seeing her inside the old house—entering the hall where the one naked light bulb would shine on her flowing hair, and the man under the stair would stand quietly inside his doorway, extending toward her his shadow and his surveillance; where for all her burden she'd rise lightly and soundlessly on the stair, trailing the fingers of one hand above the murky banister without ever touching it; where she'd open the door of her room, in which Johnny would wait. Johnny in his uniform, cap cast to the bed, hands reached to her, lips saying, "This is where I've been—all the time, waiting here. That other—none of that other was real at all. Not the car, not the whiskey, not the accident; that was never me. I've been here, always here——"

Sanity, the cold harshness of fact too well known, pulled me out of that, only to plop me into a different sequence. The entry, the climbing to the second story, as before. But then the shadow moving under the stairs, the little man emerging quietly as he'd emerged for me, soundlessly rising, opening the door without knocking, sliding in, closing himself upon a coalition unholy and unknown.

I fought that off too. Just because she was her kind of girl, just because it was that kind of house, just because the man was there, didn't mean——

I got through a fair list of just becauses and didn't means, approaching closer to what I suppose are the bases on which most decisions are eventually made. Bases almost entirely selfish and personal.

I might say that what I had come for was to discover the facts of Johnny's marriage, to find out what sort of person the girl might be. If I were an especially good liar, adept at face-saving dishonesty, I might even say I was here to do my scrupulous duty about money. But that wasn't why I had come, really. My true cause for coming was that, out of all expectation, I was being given a choice. Not between whether I should ask the girl home or leave her here—that was merely exterior. My choice was between which of two things I myself most dreaded—being alone and having no one, or starting over with a human being who mightn't be one I'd pick but who at least was linked to me through Johnny. Who'd be bringing forth a stronger link.

As soon as I knew what the choice was, I also knew what, against any contraindications whatever, the answer would be as far as I was concerned.

By the time my proffer was made, I'd swung as far as a little humility—not a quality I necessarily cultivate, but with my final views of what I was doing and why, it wouldn't have been possible to be less than diffident. She hadn't asked that I impinge on her; the least I could do was give her, as well, a free choice.

She plumped for alliance with little more demur than she'd shown for accepting dinner the night before or the lunch I now tendered her.

Tangled lashes confining her glance to her plate and the slender hand holding her fork, she asked slowly, repeating and clarifying, "You mean you want I should get this allowance of three hundred a month, and I'll be getting it whether I stay here or go back there up North with you?"

I defended, "I don't mean live with me, if you come North; you'd find it uninteresting, being cooped up with a woman of my age. But somewhere not far from me, an apartment, it might be, where you could see me when you wished, and where I could sometimes help with the baby."

She said, "You're being terribly nice to me. Really you are. I didn't think you'd be this nice."

She didn't lift the lashes, saying it. Her voice hushed; for the first time in my acquaintance of her there might have been a break in it, a break that caused a quick half wheeling of my heart in my breast. Maybe, my heart said right then, maybe, meeting decency, she'll be decent too. But if she'd been moved she quickly overcame it to return to composure; the rest of her acceptance was spoken with the same slowness but quite coolly.

"It don't seem to make too much difference. Not to me; I don't have much kin around here any more."

It was my turn, of course, to have my voice break. "Oh, you'll be coming then." My hand went out again; I wasn't able to hold it back. Once more, as in her room the first evening, she suffered a touch but didn't respond to it. She said only, practically, a little nervously, "It'll take me awhile, getting ready. Would day after tomorrow be too long?"

I told her day after tomorrow wouldn't be too long. And what I felt—heaven help us all for the way hope can triumph over almost anything on earth—was that old sensation of having been handed wings. Not for soaring; my soaring days must be pretty well done. But at least for low skimming flight.

There wasn't anything more in that trek down to Georgia; not one thing more at all. Maybe an additional sidelight or two on the girl—I remembered to ask if there were bills she would like to take care of, and in a sudden sharp increase of her look of defiance was certain I read her exact answer— "I'm getting out of here, why should I pay those bills? I can skip those bills." On the next day, though, she let me drive her around, while she paid at least some of them; there seemed to have been a little over two hundred dollars' worth.

I didn't again see the man under the stairs, not there in

Georgia. Wasn't introduced to anyone else she'd known. Didn't glimpse a single other occupant of the rooming house, not the old woman who railed, or whoever else it was who clinked dishes and fried hamburger, didn't see a single door any way but closed. My remaining few minutes in the house, in fact, covered nothing but two eventless calls, to pick her up again for dinner, and an equally eventless carrying down of her suitcase the last morning. Eventless, that is, in the light of what came later. I wouldn't have used the word "eventless" at the time, occupied as I was by the small, careful foundations I thought I was starting to lay. Establishing confidence, outlining tolerance but also implying its limits, erecting attitudes.

Toward the house, when the girl closed the door of her room—she herself displaying no emotion in the act, not for the room or its memories—I had only the briefest of pangs. Johnny had been there, but it wasn't a setting in which I wanted to think of him. Taking the girl away, it seemed, I took Johnny too. His shade followed us, abandoning the grape-pattern room to its future inhabitants; he descended with us for a final time down stairs whose carpet was worn to thin warp and dust; he too passed without pausing through the hall below, even if one fleet glance was cast backward toward the rear where, in morning dusk, no vaguest outlining of light appeared, and where, except for our small rustlings, silence was as complete as it had been abovestairs. So to the porch and my waiting car.

The ride north held no happenings either. Continuingly informative, in a limited way, but unbroken by related incident. It wasn't until the first night we were home that we heard the whistling, not until the next morning that the doll rested against the door.

## CHAPTER FOUR

IT'S NOT TOO UNUSUAL for young men, boys in their late teens, especially, to whistle as they pass along a street at night; if I'd been by myself the sound would have fitted so well to a pattern I mightn't have heard. With the girl there I heard, all right. I unquestionably heard.

We were late, getting in. Later, much later, than I'd thought we'd be; it had been only eight in the morning of Saturday, November fifteenth, when we left La Crosse. The ten days of my absence, though, had included those in which winter fixed its grip; past Winona we came on sheet ice, and for the rest of the way could do nothing but creep, soon harried further by a chill rain which clung and solidified where it fell, pebbling the windshield until there was almost no visibility, forcing me finally to drive with window down and head out.

By the time I had the car in front of the house—so grateful to reach it I didn't even try for the garage—I thought it was midnight and it actually was nine. I was weak from exhaustion and taut with strain, my face burned half raw from dampness and wind. Before doing anything but flick on lights and turn up the thermostat, I pointed out one source of hot water and cold cream to the girl and made for another myself. Inducting Johnny's wife into his home, right then, didn't bulk nearly as large as being in off the road, safe and unbuffeted, havened by my own bathroom.

For the next hour that didn't change too much. In a way, through that long Saturday, I'd begun feeling a little camaraderie toward the girl. She hadn't enjoyed the day's driving; no one could. She'd sat pinched in her far corner of the front seat, not saying much, hands gripped. But she hadn't complained either, hadn't screamed when we skidded—— Once or twice I'd grabbed time to think, "She has her own kind of fortitude. Not an active type, more the passive, resistant kind. But it's there." Getting on the percolator, rustling food from the cupboards, wolfing a late supper in hit-or-miss picnic style, we both had so much relief to convey—"I thought we'd never make it. Never, never"—that we might have been companionable parrots.

But after we'd carried in our luggage we stood in the living room, she with her coat back on and her suitcase at her feet, I with my coat on again too and my suitcase in the hall, all downstairs lights off except the one toward which I was reaching, when I felt her stiffen. No, stiffen isn't quite the right word; what I felt was a flying alert. Not anything seen; she was behind me. One moment there'd been that somewhat lightheaded, fairly relaxed degree of openness, better than anything previously reached. The next, without any word spoken, quick reversal. Chill, tautness—so evident that my hand dropped from the turnscrew of the table lamp and I questioningly turned.

She must have been half bent to pick up the suitcase; she was straightening, leaving the suitcase where it was, her hand open. On her mouth, in her barely revealed eyes, a look of being caught. Over her entire person the same effect of—what was it? The unobtrusive cringing she'd shown when I first told her who I was, twelve hundred miles away in that Georgia rooming house.

Then, because it was so quiet, or because she was listening, I heard the whistling too. From in front of the house, where only a few minutes before we'd been taking bags out of the car. A tune which was that of a familiar and whining old ballad, "Oh, I wish I had someone to love me——" Only, the way it was being whistled it didn't sound whining; it sounded, instead, rather mocking. High and piercing, with a sharp, drawn-out emphasis. "Oh, I *wish* I had someone to love me—just *someone* to call me their *own*—Oh, I *wish* I had someone to love me—I'm *tired* of living alone." At once rebeginning, shrill and flaunting, "Oh, I *wish* I had someone to love me——"

Whoever was out there was taking plenty of time to pass by. Plenty of time on such a dismal night, when you'd think any sane person would scuttle.

If you ever want to annoy yourself with reflections on how stupid you can be, try recalling the inanity of remarks you make, under some circumstances. What I contributed, at that particular juncture, was "It's somebody whistling."

She said tonelessly, "I can hear it is."

There wasn't any evading the inferences; I made them willy-nilly.

"It could hardly be anyone you know, could it?"

That seemed the query to snap her out of whatever she was in; rather rapidly the look of tightness began leaving her cheeks. Her mouth relaxed, the lashes lifted at least a little. Still tonelessly she parried, "Nobody knows I've come back here. Except you." Again, though, she apparently felt forced to add explanation where none had been explicitly asked. "It just made me jump, that's all. Roke—that man I used to know—he always was whistling a lot."

The whistling had diminished in the night, sounding now both more faintly and farther away. "If you need it, here's another reminder"—that was what I said to myself. "She had her own life, of which Johnny was only a part. It's bound to crop up here and there."

We were strangers again. Almost entirely cut off from each other, when a moment later we mounted the stairs toward bed. I didn't put her in Johnny's room. I showed her to the guest room.

And in the morning, before she was up, when I went out the front way for the double purpose of bringing in the Sunday paper and chopping free a mess of iced-in papers that had accumulated during my absence—there sat the doll, propped, falling sideward as I opened the door.

I didn't do anything, for a while, but look down at her. Then slowly and carefully, still hanging on to the hatchet, I picked her up. I can't say I expected her to be a shroud for a bomb, exactly; I can't in fact say what I expected. There'd been times in my life when I almost habitually came on odd items at my doors—once, as I well recall, a shoe box holding a garter snake. Johnny'd never have left a doll.

Johnny'd never be leaving anything at my door any more, not dolls or anything else.

She wasn't a small doll; she filled my arm. As big, almost, as a child of four. Dressed as an adult, a female hillbilly, with a blue and white sunbonnet, a matching blue and white calico dress. Strangely weightless for her size, limp, in certain ways, especially about the legs. The face, the head, seemed to be made of wood, painted; the face was almost startlingly lifelike, in a fixed way, the flaxen hair in braids——

I turned her a little in my hands, and her lower jaw dropped.

I knew then exactly what she was, a ventriloquist's dummy. Well worn. Both dress and bonnet were faded and fuzzy, the dress had two rents in the skirt. Here and there the paint on the face was chipped, showing the wood beneath——

The mouth held a faint pucker, as if its owner were waiting to be kissed. Or as if, inspirited, she might whistle.

I think it was this last detail which, when I got to it, made me draw in a good long breath. I took the thing inside, settled it in a corner of the davenport, and came back for chopping out the newspapers, somewhat more vigorously, I suspect, than I'd have chopped if the porch hadn't yielded its other discovery. When the girl finally came down for breakfast—back in the blue satin negligee, feet still in blue satin and eiderdown at eleven in the morning, looking as if she hadn't slept too well, but ready to be politely apologetic, "I guess I should have told you I usually sleep late"—I had a question and a fact to put.

"This man you say you used to know. Bradsher, you said his name was, didn't you? He didn't happen by any chance to be a professional ventriloquist?"

She was ready for anything, instantly on the defensive. Her breakfast had been waiting on the diningroom table, or at least such of it as could be laid out beforehand was waiting there; she'd seen it and was moving forward to the chair. At what I offered she paused and half turned, in a sequence of movements I was beginning to know as familiar—the twisting of her body, a sliding swift glance from under the covert lids which immediately drooped lower, the thinning of her cheeks, the sharpening of her mouth, the bending aside of her head to let the deep blonde fan half hide it.

She said, "What made you guess he was?"

"A gift," I told her. "One undoubtedly meant for you."

At the davenport, when I'd led her there, she gazed down at the doll more or less as I had. More or less as I had, too, she took it up. For her, though, it had an aliveness it hadn't had for me; one of her hands slipped up along its back, endowing it with body, closing the mouth; the other familiarly straightened the dress and the bonnet.

With the woodenness which also came over her when she was in any way besieged, she lingeringly but quite voluntarily began an admission.

"It's Roke's, all right. Not his good one. His old one, his Hillbilly Sis. I didn't know he had this one around any more; I thought he threw her away. Not everybody could make a dolly do everything Roke could make one do. He could make her whistle. It's hard to whistle without you pucker up your own face."

Long memory, pride, some faint ring of regret—was I hearing them or was I, once more, imagining? I don't know why I should have felt I was making a charge, exactly; if this man meant anything to her and she'd gotten in touch with him—if she'd written to say she'd be coming, adding my address—why shouldn't she do so? She wasn't a girl to be long on the market unmarried. Or not part of some other alliance.

Whistling in the night. This token left at the door. All I could say of it was that it was a secretive and peculiar way of establishing contact.

I said, "He certainly knows you're here."

She was slower about replying to this than she'd been about answering anything else put to her. Even back there in Columbus.

What she finally said was, "Not from me, ma'am. I didn't let him know."

How could I have believed her? If she hadn't let him know she was coming, how could he have indicated his awareness of her arrival inside two hours, if he was the whistler? No other explanation appeared, then, as sensible. Certainly I had no reason to believe Roke Bradsher had lurked and watched—as that other little man in Georgia had lurked and watched—ever since he'd accosted Bunky in the Palladium parking lot. He couldn't have guessed, from that one act on his part, what I'd do. He was no familiar, not of mine.

Until then the person of Roke Bradsher had stayed in my mind only mistily; now he began emerging as much more close. A man of not too well described lineaments, descending on Bunky—what was it Bunky said of him? By Bunky's college-age standards he'd been an older man, twenty-eight, thirty. Bunky hadn't used the word "scrawny," but there'd been an effect of scrawniness. Ragged hair, foxy jaw, adam's apple bobbing. Drunken and surly. "He's the one got my girl out away from me. He's the one married her." Glad of what had happened to Johnny because for him it was a personal vengeance.

A man such as that might very likely want to make some reprisal against the girl. Might enjoy knowing he frightened her——

The next thought I had was that if Phil knew any of this he'd be shooting himself all over the place.

After we'd eaten, the night before, I'd called to let him know we were there and safe. He'd offered to come over; I'd pleaded our weariness. But he'd turn up at some time on this day, unquestionably. I'd already had both adjacent neighbors, and one from across the street. "We didn't know you were going away—who's the girl that came home with you? Oh no, *honestly?* You mean Johnny was *married*, Gail? But you never——" I was working a formula out, one for broadcasting. For Phil, though, the story must have more insides.

Should I tell Phil about the whistling and the doll? Try giving some account, too, of the man under the stairs?

It's odd in what ways, now and then, the cement of family cohesiveness sets. During most of Johnny's lifetime there'd been few problems I hadn't taken to Phil. I hadn't wanted to keep secrets from Phil. In the last years we'd usually been three—or four—talking difficulties out. The time when the boys were fifteen, for instance, and Pat Evers accused Bunky of shoving her from a grandstand. The time when, as high school seniors, both boys were hauled in for piloting a speedboat on Minnetonka with no one in the driver's seat. But just as Johnny had been chary of making his relationship with the girl known, so now I too——

The doll sat on the davenport where, after her last statement, the girl without further comment replaced her. When she was rising from breakfast I asked pointedly, "You want the doll in your room?" She answered, "I guess not, especially," and went back up the stairs without so much as returning to the living room. Passing in my Sunday comings and goings, I noticed I skirted the davenport a bit widely too. That presence there: the blonde inane smirk, the sunbonnet half obscuring the face, the limp body, the mouth pursed for a kiss or a whistle, stayed sharply enough in my mind as it was. When the chimes rang, announcing Phil, I swooped in, snatched the wooden visitant from her seat, and stuffed her on a shelf of the hall closet on my way to the door.

To almost everything else I did make Phil privy. The kind of house the girl had lived in, our meeting, what I'd learned of her, the results of my descent on the courthouse, the justice of the peace, the Fort. When I called the girl down she came readily, dressed, by that time, in the navy-blue crepe with the white Peter Pan collar.

For Phil she spread out her best wares—the blonde fall and slide of that sleekly waved hair, the half raising and lowering of the gummy lashes, an uncertain asking smile—— Many men may have been taken by her, including Johnny. But there'd been others, too, who hadn't. When Phil, instead of quickening, merely grew tighter and grimmer as the hour progressed, she relaxed to nothing more downcast than a meek equanimity.

With complete equanimity, also; in fact, with what might have been called superb aplomb, she allowed Phil time for a concluding word. Rising, after thirty minutes, saying, "Would you mind if I go back upstairs again? It seems I'm still tired from yesterday." She lifted her well-carried burden with that effect of lightness up the stairs.

Phil stayed silent until the door above closed. He was seated in one of the large chairs for this visit, bent forward, twisting his hat in his hand.

He said heavily, "What we expected, isn't she? Not what we hoped. Well—there'll still be the child."

Heaviness and somberness weren't the expressions that went with his long humorous upper lip; tiredness wasn't either, nor strain. Looking at him then, though, I saw tiredness and heaviness settling in. To me he'd never seemed anything but young; his hair had begun graying in his thirties but that made no difference; the spring in his body had been that of strength, the planes of his face had stayed firm. Now face and body both were softening, sagging——

I should know how he felt. The same drags pulled at me.

The last thing he said before he left was "What I still don't understand is her not applying to you for support. She's accepting it readily enough now, isn't she?"

I suggested timidity. Not really believing, myself, that it was an answer, merely giving it as a single possibility. After all, a man lurking, a whistle in the night, a doll left on a porch—those added up to no adequate explanation either.

If that had been all there was, I'd gladly have left things there. Whatever the girl's past might have been, it wasn't for me to explore. Not closely. Better, much better, if we left much of that past tacit.

That, though, wasn't all. That same evening the whistler was back with us, and this time I was pushed into what, if I hadn't been so taken aback and uncertain, I'd certainly have arrived at earlier. Irritation.

The girl, I was finding, had what amounted to a genius for staying closed off by herself. She made the one voluntary sortie for breakfast, descended again not long afterward for Phil's early afternoon call, but before she came down for dinner I had to climb the stairs and announce it with a second knock at her door. When I did so and she'd answered, "Come in," she was doing exactly what she'd been doing when I got her down for Phil, what she'd been doing when I came upon her in Columbus. She sat at the dressing table, cigarette at hand, brushing her hair. Smoothing it, drawing the brush through it lingeringly, shaking it back, resmoothing it, swirling in a deeper wave at the side, with the absorption of a votary priestess dedicated to a single god.

As in the afternoon, however, she rose willingly to follow downstairs, eating with good appetite, entering a little lethargically, but still adequately, into a discussion of what she'd like in an apartment. Finding one, her replies inferred, was an activity in which I'd play a major role; she wouldn't know how to begin. Thinking it might make her more at ease, I suggested, after dinner, that she wipe dishes; she couldn't be said to fall with delight into this suggestion; in fact, the look crossing her mouth when I made it might have been classified as mulish. But she complied there too, coming along into the kitchen, performing her task awkwardly but well enough. Still on the tack of making her at home, I asked if she played Russian bank and, when she said no, offered to show her how. There also she acquiesced. As soon as the kitchen was in shape we progressed to the living room. Where we met the whistle.

It might have been going on before we got there. The effect, though, was that it awaited us. That whoever produced it had been standing somewhere beyond the wide unshaded front windows—I'd seldom in my life pulled the draperies over those windows—waiting for the sight of our persons in the room and my hand on the table lamp turning up its candle power. Shrill, clear and teasing, the same tune as before. "Oh, I *wish*——"

I wheeled toward the girl. Standing, just behind me, in very much the same mute, caught quiet in which she'd stood the night before. Then, without saying anything, without stopping for so much as a sweater, I ran for the door and outside.

It was a perfectly clear, cold night, the kind of night which makes dyed-in-the-wool Minnesotans deep lovers of winter and home. The previous day's rain had all blown away, but its moisture had stayed where it fell, covering an earlier snow with a crust which in sharp moonlight threw back twinkling gleams, casing each bush twig and tree branch in an equally glistening round, seeming to lie fractured in the very air, forming splinters of sparkle there too. If there'd been anyone along the shallow uncovered tunnel of the sidewalk I couldn't have missed it. There wasn't anyone on the sidewalk. No bulk of a human being near the car still parked at the curb. Or, that I could see, across the street. No one on my side of the cedars lining the sides of my lawn. No one—yes. A couple appeared at my right, walking rapidly along toward the lake. Two unfamiliar young people, both carrying skates. The girl laughed, the boy answered, rumbling. They weren't doing any whistling, but all the time the sound continued from somewhere. Farther away again, mockingly. Dying, but seeming to remain as an echo.

Not for me to run about in the neighbors' yards, hunting someone who hid behind a tree. I had that much sense. Maybe being chilled to the bone helped some. I got back into the house, rubbing a current into my arteries. Ready to issue a few rather stern ultimatums.

"Look. I don't like annoyances of this kind. Whoever this Roke Bradsher is, wherever he is, I'd suggest you get in touch with him. Tell him to stop. If he doesn't I'll——" I hadn't gone in my own mind as far as the threat I next found myself uttering, but I found myself uttering it. "If he doesn't, I'll have to call in the police."

She wasn't caught any more; she'd again recovered from cringing; she sat on the davenport, fingering the shell-handle top of a candy dish from the coffee table, in the same way she'd fingered the tray in her room. The hair drooped forward as she meekly answered, "I wouldn't even know where he lives now, ma'am."

If people look recalcitrant when they're faced with a dictum, they're usually willing to argue—or shout—matters out. But if they start looking meek, then they're usually obstinate with a kind of obstinacy you can't do a thing about. Faced with that meekness, I managed to swallow some of what I was ready to say, but I wasn't entirely ready to lower my colors.

"You know where he was last year."

"Oh, sure, I know that. He went off away from there, though. He was gone when I went down to Georgia."

"He said nothing of where he was going?"

"No, ma'am, not to me. That's how Roke always was. He'd just pick up, sometimes, and leave. He had this job in a tavern, a night club, like. With his Sis, his new one. But then he said he was going, and he

47

went. He often did that. He'd take his Sis, and his traps, and be gone, sometimes three or four months. He could always get him an eating job, anywheres."

I pointed out, "It's obvious he's not gone now. He's back."

She asked helplessly, "But how could I go about hunting him? This town here is too big."

Fretted I might be, but that stopped me. I couldn't, offhand, think of any method by which she might track him down. What I'd spoken as a threat, I began suspecting, covered a course I might well be following. That was why a police force existed. I wasn't actually ready, though, for that much fuss.

Not that night. Or the next day, Monday, which was spent on the first leg of apartment hunting and which didn't end until after ten o'clock—we ate in a restaurant. Through the hour or so after our homecoming, in spite of anything I might say to myself, such as that even if there was whistling it was the girl's business, not mine, my ears stretched until their tops should have developed points. If there was any whistling that night, though, it was earlier while we were away.

The next morning the card was at the door, and I was readier for a fuss.

## CHAPTER FIVE

AGAIN THE TOKEN turned up in the morning before the girl was around. I came downstairs on my way toward the kitchen, and noticed the card on the hall rug below the mail chute.

During the previous day without incident both irritation and expectation had fallen a fair amount. While I was walking toward the card I can't say I foresaw it would concern the girl; it's too common for advertising of various kinds to come in through the chute, even that early in the day. If thought had run in words it would have probably been, "Now, this will be the most ordinary——"

At first view, that was the anticipation which would have been met, too. In fact, the address side, which lay uppermost, carried nothing at all. Merely blank space, the government printing, in green, and the green government stamp. The old stamp, for a single cent. The other side also might have appeared messageless to a careless glance. Only in the lower right-hand corner was there anything to stop the eye. A very small strip of paper, grayish white against the pale buff of the card. Paper half transparent, attached by glue, dimly revealing the darkness of its underprinting. But entirely clear on the upside. A numeral, 20, and then the words, "Lo, I am with you alway, even unto the end of the world."

I don't know if I classify as religious. Before Johnny died I was active in church, teaching Sunday school when he was little, helping at suppers, directing—these last years—most theatricals put on by the teenagers. The Reverend Mr. Raeburn once told me, half joking and half sad, that he hoped my faith was equal to my works. In what he hinted he may have been right; when Johnny died I couldn't go near the church.

The funeral was from a chapel. I hadn't attended a service since. That didn't mean, though, that there weren't things I respected. Looking at the biblical verse on the card, one of the things I saw was the desecration of the page from which it had been cut.

"I'm just a terribly late sleeper," the girl had apologized on her second morning, more or less as she had on her first. Until she put in an appearance, now, hours might pass. Determined, this time, to be calm and judicious before anything else, I took the card with me to the kitchen, propping it against an edge of the toaster while I breakfasted from the top of the stepstool.

My fright at the shadow under the stairs—with time I'd come to a place where I was willing to write that off as unreasoned. The whistling and the doll—those, once the original impact was over, might just possibly be filed under the heading of unpleasant playfulness. This card, though, was hard to squeeze into any such category.

"Lo, I am with you alway, even unto the end of the world." In its original context a promise compassing the heart of comfort. But one which, arriving in this way, hinted at something quite opposite.

In my mind, bulking ever more clearly, loomed the man seen by Bunky. Coupled with these words, he was menacing.

When it was eleven and the girl hadn't yet appeared, I wasn't able to hold myself back any longer; I knocked at her door. She couldn't have been sleeping but she also wasn't out of bed; her "What is it?" emerged as half smothered.

I spoke; she invited, "Come in." When I pressed the door inward on the darkened room her head still lay back on the pillow, her mouth was half open for a yawn and her arms halfway upward for stretching. My appearance must have halted the stretch; instead of completing it she shoved herself upward until she sat, smoothing the blonde niagara of free tousled hair, asking, this time, "There isn't anything wrong, is there?"

I answered, "That's really for you to say," and showed her.

Running up a shade so she'd have light, giving her the card, telling her where I'd found it. She didn't bother looking at the address side; she kept the verse side upward just as I handed it to her, looking downward with gaze hidden by the lashes which were stickily adhesive even at this time of day.

Why did she cringe at me, at the whistling, at the doll, but not about this? There wasn't any least sign of her being under any kind of fire while she took in the card. None of the obvious tightening, none of the chill. She merely acceded, "That's Roke, all right. Cutting little snips out of books, that's one thing he purely was fond of. When he got him a Bible out of a hotel room, or like that."

In only one way might unpreparedness have let her down. For the most part her speech wasn't entirely illiterate; in fact, at times she made comments both fairly well phrased and shrewd. It was only in some circumstances that she took on the childishness, a manner consorting not too badly with her years, but also carrying a slight air of being deliberate. Whatever the reaction being handed me now was intended to convey, what stuck out was its insufficiency.

I supplied, "I'm not mistaken, am I? The man's threatening. He means to get back at you——"

She said, "I guess so. I always did guess Roke would take his mad out on me."

I couldn't ask, "Then *that's* why you didn't get in touch with me?" Our relationship wasn't one to include that much intimacy. Instead, I skirted the area—"If you're better off away from Minneapolis, you know you can go back to the South. We'll arrange——"

Eyes still fixed to the card, she returned, "I guess that wouldn't make no real difference. He could find me there too."

What was there for me to say? Now ready for another subsidence, for seeing this, too, as a magnified will-o'-the-wisp, I began a retreat while one still might be dignified.

"You're the one to judge. If all that's involved is a—quarrel, if you think the man wouldn't be dangerous, then I won't be too worried, whatever——"

She cut it. With the drawl. "Oh, Roke can get dangerous, all right. He killed a man once, he said. They just got in a fight and he knifed him. He always did have a knife, had it on, all the time. Sometimes he played with it, funny like. He just liked to know he could make people scared, I guess."

If she'd shown herself a little more upset, I might have been less so. I stood where I was in a half turn, and I admit I was pretty well thrown for a loss. My connections with crime had all been confined to a reading level; I hadn't had as much as an ancestor who'd been hung for horse stealing. Johnny and Bunky were hauled in, the one time, for the boating misdemeanor, let off with a lecture and a fine. Any close knowledge of criminals was as foreign to me as the habits of cobras in their retreats.

As usual, what I brought out in such a situation wasn't distinguished for brilliance. I objected, "You can't mean that. Not actually. If he's a—if he killed a man, he'd be imprisoned. He couldn't just——"

She said, "You don't know Roke, though, ma'am. Roke could do anything. Roke could get out of anywhere. Sometimes I think Roke could be dead, even, and get back if he wanted back."

While all of the foregoing was being said—the whole while, without a break—she'd kept her gaze fixed on the card; it was only for this last she lifted it. Not high, just enough so the gummy lashes allowed a glimpse of the dark glimmer they'd hidden. In that glimmer, and around her mouth, too, what I read was a kind of somberness.

*Somberness.* What response was that? It was so incomprehensible and yet at the same time so patent I tried making one of the flights of which I'm sometimes capable—leaving my own skin to get into hers. Orphaned at two, or so she'd told me during the drive north. Taken in by wealthy but disinterested foster parents who had older children of their own. People owning a large corn and cotton plantation. Running away at fifteen to take up with a carnival, staying with the carnival until it dissolved—that was the route by which she'd come to the Midway at the Minnesota State Fair, and to Johnny.

Some of it—the last part, especially—I'd pretty well taken at face. On the rest I'd reserved judgment. Even if she'd been left to servants, as she also said, she was remarkably rough around the edges for having lived in a family of means. In a life such as hers, there might well have been occurrences to which my imagination scarcely would stretch. Violence, for her, might wear no stranger's face. Toward it she might have built the stoicism she'd displayed toward the dangers of icy roads, and that she apparently was able to call upon now. Yet she also had shown herself capable of fear.

Bafflement wasn't to be dislodged by thinking, or even by a physical shaking of my head. With anything else beyond me, I fell back on possible action.

"If any of this is true, if the man is a—a killer, then we haven't much choice. I'll call Mr. Sawyer; I'm sure he'll advise the police."

In the little interim before I began on this, she once more was shaking back, smoothing back, the thick fall of her hair, leaving the card on her lap. Just as I spoke the word "choice" she was reaching a hand toward the dressing table, asking courteously, "Would you mind if you gave me that brush, ma'am?" I automatically did as she asked, and by the time I'd finished she was already at work on the tangles, face tilted away from me.

Against that much calm it was almost impossible to keep determination at a peak. When I brought out nothing further she made comment, and comment is what it was, too. Nothing more. She said, "Roke won't like it if you get the police on him; I was thinking that yesterday. He always said he'd kill me if I called in the cops on him."

There was more or less only one return to make to that, and I made it.

"What would you wish to do? Sit waiting here for whatever he dreams up next?"

She didn't reply, didn't answer one word at all. Head turned away, brush continuing its steady strokes, she fell mute.

Judicious care may have described the attitude with which I approached this interchange, but not the spirit in which I ended it. The muteness was too much for me.

"You may be accustomed to situations of this kind," I snapped, "I'm not. Your nerves may be up to it. Mine aren't."

I was at the phone as soon as I got to the foot of the stairs.

I can't see how we could have applied much sooner to the police. Upsetting as the earlier events might have been for me personally, they hadn't been of a kind to demand intervention. The second time we heard the whistling, even, Roke Bradsher had been little more, in my mind, than disgruntled and surly.

If it comes to that, too, I can't see what difference the police would have made if they had come in earlier. Certainly their knowledge and assistance didn't prevent what fell over us afterward.

At the time, necessarily, that was all ahead. If I'd been asked for an opinion of Phil's response, once I got to him, I'd have said he was moving unduly. As usual, once I'd taken a step, I was ready for backtracking. Call for official help, yes, but not quite so far up the line. Accompany me, yes. Insist the girl be along, yes. But not necessarily yank Bunky from his classes, just so the antecedent incident might be related at first hand.

When the four of us foregathered in what, we were told, was the common room of the police section at the back of the courthouse on Fourth Street, it was exactly two minutes to two, the same day. What the others were expectant of there I can't say; all I know is that Phil's pacing and the settled lines around his mouth said he was roused and determined, the girl's huddle on a brown leather settee said sullenly that she'd never have been there if she hadn't been forced, Bunky's traveling glance and the tendency of his mouth to drop open spoke a lively inquiry mixed with astonishment. For my part, I was thin and uncovered as far in as my bones. Justifiable complaint might cover my purpose in being where I was, but what I somehow expected was that only Phil's influence would keep me from looking ridiculous. Foreknowledge of our exact destination didn't help, either, even if, as had been explained to me, that destination was largely occasioned by circumstance. It continued not helping when, after seventeen minutes of waiting, a large man in civilian clothes emerged from a corridor, asked "Sawyer?" of Phil, and led us back to a door with a frosted glass pane where a single black word announced *Homicide*.

Phil, entering first, greeted the man inside. "I guess I could have taken this elsewhere, Vince, but since you say you're a friend of mine——"

Vince, rising, was answering easily, "Sure, Phil, any time." He was a large man too; every man I'd seen in the place was big. Looming, when he stood over us, not just upward but toward both sides. Dressed in well-pressed oxford gray, compactly hard, healthily ruddy as to skin, balding, obtruding a nose tight and high at the bridge, widely flaring at the base, in the way that seems to be a pattern for police noses. Sharp around the eyes. Increasingly sharp when, from Phil, he passed to me, being introduced.

Lieutenant Winterung. Lieutenant Winterung, it turned out, had sat near Phil through eight grades of school, cracked one of Phil's shins with a hockey stick, accompanied him on dates—Lieutenant Winterung, his manner said, was as ready as I to discover that our tokens had been planted by an eight-year-old scamp from next door.

Just the same, during the instant he held my hand, his scrutiny enveloped and isolated me as completely as a diving bell.

"Mrs. Kiskadden," that scrutiny repeated to itself. "Small, dark, not badly off." From me the bell was lifted to clap down over Bunky. "Horace Lorimer Knowles, Jr. That'll be Pam Knowles's kid. Horry Knowles's. College boy, right age for larks." After Bunky, the girl.

"Mrs. John Kiskadden. H'm." On Sherry Lee the scrutiny didn't stay appreciably longer, but when it lifted there existed somewhere in Lieutenant Winterung a mental ticket carrying a good deal of salient data.

Casually but directly he channeled our business with him.

"There's been a card and a doll, I hear. Someone's been whistling around your house at night." He listened well. Heaven knows, as I've said before, he was scrupulous. The card came from my handbag, the doll from the carton in which she'd been packed for the journey. He examined each, laid it aside on his desk without commenting. Elicited an account of the whistling, of the man and the shadow under the stairs.

After me, again, Bunky; after Bunky, once more, the girl. She, of course, was the one against whom he moved in. Courteous, but not hesitating to be invasive.

"You say you were fifteen when you ran away from this family—what was the name again? Slade. While your maiden name was—thanks. Givens. You left the Slade family, by which you'd been raised. The man Bradsher, that you've named, he was concerned in your running away? No? I see. You went to the carnival with whom? The Slade family made no efforts you know of to——"

She wasn't any more willing than she'd been in the anteroom. If she could have managed, she'd have broken away and vanished while we were yet in the corridor. That noon when I told her what would be asked of her she'd flared back, "Me? What would I do that for? I'm not complaining about anything; I don't want no truck with cops. I told you what Roke would do to me——"

She'd apparently developed an illusion, somewhere, that when I said police they'd be my concern only and she'd be left out. It had taken Phil's knock at her door and his steely "Ready?" to get her out. She'd come then; she was so far prepared as to be wearing the navy-blue dress. But she wasn't to be won over; she sat alternately brushing a hand under the roll of her hair in the back of her neck, and inching the fingers of that same hand along the surface of the large tooled leather handbag in her lap. With every word forced from her the covered eyes and sharp mouth grew more sulkily mutinous.

Yet she wasn't departing from the story she'd given me, she merely elaborated. No, the Slades hadn't tried to get her back. The carnival's name was the Len Feasely Carnival. It had broken up since, but that was its name then. The Leonard Feasely Shows. She'd stayed, for a while, with Len Feasely's wife. Then paired up with another girl. Afterward, she'd lived by herself. Roke Bradsher had his own show, then, his own tent. He was one of the stars. She had gotten to know him. She had gotten to be his girl. He was jealous; he'd beat up Len Feasely once——

Obvious where the lieutenant was heading. We might by this time be seated almost informally about the room, he might be resting, half sitting, against the fore edge of his desk, playing with a ring of keys from his pocket, but his path was a bullet's path.

Yes. Admission on this was obviously more reluctant than toward anything previous, but, pushed by insistence, it came. She had told Mrs. Kiskadden that Bradsher had knifed a man. She couldn't know for certain; she hadn't been there. She just believed he had. He'd said so. One night they'd been in a small town. Andalusia, she thought it was. Alabama. A kid had come around; Bement, he'd said his name was. Bill Bement. She'd been a little mad at Roke; not much, just a little, so she'd gone out with Bill Bement. After she was back at the trailer where she lived, Roke had come around, waking her up. He'd said she wouldn't be seeing that kid any more, not that one. He hadn't added more then, but a couple of months later, when they'd been somewhere else—Mississippi, or Tennessee—they'd been having some drinks one night and he'd said he killed the boy.

"We were over in his tent that night; it was after the show. He had out his knife, saying it; he laughed. He said, 'How come you're not running around any more? Don't you want that your boy friends should go the way that other kid went?' That's when he said about killing him. He laid for him and knifed him, he said, and then hauled him away in his car trunk. He said he left him under a straw pile out on a farm someplace. He said, 'Any time you want to talk on me you know what you'll get, too.' If he knew I'd been telling on him——"

Through the last of it there wasn't any mistaking her inner state; her always pale skin was taking on the waxy green tinge of a bayberry candle; she was shaking enough so the tremor was visible over her shoulders, her hands, her knees. Appearances said that she'd given up hope of support from me; less and less often, as the questioning went on, did the liquid dark glance come my way. Or Phil's. For the most part it stayed fixed at the level of the narrow gold tie clasp affixing Lieutenant Winterung's neat, navy-blue four-in-hand to his white broadcloth shirt. When it strayed from there it bent, more than anywhere else, toward Bunky. Out in the common room the two had met, Bunky awkwardly offering, "I think I saw you, out with Johnny once." She pallidly returning, "I guess that you could of." Under the circumstances they couldn't have been anything but strained. "You're cut off, away from me," her glances now said. "You don't want to know me. But you're the one my age; if I'm to get understanding from anywhere——"

Bunky was aware of the supplication; under the freckles his

broad face slowly deepened in color until it was redder than his stubbled hair. He sat with leather-cased shoulders loose, fingers laced at the height of his diaphragm, elbows back on the chair arms, gaze for the most part directed at his feet, but now and again he wasn't able to keep from looking at the girl, either. I felt what I thought he must feel.

You can't forever stay taken aback, not twenty-four hours a day. In a way, a peculiarly inclusive way, I'd come to accept her as what she was. Sitting beside her as I now did, though, hearing her recital, I had to see her, freshly, as she appeared to unfamiliar and judging eyes. To Lieutenant Winterung's. Phil's. I wasn't—a fact I perhaps should admit with shame—able to lift myself above being mortified that the two of us, she and I, made up a family. Yet I squirmed exactly as Bunky squirmed: what she was she'd been made by social circumstance; in what she'd experienced she hadn't necessarily been an accessory. The very fact that she wasn't expecting me to yield her any sympathy made compassion bite deeper.

Whatever fellow feeling might exist in the room couldn't temper her ordeal, or shorten it. When he'd led her back over the facts of the killing, the lieutenant passed on to the man I'd seen at the Columbus rooming house. There—out of all reason, I'd have said—she showed herself more recalcitrant, more reluctant, more beset than in talking about Roke Bradsher. Yes, she had known there was a man down in that room. Yes, she'd known him. No, not known him, exactly, not well. He was just someone Roke once knew, that's all, a man who used to go around with the carnival, mostly working the ponies, the riding ponies for the kids. Ed Toomey, his name was. It had just happened, by accident, that she'd run into him, one day, in a Columbus diner. One night late when she'd gone out for coffee. He'd moved in, after that, to the same house she lived in. No, he hadn't bothered her, not too much. He'd said he wanted to see Roke; he was waiting for Roke to come around.

At Winterung's "Any reason he'd want to see Bradsher?" she sat wordless so long I thought she might be trying out the muteness on him too. When he repeated the query, though, she answered.

"It wouldn't surprise me if he wanted money."

"You mean he may have been blackmailing Bradsher over the killing." If she wasn't quick, the lieutenant was.

"I don't know. I just guessed, that's all."

The scrutiny settled over her again, but after an instant or two rose; abruptly he abandoned the question of the little man to return to Roke Bradsher. She had no idea where he now was? Where had he lived when she last heard from him? Did she own a picture of him? Well, that was a pity, but——

Addresses, facts. Police descriptions, or at least Lieutenant Winterung's descriptions, covered a good deal more, I found, than color of hair, black; color of complexion, sallow; build, thin and tall; eyes, bluish gray. They covered theatrical agencies with which he might be registered, skills other than professional ventriloquism by which he might earn a living, places he might frequent for amusement, make of car driven, license number of car, where car was registered, any likely aliases, any chronic complaints which might take him to a doctor, any dental difficulties which might bring him to seek oral care. By the time he finished, Roke Bradsher was pinned by definition at every point you could think of a pin being applied.

"I guess that's it, Phil." When he was done with this—during the last of it he'd sat behind the desk, methodically noting answers as the girl supplied them—the lieutenant turned again to Phil. "We'll get the fellow in. Ought to have him inside a few hours. I'll contact the Alabama police, of course, see what they have on this Bement story. I'm glad you came around; if more people——"

We were ushered to the door by reflections on civic duty, dismissed with encouragements directed mainly at me.

"Don't worry any more, Mrs. Kiskadden. Keep your doors locked, but you won't be in any danger; I'll put you on the patrol car alert schedule; there won't be any unidentified men in your neighborhood."

There's no doubt that he held to this promise, at least the part about putting us on an alert schedule for the patrol cars. No whistling fretted us that night. Every time I went to the door during the evening, it seemed to me, there'd be the two blazing eyes rolling nearer along the street, revealed, at the moment of passing, as forerunners for a white and black car. We were having an otherwise busy evening too. I'd felt I had to tell the tale of the girl's existence and her arrival to Dorothy Albiguard, and from that, and the neighbors, the news had got around. The phone had rung on and off all day, and that evening no fewer than eleven sets of people dropped in, to repeat exclamations, and employ covert stares, and hug me expressionlessly as they left. The last set was just going when Phil called, about eleven. Winterung, he said, wished the girl and I would come back to the station, if it wasn't too late; his men had picked up someone.

# CHAPTER SIX

"YOU DIDN'T GET the wrong impression?" When the three of us, Phil, the girl and I, turned up at the door of his office, Lieutenant Winterung's greeting was a careful putting right. "This man's not Bradsher. For some reason we haven't yet rousted Bradsher out. One of our patrol cars, though, turned up this other fellow, hanging around in your alley between a garage and some bushes. He hasn't given much reason for being there. It might save time, I thought, if you'd take a look."

I was willing enough to look, even if I was half expectant, half fearful—though why I should have been this last, I don't know—of what we'd see. We were led, not to the office where we'd been that afternoon, but to another one farther back, a larger one containing in the way of furniture four desks instead of two, half a dozen chairs instead of four, a greater assortment of filing cabinets and stacked sheaves of curl-edged papers, but giving off the same air, even when well filled, of being somehow empty. Its population, before we got there, had been composed of three people: two men, standing, whose build was such that they fell immediately under a tabulation of plain-clothes men, and another smaller man in a chair.

Lieutenant Winterung was entirely right. The man in the chair wasn't Roke Bradsher, not as Roke Bradsher had been described. A draggled overcoat had been added to encase the whole, but suit, polo shirt, swagger and smirk belonged to the man I'd last seen in the hall of the Georgia rooming house. Whose shadow, I was certain, had lain in the rectangle of light.

It wasn't hard to recall the start I'd had, seeing that shadow; the remembered emotion seemed to blend and merge with the half expectancy in which I'd come. Yet, looking at the man in the unobscured light which now circled him, it again was almost ridiculous to consider him as a cause for fear. Whatever effect might have been supplied by his swagger in that dimly lit hall, here any hint of youthfulness was gone, obliterated by the blue-red of his skin and its sharp fissuring; he must have been well into his sixties, and badly weathered for that. He still could be dapper, though. When, at a nod from Winterung, the two plain-clothes men fell back for our clearer view, the object of our attention pulled at once to his feet, raising his right hand in a gesture of sweeping off a non-existent hat, offering a bow.

"Roll my bones." The voice, expressive of astonishment, also carried the humming purr I'd remarked before. "Mrs. Sherry Lee Kiskadden. The other Mrs. Kiskadden too. You sure had lots of company tonight, your place. You never come down here for *me*."

Nothing that would ensue, so his manner implied, could affect him in any way; certainly nothing would dent either his sangfroid or his impudence.

Lieutenant Winterung, behind me, asked, "Who is he?" and when I'd answered, commented in satisfaction, "I thought so." Then to the girl beside me, just in front of Phil, "You recognize him too?"

She'd been quiet all evening—quiet against my friends' inquisitiveness, quiet against their obvious if unexpressed dismay. When I'd informed her of Winterung's request, she'd responded with a bleak "Do I have to?" On emerging from the house she'd shivered an even bleaker "It's cold out." Through the drive in Phil's car she'd not added a word to that, huddled in the front seat with Phil on one side, me on the other, head bare but coat clasped close, hands in pockets, shoulders curled forward for conserving warmth, thin face tight with strain. That strain wasn't easing as she gazed at the man who stayed standing before her; once again her pallor was turning transparently waxy, and the flesh of her face had pulled so close to the underlying bones that when her lips moved the ridge of her toothline was visible. Yet she spoke straightly. Tonelessly, but evenly.

"That's the one I was telling you about, all right. Ed Toomey. He's the one was down there in Georgia, just like she says."

Lieutenant Winterung offered to the man, "Gave us your name as Ed Martin, didn't you? What're you saying now?"

"You know how it is, Officer." The thin shoulders lifted the overcoat for an apologetic but unperturbed shrug. "Toomey—it's a name ain't so common around here. Sometimes I got to spell it out. Edward Martin Toomey. Sometimes I use all of it. Sometimes I don't."

"You'd like to add a little something to your story of what you were doing in that alley?"

The eyes in the gullied dark face—eyes small, glinting and light—seemed to eclipse momentarily while the mouth pursed for deliberate, reflective thought.

"Well, you know how that is too. I can be frank to say now, I guess—I didn't want to drag anyone into anything. A gentleman don't drag in a lady's name. I guess I can be free now to say, though, I got a little interest in Mrs. Kiskadden. Mrs. Sherry Lee Kiskadden." A superbly courteous glance, sent my way, implied that I need never have a worry, not from him, that he would particularize the girl by comparative age. "Not very much business, just a little business. She was friends once with a friend of mine. She says she don't know where that friend is at, but I figure—well, I figure sooner or later he'll be around where she is. I don't want to *bother* the lady, you understand that; didn't want to bust in on their company. That's why I was keeping so quiet, like. Just waiting around. I'd be the last one would ever bother——"

Winterung, in the midst of this, delivered himself of an outgoing breath whose velocity was enough to strike like a blast against the back of my neck.

"You were waiting for this friend of Mrs. Kiskadden's to turn up after ten o'clock? You'll have to do better than that."

"You caught me just leaving. I was there eight o'clock. I thought this friend might be coming then. I was looking over whoever come around. I was giving up——"

"You were giving up, hell. Why'd you leave the doll on the front porch?"

I hadn't been aware, exactly, that Winterung had pushed past, but by the time this question was put he towered in front of me, half obscuring the little man, who blandly stood his ground and who, to this last charge, returned a mild "Doll? What doll? I don't know nothing about any doll."

"One of Roke Bradsher's dolls. His talking dummy. It's Bradsher you're looking for, isn't it?"

Reflection for this was shorter—visible once more in the temporary optic eclipse, but soon ended. "Now you give the name, I guess I can be free again. You're right. Roke Bradsher. He's the one I'd like to see."

"Blackmailing him, aren't you? You know about that man he knifed in Alabama; you've been hushing it up, cashing in. That's why you——"

"Nothing is going to astonish me," Ed Toomey's manner had continued to say. "Nothing I can't handle will be brought up to me." In this last charge, though, he was meeting something he hadn't anticipated. Which swept up and slapped him like the backlash of a whale's tail. Ruddiness drained from his face, leaving an unalleviated blue that had a tinge of actual cobalt. The shoulders fell to a line that held no hint of swagger, the lips thinned and the polo shirt receded from the lapels of the overcoat, leaving a hollow.

He said, "Who said that? Who said Roke Bradsher knifed anybody?" The tone was as stripped as he.

"That's none of your business; we have full information. You knew he'd committed that murder; any knowledge you have must be——"

The silvery eyes weren't retiring for reflection any longer; they were slipping and darting like minnows. From Lieutenant Winterung to the girl, to Phil, to me. Undeflected by Winterung's response, he continued speaking. "Roke never killed nobody. I don't know nothing about Roke killing nobody." Denial, though, seemed merely negligent, a surface activity to cover something more important. Something which as soon as it was sure made him raise a finger toward Sherry Lee in what, while incredulous was no question but a statement.

"*She* told you Roke Bradsher knifed somebody."

"If you need a repeat, who gave us our information is none of your business. What we want of you——"

With a small, forward stagger, the little man began recovering composure. The shoulders came back up, defiantly, the polo shirt filled, a warmer color tinted the blue. He wasn't to be so shaken again. Stoutly, over and over, against questions shot at him now from one angle, now from another, he insisted he knew nothing of any killing. He knew of nothing whatsoever illegal in connection with Roke Bradsher. His business with Bradsher—well, if pressed, he might admit it did concern money. Roke owed him some. A debt. From a poker game. Not much, not much for anyone else, maybe. Just (reflection was visible here once more) around a hundred and twenty-five. Dollars. Peanuts for Roke; Roke was a boy who could haul in the coin.

Shown the doll, he was half moved, half indifferent. A little the same as the girl had been. He used several of the same words. "That's Roke's, all right. I seen him put on a show with her, many's the time.

He could make that Sis really talk. Sing, whistle—he sure could make her whistle pretty."

In proof of his statement that he'd done no whistling himself, he essayed a note, definitely weak and flat. "See? Never could whistle. Just one of those things I purely never could do. Ask anybody knows me. Ask Len Feasely. Ask this girl right here. Never did do no whistling."

Shown the card, he said he'd never seen it before. Asked how he'd come to know where the girl would be in Minneapolis, he replied reasonably, "Well, now, you take a lady leaves her car, with a car license, parked right out in front of a place, it ain't so hard to find out where that lady would live at."

Lieutenant Winterung, we were learning, was a man for fast finishes. As soon as he had this last he spent a split half second looking down at the contents of his hands—while the questioning proceeded he'd found a desk edge and his keys—then, after no more pause than this, turned to the two men who all this time had remained in the background. With a curt nod, he said, "Okay, you fellows," and stood up, from then on ignoring Ed Toomey completely, turning to the straggling row in which Phil, the girl and I had been left.

"That's all here, I guess." He had us at the door and through it before I scarcely was aware of moving. In the corridor he spoke again. "Step this way a minute, will you?" Leading us on toward his office, riffling through a stack of papers there until he came up with an unmounted three-by-five photograph, which he held toward the girl.

"That's a fairly good likeness of Bradsher?"

As bidden, she took the white-backed, dark-fronted rectangle into her hands, gazing downward for no more than the briefest of instants, before she said, "Yes, that one's pretty good. It's the one he had taken when he got on at the Black Rose Club. About a year ago now, I guess."

You'd have thought it would have held her, fascinated her,

seeing a delineation of the man who'd been her lover and who now was a threatening tormentor. Yet she spoke almost indifferently; her thin face had become wooden and stayed wooden. She reached to drop the picture on the desk, face down, fingers curling upward from it. Winterung's eyes on her were sharp, and there was a short silent hiatus before a gesture said it was Phil's turn and mine.

"Picture give you any ideas, Phil? You, Mrs. Kiskadden?"

Phil picked the thing up, holding it for me to see. Thin, tall, dark, adam's apple—the words had made pictures in my mind, here had been a reality joined in flesh. I'd been right in the term "scrawny"; the photographed man was young but gaunt. Shoulders bent slightly forward over the dummy in his lap, a dummy which was a fresher replica of the one Winterung had just shown to Ed Toomey down the corridor. But head back, chin belligerently up, a foxy jaw belying the thin smile on the mouth. Side-parted hair slicked smoothly, but a pointed strand edging forward, promising to fall the minute the tilt of the head was changed.

I stood looking for the thing that was different, setting him apart from normal human beings, the thing you always look for when you see pictures of murderers. There wasn't much: the only feature at all out of the usual, perhaps, was the glance of the eyes, hot and proud. Not eyes to meet in a dark alley.

Phil said, "Never so much as glimpsed him, I'm sure of it," and I shook my head too. Adam's apple, hair, jaw I might have passed somewhere and forgotten. I didn't think I'd have forgotten the eyes.

Lieutenant Winterung commented laconically, "You two don't get around. You don't even watch television. The fellow's no stranger; I guess he was a pretty good attraction at the Black Rose. Anyway, Joe Golies says so; that's where I got the picture. It's the one they had blown up for posters. If you women want to go on out—Phil, I'll have one more word with you."

Gallantry—another discovery we were making—could never

be said to be one of his attributes; the girl and I found ourselves shoved out, left to hang about in the corridor for as long as two minutes, while the men conferred behind the closed door. When they emerged Phil was newly grim, if he'd needed impetus in that direction, and Lieutenant Winterung's eyebrows said he was mildly astonished to find us still about. Yet he took time off for more official comment, again addressed to me.

"Not too much we can hold that fellow down the hall on, I'm afraid, Mrs. Kiskadden. Not until we get Bradsher too. Not for vagrancy; he admits not having worked since last spring, but he's got over forty dollars on him. For loitering maybe—that might give him a few days. We might do better turning him loose, tailing him to see if he manages to nose out Bradsher. I don't understand about Bradsher; with that picture to go on we should have had him by now. He must have been in town if he was the one put that card and that dummy on your porch. Don't worry, we'll get him, though——"

Perhaps gallantry, in Lieutenant Winterung, merely took a stern official form. Once home, Phil declined coffee but pointedly waited until the girl, having once said yes, she would like a little something, changed her mind as soon as I started for the kitchen. "No, wait. I guess not. I'm so tired I can hardly stand up. All I want is to get back to bed." Poor child—compassion for her ebbed and flowed, and right then it was flowing—she didn't look as if she wanted to do any talking. Between my friends and the day she was drained. I said I'd bring her up something. Phil waited until she was well away, and then brought out the upshot of his interlude with Winterung.

"I want that girl out of this house, Gail, and the sooner the better. Tomorrow we'll get her to a hotel where she can stay until we find her an apartment. Winterung's arranging a patrol here tonight, but that can't go on forever; he hasn't enough men. The girl will do as well elsewhere as here; she'll be safer, if it comes to that, than she is here with you. We'll see that she's made safe. A man like this Bradsher—the mess is the girl's mess, none of yours. I want you out of it."

A Sawyer reaction so typical I might give it attention, but not perhaps its full weight. When I'd got him away, when I'd brought the girl hot milk and a sandwich and tucked her in, when I had the lights off and drew near my own room, I was so tired I scarcely cared about anything—whether she was threatened or not threatened, whether there was danger of my being involved or no danger at all, what my friends thought, whether Lieutenant Winterung's men were playing ring-around-the-rosy on the lawn outside or whether they weren't anywhere near us, whether, in that night, the man I'd seen in the picture lurked somewhere near——

No, I wasn't indifferent to that last, not entirely. In pajamas and slippers, when I opened the window the regulation winter three inches, I looked out in the once more moonlit night, to the blue and white expanse of my snowy lawn, to the dark rise of the cedars, the farther loom of the neighboring houses and the crumpled gray of the sidewalks and streets; it was late by then, almost one. A car came past, not a police car, but following the patterned progression: intensifying shine of light, swift rush and roar of a dark low shape, then the sudden vanishing of that alien and fleeing brilliance, a returning to the softer and more static glow of the moonlight. Behind the walls of the houses, now, people slept. No one, not even a young couple, passed along the sidewalk; the only shadows were those immobile—tree, bush, house, telephone pole.

As soon as the blanket came over my shoulders I slept. A few hours later I woke, though. No sight or sound rousing me, merely the yeasting of a thought process which had proceeded while I slept. Ed Toomey had lied in that office. Must have lied. His very attitude said he'd lied. Except once. He'd been flabbergasted by the idea that the girl had informed Lieutenant Winterung about the Alabama killing.

It was only my mind that worked; against its pillow my head lay so heavy I couldn't have lifted it; my body was drugged. When I managed to turn enough to free the right arm on which I'd been lying the fingers of that hand were so rigid it took minutes of flexing before they began feeling like fingers.

Ed Toomey had been staggered by the fact that Sherry Lee had talked about Roke Bradsher's crime. "One of those little lice who prey on bigger lice." That had been Phil's contemptuous, dismissing verdict on Ed Toomey. It was a fierce-eyed man with a knife in his pocket who worried Phil. Phil might be right. Lieutenant Winterung's attitude had been more or less similar. Just the same, Ed Toomey was no man to be easily staggered.

I rolled entirely over and considered the little man. Following the girl to Columbus, hunting her out. Moving into the house she lived in—on this they concurred. Watching so closely he was there in the hall before I had the door all the way open. Yet willingly and without question directing me to her. Getting the license number of my car, watching under the stair until I left. Or listening, it might have been, outside the girl's door until he heard me getting ready to depart. Following us here. Watching here as he'd watched in Columbus. Imparting his cryptic reminders—the whistling, the card, the doll.

He wasn't acting in this on his own behalf. Behind him loomed the taller and more dangerous figure. He was Roke Bradsher's spy. The girl might have spoken truthfully when she said, "Not from me, ma'am. He didn't find out from me." Toomey might have sent Bradsher the license number or my address. Toomey, in that case, might have told the truth some of the time too. Bradsher might have been the whistler, the one who deposited the doll and the card, as we'd thought earlier.

Only why? Just as threats? It was all so elaborate.

Lying awake in the dark, mind alert, body detached, I considered that elaborateness with the solemnity belonging to night thoughts.

Bradsher, if what he wanted was vengeance, could have had it so easily. A man who laid for a fellow male, knifed him, hauled his body away to the concealment of a straw stack, was a man for succinct action. Not one for whistling mockingly along a street, leaving his castoff dummy at a door, sending a sacrilegious reminder of his presence.

It was almost as if there were three shadows. Ed Toomey's. Behind Ed Toomey's, Roke Bradsher's. Then, behind Bradsher's, another's. Darker, larger, spreading——

It was sleep, I thought. The sleep I'd so lately left, drawing me. I was growing adept at explaining myself. Phil, of course, was the one who was right. There was one principal in this thing, one only. Bradsher. Engaged in an activity which for him, with those eyes, would be perfectly reasonable. Getting even for what he considered an injury. In the morning I'd do what Phil said. Get the girl to a hotel. The Radisson or the Nicollet. A good big hotel with a doorman and a house detective. I'd find her an apartment. Lieutenant Winterung would have Bradsher halfway to Alabama. The whole thing would be over.

I slept again.

The next day, though, I didn't take the girl to any hotel. Lieutenant Winterung didn't have Roke Bradsher halfway to Alabama—he'd still failed to get him in custody. The tide of occurrences in which I was floundering was far from its ebb, it was barely in flood.

I found out the first in the early afternoon when, performing an action I resented but into which I seemed continually being pushed, I made my way to the girl's room. Eleven and no appearance all right; eleven was no more than her ordinary rising hour. Twelve and still no appearance—that I ticketed as deliberate seclusiveness, meant to indicate resentment of the performances into which she'd been forced on the day before. I'd called the Nicollet, long before then, to reserve her a room. An hour later I was telling myself that I could last better than she;

one midnight glass of milk and a sandwich wouldn't hold her forever. When it was two, though, and she hadn't as much as set audible foot to the floor, I began having heart-stricken visions of something amiss.

Self-guilt, already beginning, shot higher as soon as her invariable "Come in" allowed me a sight of her. She didn't have to say feebly, as she did, "I'm sick, I guess." Against her pillow the blonde hair lay limply, an aureole. In the midst of it her face was pinched, bluish—not the dark blue of Ed Toomey's weather-and liquor-ravaged countenance, but still blue. Dark half-moons underwrote the sticky lashes, and the hand she lifted to pull down the blanket moved as if there were nothing inside it but melting gelatine.

There's something amiss between me and pregnancy. Other women manage to keep it in mind. They can discern such states at times when I, told, see nothing but a usual slenderness. They can tell to a week what the limits are. Oh, faced with an absolutely incontrovertible fact, I can usually see that much; I never have any idea, though, how much time has elapsed backward or must elapse forward.

During the long drive from Georgia I'd remarked, desultorily, that as soon as we were home we'd have to get her set with a doctor. She'd answered, I thought comfortably, "Oh, there's no hurry yet." Monday, during the apartment hunt, I'd again offered to arrange a medical visit; she'd been in no haste then, either. Now, seeing her wan face and bumpy figure, I was forcefully reminded how ignorant a girl of her age might be, and how much I might mistakenly have taken for granted.

I asked, "Why didn't you call me? You're not having pains, are you?" Even to my own ears my voice sounded sharp; heaven knows what sharpened it was conscience; there I'd been, defying her to outstay me, when all the while she'd needed help. She couldn't know of my self-reproach, all that could have been audible to her was the tartness. Her own brand of stoicism flowed up over her face to set like an enamel mask. More than ever our relationship was such I couldn't rip constraint aside. "Get her out of your house," Phil said; an hour ago I'd been at the phone arranging that very removal. Over the phone I'd begun telling callers, "She'll want to be by herself, of course——" I couldn't be a person who, however doubtfully, concurred with Phil, and at the same time another who'd hold out warm arms, saying, "Child, there'll be nothing to worry you."

I did get the right queries made, more compassionately, I hope, than the first two. I did immediately get the right thing done. No, no pains, she said. The baby wasn't due for six weeks yet. Just—she'd been all right, really, until a bit ago. There hadn't been any need to call. Now she was hot for a while, cold for a while.

Dr. Grellman, who's our family doctor, has office hours in the afternoon; he must have cut some of them when I called. He didn't say much at his entry, little more at his departure. Just "I think she'll be comfortable. Get her in at my office tomorrow, though."

It was next day, in his office, that I found out how from then on the land would lie.

There'd been no question, necessarily, of the girl's going to a hotel that Wednesday; before Dr. Grellman so much as got there, I'd canceled the room. Too, I'd called Phil, whose very paucity of answer had sounded combative, but what was there for him to say? Under medication the girl improved, perking up enough in an hour or so to lie languidly against a bedrest at her constant occupation of hair brushing. On the Thursday she was able to dress for the office call which, instead of a usual twenty minutes, went on for an hour. And when Dr. Grellman ushered her out it was to beckon me in.

In a city such as Minneapolis you know your doctor; you don't chop and change. Dr. Grellman had been Howard's physician, he'd piloted Johnny into the world and gotten him through measles, the broken arm, innumerable gashes, a tonsillectomy and a more serious strep throat. I was accustomed to seeing him move with alacrity but also with a fair assurance. Right then the assurance seemed to have declined. When he sat he slumped, pulling off his glasses, rubbing eyes that looked tired and, more than a little, exasperated.

With the peevishness uppermost he asked, "Why didn't she get in to me sooner?" I was ready, I suppose, for self-defense; I began, "She's only been in my house these few days," but his interest wasn't in me, the hand with the eyeglasses brushed me aside.

"I don't mean you, especially. I mean her. Good Lord. She says that she's Johnny's wife. Do you know she admits, herself, she hasn't been to a doctor except for an original visit, back somewhere in May? It's almost inconceivable, these days, that anyone can hold an own life so cheaply. If she did make later visits she hasn't acted on advice. What she has now is a kidney infection. Well rooted. We may get an eclampsia. The blood count is 63. The pelvic aperture is unfortunately narrow." He was moving toward outrage. "In my practice I don't get cases like this, Gail. I'll want a specialist in for the birth; in fact, she should see one immediately. Dr. Legge, I think, if he's available. She's malnourished; if the baby comes through alive it'll have bones like chalk or gristle, I don't know which."

He broke complaint to be pathetic. "Sixty-nine. Seventy in the spring. Did you have to load this on me?" Smiled ruefully to indicate he didn't mean it, and turned to the sternly practical.

"I got enough of the background, I can guess how you feel. I'm afraid that can't make any difference, Gail; if you've a heart in your body you'll be putting everything else in your life aside to get that child through this next month. She says six weeks, but my guess is for less than that. She had a massive penicillin shot yesterday and another today. As soon as I get her an appointment with Legge she'll probably be seeing him daily, at least every other day. She'll be taking seven kinds of pills seven times a day. She's to have liver not once a day, twice a day. If she can get it down, give it to her for breakfast. If

I thought that the hospital—no, no, the only place for her is a house, moving around. Get her outdoors, see she has rest. Encourage and cheer her up, get her to relax——"

As if he hadn't already been impressive enough, he halted to begin over.

"Your every waking thought, Gail——"

Ed Toomey. A man who used a knife. Whistles in the night and a dummy at the door. Threats.

I didn't so much as bring them up. What would have been the use?

# CHAPTER SEVEN

FOR THE ENSUING six days it's not easy to get the right emphasis. Where there'd been mainly one course of distractions there now might be said to be two, keeping pace. On the one hand our efforts concerning the girl—her visits to Dr. Grellman, and, by Saturday, to Dr. Legge. Her diet. Scheduling her medications and checking on that schedule, a task she never took on for herself. If I left so much as an iron capsule to her memory she'd sooner or later be answering, "Oh, I guess I forgot."

Since she also was supposed to be active I forever was prodding her. For walks, for a movie excursion, for informal calls on the neighbors and on friends such as Dorothy Albiguard. To take up light tasks about the house. Toward one of these, the walking, she was blankly amenable; each afternoon around three-thirty she'd put on her coat and be off. A breathing space, I might add—not that it figures anywhere—which I spent at my solitaire in a kind of frenzy. She wasn't too bad at meeting people. It was activity inside the house which was least to her taste. There was one afternoon, in fact, when I suggested she might scrub baking potatoes for our dinner while I scraped her beefsteak; she got as far as holding the small brush in one hand, but instead of progressing from there merely stood at the sink looking more and more sullen.

I asked, "Anything wrong?"

She rolled out, "I never aimed to do nobody's dirty work," dropped the brush and stalked off, head bent for the fall of hair to hide her face.

Under the circumstances I'm afraid I was guilty of a reaction—not that this is important either—which kept me in the kitchen a good hour and a half before I was able to face her without opening my mouth. Encourage and cheer her up, Dr. Grellman also said. Get her to relax.

If this last hadn't been difficult enough as things were, it would have been kept difficult by the second series of distractions, which in a way now was out of our hands and which until the sixth day didn't climb to any new apex, but which just the same impinged daily. Ed Toomey, or so the newspaper briefly noted, was given five days. The Alabama state police didn't wait to answer Winterung's query by letter or wire, they riposted by long-distance phone. Yes, they did have an unsolved killing as described. In the spring of 1950 the body of a young man, later identified as that of William Bement, an itinerant farm hand, had been discovered under straw in a field four miles south of Andalusia. Further information which the Minneapolis police or anyone else might have on this killing or its perpetrator would be heartily welcomed.

Dropping this information in passing, Lieutenant Winterung and one of his cohorts pushed in through my house on Friday morning—that was November the twenty-first—to spend most of two hours with the girl upstairs. When they came back down for a departure they obviously planned to be as unceremonious as their entry, I managed to get in the major query. To it Winterung snapped, "Not a thing," and then added, glowering, "That girl was in any other shape, I'd be taking her in." Not a hint, I gathered, was being turned up as to the whereabouts of Roke Bradsher.

Yet twice, in those six days, I thought I heard the whistling. Not so near, it's true. From the next block, perhaps, or the alley. The same unmistakable tune, though. "Oh, I wish——" Each time, jumping for the phone, I got Winterung's office. Each time, afterward, there'd be so many police cars in the neighborhood, one went past every two minutes.

Phil, who had the callousness to ask, "She couldn't be putting on, could she?" about the girl's illness, and who hadn't been pacified even by a talk with Grellman direct, had taken to driving past the house three or four times in an evening; he was stopped, as he concurringly but yet resentfully admitted, twice. Bunky, as he also reported, was halted for questioning any time he came home late from the university library or a date. Neighbors began a more cautious tune, "Gail, what *is* with you, anyway? Last night when Carl got in——"

The laundryman, the dry cleaner, the towheaded grocery boy, usually so talkative, began being curtly businesslike except for long covert looks. Few men, I gathered, came into our vicinity unless they encountered scrutiny.

Except the one sought.

I suppose it is impossible to convey the tension, the urgency, the restlessness, the feeling of things-can't-go-on-this-way, which began possessing me. Personally engaged in the hunt I might not be, but it was so patent around me I couldn't have stayed unaffected even if it hadn't touched me so nearly. I'd have been happier if I could have engaged in it personally. The strain, the uncertainty, the anything-may-happen were too corseting to bear. Going to bed my last thought would be "They must find him tonight." In the morning it was "There'll have to be an end of this today." I wasn't the only one; Phil, when I saw him, acted like a Hindu novice who was never going to get used to the hot-coals routine, and even Winterung, I gathered, was beginning to be edgy.

"He can't understand it." Sunday evening Phil dropped around for a somewhat fuller report, after Winterung that morning had taken time for a talk with him. "If what Vince tells me is true, then the dragnet by this time is one you wouldn't think a guppy could get past. What's especially annoying is that until the seventeenth of May, this year, Bradsher's whereabouts were so open and aboveboard. He was living in a rooming house on Cedar Avenue. Winterung visited the house. The girl lived there too, at the time, in a separate room. She seems to have stayed there until she went to Georgia early in June. Bradsher's act was a regular part of the dinner and evening show at the Black Rose Club on Hennepin, where Vince got the picture. Joe Golies, who runs the Black Rose, says the guy is an alcoholic and can get ugly, but he had a good act. On May seventeenth he came around to Golies in the afternoon, said he was taking the night off. No excuse, no explanation, no effort to supply a replacement, just that he wouldn't be there. Golies told him in that case he needn't come back. Bradsher appears to have been half seas over; Golies says Bradsher retorted that would be all right with him, he was ready to move on anyway. Drove off in his car, a banged-up 1941 Ford, and that's the last there is until Bunky saw him at the Palladium a few weeks ago. The landlady at the Cedar Avenue address says he must have been around, say, May twentieth or twenty-first, because his belongings were taken from his room, but she didn't see him take them. That kind of vanishing apparently didn't seem unusual to her; he owed her a little rent. May seventeenth is the last your girl upstairs will admit seeing Bradsher. Winterung has turned up Len Feasely, the man who ran the Feasely Shows until they broke up here; he's got a restaurant now, a diner out on South Minnehaha. Feasely says Bradsher used to drop around once in a while, but not since May. There's a chiropractor on Lake he used to go to for something in his neck; he hasn't been there since March. He hasn't listed himself with any of the theatrical agencies, isn't working as a professional ventriloquist anywhere—that sort of thing's easily checked. If it weren't for the glimpse Bunky had, if it weren't for that infernal dummy and the card, we could believe he'd left town to hole up. He might be in Kamchatka. Even if he left after he ran into Bunky, though, who then's been leaving those messages? Toomey? It's a merry-go-round. Vince isn't fiddling with this thing; he's a friend of mine, and he's out for business. But if there isn't something soon he'll have to let up somewhat. He's got too much else on hand. I wish——"

His wish was the same as mine, his wish was such that two or three minutes was the most he was willing to spend in a chair; after that he was up to steal glimpses past the draperies. Sinkingly I considered what life might be if, instead of the constant surveillance we now had, we were returned to the casual policing of normal times. While a killer with a grudge and a knife roamed at will, and the object of his grudge was in my care.

That eventuality, though, wasn't what met me. Not exactly and not then, at any rate. What happened next was that Ed Toomey, on Monday, was released from the workhouse. And on the morning of Tuesday, November twenty-fifth, he was found dead in one of the lesser-used sections of Glenwood.

It was Phil who told me. Before then, though, there'd already been half notice from a different quarter. Toward eleven in the morning of that Tuesday, the phone rang. Lieutenant Winterung, sounding freshly brusque, freshly determined, asked for the girl. He was never as polite as Ed Toomey. What he said was "Mrs. Kiskadden? Let me talk to the other Mrs. Kiskadden, the young one."

When I told him she wasn't yet up he wasn't deflected much. He merely threw curt orders at me. "Get her up. Get her dressed. I'll be around in half an hour. I want her ready to go with me."

Duty was so impressed on me that before anything else I began, "Dr. Grellman won't like it; he doesn't want her excited, doesn't want her under any more strain. I can scarcely——"

He cut in, "I'll call Grellman."

Need to know rising over responsibility, I began, "What——" but he wasn't waiting for query; a silent line said he'd hung up as soon as he'd made the promise about Grellman.

With this much to go on I did as commanded. "They must have that man Bradsher finally," I told the girl. That, of course, was the likelihood shooting to mind. "At last there's an end of this waiting; I don't myself see how we've stood it." In mistaken relief I not only was willing to chatter, I was ready to disclaim personal unsettlement to concentrate on what the ordeal had been for her. "You can be so much more easy from now on, you'll have nothing on your mind whatsoever except keeping well and getting the baby born."

Through all of the six days past I'd been doing my best to muster encouragements; she hadn't been entirely unresponding. At least when I said things such as "Thank goodness we have police of the kind we do," she'd answer tepidly, "I guess that's right, ma'am." If anything—and this was one of the things hard to understand—taut as she was, turned in on herself as she was, ready to fall into tremors as she was, she also continued evincing her remarkable hardihood. The first two times she'd heard the whistling she was shaken, the last two times, when I appealed to her ears, she'd done little more than listen with what might have been studied care, and then comment, "It's so far away. I wouldn't know if it was him or not." She seemed able to sleep nights, which—another admission—was more than I always did. I'd taken it for granted, at first, that when she walked I'd walk too; she'd dismissed me. "You don't have to go if you don't want. I'm not afraid daytimes."

If it came to a comparison of alarm—I'd had the actual thought—I'd have said in confoundment that I was prey to quite as much as she. Yet now when I waked her with Winterung's order, when I said, "They must have that man Bradsher finally," what she evinced looked like panic terror. She tried pulling herself up on one elbow, fell back, struggled to rise again. Over her face passed that effect of shrinkage which was getting to be familiar. Halting my congratulations in mid-flight, she croaked, "Who said so? Did anyone say so? Did anyone say they had Roke?"

It was so back-thrusting that I was able to do no more than

flounder. "Why no, no one said so. What else, though, could it be? It must be that. Why would Winterung——"

The hand not attached to the supporting elbow went up to her face, brushing it, beginning at the mouth, ending at the forehead, where it deflected to the characteristic smoothing of her hair. In its wake some of the shrinking passed. When she next tried to push upward she made it. Drawing her knees slightly outward for balance, she sat in her bed tossing back the hair.

"They never got Roke, then. They won't find him. They can't never find him." In the moment between this and the last of her questions the waking jet of terror seemed to have gone the way of the shrinking. She continued tense and uneasy, though, when I left her for dressing, and she still was tense and uneasy fifteen minutes later when, pre-breakfast cigarette alight, coat on, hair forever asking attention from a hand that forever gave it, she came downstairs. There's a difference, just the same, between tension and uneasiness, and the kind of emotion that had spurted, however briefly, as she woke. She got down orange juice, coffee, and a slice of toast. I doubt if a throat in the state hers had been when she choked out, "Who said so?" could also have allowed passage for toast.

Again, inescapably, I was caught in a whirl. One in which I said to myself, "Of course she doesn't want him captured. When he is he'll know she's informed on him. She's more afraid of that than she is of his being at large." *What manner of human was he, this man who aroused such terror?*

To underwrite my expectancy, not one car swooped to our curb, at this juncture, but three. When the men—Lieutenant Winterung, Phil, Dr. Grellman—came in through the front door, Dr. Grellman was arguing.

"—no sense or purpose in it. I don't see why I should stand for it. I'm on record right now as objecting." One thing Dr. Grellman usually is meticulous about is putting on his hat; he wears strands of side hair combed over a bald spot. That noon he must have jammed on his headgear; one of the long gray wisps straggled sideward from under the brim. Phil, behind him, wasn't distracted in quite the same way; he merely looked tight and alert. Winterung, entering last, was the one who was more charged than Grellman. The forward push of his body was ruthless and the line around his mouth was as hard as brutality.

In reply to Grellman he said flatly—the girl had gone back upstairs for her handbag—"She knows where Bradsher is, I'm convinced of it. I don't have to be told when somebody's holding out. I'm going to shake her into coming across if it's the last thing on this earth I do. Rustle her down, Mrs. Kiskadden, will you please? I've had enough of this niff-nawing."

Dr. Grellman was again objecting when, obediently, I ran upstairs; he was still objecting and following when, with a hand under her elbow as soon as she descended, Winterung told the girl grimly, "I've got a little something more for you to look at, young lady," and impelled her through the door.

Left behind in the hall with Phil, I at last got a question in, and it was then he told me.

"Toomey's dead. Some man living up back of Glenwood couldn't get his car started this morning. He cut across the park to the bus line, at the end, there, and noticed a foot sticking out from under a little brush. If you don't mind, I'll go too. If there's ever going to be any break in this——"

I didn't halt for thought, or for considering how grisly might be the sights I'd encounter, or how far from my habits it was to push myself into surroundings of the kind into which I'd be pushing. I merely wasn't to be left alone. I think I said, "She might need me——" and heaven only knows how much honesty there was in that. When Phil went out the door I was on his heels, coat and scarf snatched from the hall closet in passing.

The police car already was halfway to the corner when we stepped to the porch; there must have been a driver in it, waiting. Dr. Grellman's car was just lurching off. With that second car as leader—the first was soon out of sight—we trailed to Franklin and across Franklin to Nicollet, down Nicollet to Fifth. The building before which we halted was one from which, in the casual passages of other days, I'd usually averted my eyes—an unobtrusively labeled structure of pressed gray brick, fronting on a small lawn and extending deep into its block along an alley. Whatever his insistence, Winterung was showing some care for the girl; he hadn't hustled her so fast that, when we pulled open the heavy front door which held in a reek of formaldehyde, the group of three wasn't still in the anteroom. Dr. Grellman held his hand on the girl's wrist; he was frowning, but apparently longer reflection or what Winterung said had somewhat altered his attitude.

"You're all right, my child," he was saying then. "Take whatever occurs here as calmly as possible. If there is anything you know which you should tell Lieutenant Winterung, let me suggest that you do so; you'll be freer for it afterward." Winterung, at a window ahead, was speaking to a small man in a white jacket. I put my hand on the girl's hand. Not the one Dr. Grellman was releasing, the other one, the one gripping the strap of her heavy over-shoulder bag. She turned at the touch, the sharp mouth again shrunken, the dark glance from under the thickened lashes moving over me as if I were a stranger. But then, unexpectedly—and I can't tell you what it did to me, having it happen—she caught my fingers under her palm, against the strap; through that palm, through the arm my arm now brushed, I felt a kind of rhythm, a pulsing which communicated itself to me as the beat of a fear so possessing it crowded out all other experience.

It was this way that we took the next steps—the attendant

beckoning, Winterung motioning us to pass in ahead of him, the girl maintaining her clutch of my hand, taking me with her, Lieutenant Winterung falling in at our heels, Phil following with Dr. Grellman. Our feet clattered on travertine in a long starkly lit corridor, empty of everything but us and the smell. Then another room, an atmosphere that wasn't to be breathed. A bank of what looked like enlarged checking-room lockers. A door opened, a drawer pulled out.

No dapperness on the shoulders now. No smirk on the mouth. No mocking courtesy on the tongue. The little man wouldn't lurk under any more stairs, wouldn't wait in any more alleys. The ruddiness was gone from the face, leaving only the blue, a little brown. The hair, still dark, was brushed smoothly back from a forehead not badly domed, the closed eyes were sunken, the mouth rigid.

The attendant pulled down a sheet and we saw why Ed Toomey had died. Wounds in those shoulders leered thinly, like small askew mouths. Gray-brown along the gaping edges, faintly blue-dark within.

Beside me the girl drew in a long shuddering gasp. I had been shaking, too, in her rhythm. When the attendant pulled out the drawer I'd told myself I would shut my eyes, I didn't have to look. My purpose here—and I thought myself much more honest about it by this time—was purely in support for the girl. Yet I trembled as convulsively, as helplessly, as she. It was only after we'd stood there for what seemed blank eternity that I slowly grew aware of a change. I was trembling as I'd been trembling, partly by empathy, partly by strain. I no longer was doing so in unison. The girl had quit shaking or, if she still had her tremors, they were now in a different rhythm than mine. She kept her grip of my hand and the strap; maybe she'd forgotten she had it. She stood perfectly quiet and then stepped back. Nobody questioned, though Winterung, beside us, waited and watched. She spoke of her own accord, tonelessly.

"I guess it could be Roke, all right. He cut up that other man too, he said. He said that he cut him up good."

Winterung rapped sharply, "You can say that—you can stand here to look at his latest work, and not tell what you know of his whereabouts? Don't you know that a man who'll do this"—he pointed—"is perfectly capable of the same acts against you? Don't you know you're not protecting yourself, you're endangering your life every minute you——"

Her tonelessness, the settled lines of her face—not, in their shrunken rigidity, entirely unlike those of the man who'd said farewell to breath—didn't loosen. She said, "I told you. I told you I didn't know where Roke is—where he's living at. If I knew where he was hanging out I'd tell you fast. I don't want him to come whistling. I don't want him around with his knife. I can't help where he is. I can't find him; you know more about finding him than me."

As long a voluntary contribution as I'd heard her make. Longer, in fact. Almost as if it were the spate that goes with letting down. Somewhere in the middle of it her grip unfastened; I found my hand falling to my side. She had turned toward the door and was moving toward it and Winterung. Leaving Ed Toomey to the attendant with no more ceremony than, a week previously, he'd left the living Ed Toomey to the two plainclothes men at the police station, Winterung drew up alongside.

"Other times Bradsher left you, where'd he go?"

"I've told you. I don't know. Anyplace. Anyplace he could get him a job." She was making fast for the corridor now, and Dr. Grellman, who'd been behind us, was wheeling to catch up with the two of them.

"You've got some post office box someplace, where you leave messages or get them. You know some relative who keeps in touch."

"He never had no post office box and I don't know no relatives."

"Then what're you lying about? Don't you think I know a liar when I see one? You think because—let me tell you, there've been women give birth at Shakopee before this. For all I know——" She was so swift, leading, that by this she was back in the anteroom; as he came to the doorway he jerked to me.

"How about it, Mrs. Kiskadden? This girl out at all last night?"

Put at bay, floundering against the appalling inference, I stammered, "B-but that's impossible. She couldn't have managed it. She couldn't have——"

"I'm not asking could she have managed it. I'm asking could she have got out last night. Yesterday."

"I don't see how she could have got out last night." Still staggered, I tried considering the possibility. "I haven't been sleeping well. She'd have had to get past my door. She hasn't any housekey. No car. It was terribly cold last night——"

"Yesterday?"

"Well, yes. A walk. In the afternoon."

"How long?"

"Maybe twenty minutes. Thirty. It was cold then, too."

He swung back to the girl.

"*Meet* anyone on this walk of yours?"

Her turn to be once more at bay. She stood in a little island of isolation which Winterung's bulk formed around her, hand on the strap of the bag as before, eyes a little wider than usual, in them a look of being drawn away, puzzled, and faintly dazed.

"Only people. I was in at the drugstore. Walker's. Bought me a soda. They'll tell you there."

"Before that happens you'll be putting in a little more time with me. If you don't mind, Dr. Grellman, I——"

It isn't everyone who, at a moment such as that, comes up against a means of evading a questioning by a lieutenant of Homicide as determined as Winterung. She, though, was against one. Instead of offering any resistance, any reply to Winterung, she just seemed to withdraw. The lashes unsticking farther and farther in astonishment.

# THE WHISTLING SHADOW

The one hand dropped from the shoulder strap. In a moment both hands moved forward to lie flat, one on each side of her abdomen.

She bent a little forward and said weakly, "I got a pain, I guess."

"I knew this would happen. That opinionated bulldozing ignorant ass. That lout of an uncivilized plowman—what does he think he is, a juggernaut? I hope he's well satisfied. If I can't get hold of Legge——"

Savagery was confined to the mutter, the driving was smooth and unhurried. Lieutenant Winterung, tossed for a loss, had been left with Phil in front of the morgue; it was in Dr. Grellman's car that the girl and I were being conveyed. At the hospital I helped get her out of the car and up the steps.

"Let's all calm down, now; there's no hurry about this, no hurry whatsoever. Everything's in order; you're plenty far enough along so things should go well. No hurry, let's remember that. Legge will be here." At sight of the hospital Dr. Grellman began forgetting what was behind in favor of what was ahead. "No hurry whatever. Just take all this slowly and easily. Relax, child——"

And so we went into that space of time too.

A space which, then, seemed set apart, when facts about Roke Bradsher and anonymous threats and shadows and the doll and Ed Toomey lying dead were something to shove aside as for later, when all that had import was the one action at hand. I was allowed to stay with the girl until she was taken to the predelivery room; after that, together with one young man complacently expectant and another young man anxiously wild-eyed, I waited in a small room across the corridor.

This is no place for comments on the crisis of birth. However cut off you may in some ways be, though, whatever barriers you may have built against its concurrent emotions, you can't be anywhere near such an event without having it be a crisis. The complacent young man, occasionally turning back his coat to run a checking finger along two rows of cigars in an inside pocket, sat about smoking cigarettes, glancing at magazines, tunelessly whistling. The wild-eyed young man walked the floor, lit cigarettes and threw them down unsmoked, twisted himself away to stare desperately at corners, jumped every time someone walked in the hall outside. I tried to sit still, couldn't. Got up to look out the window. Got out to walk in the corridor. Snatched at passing nurses to ask if Dr. Legge had come, only to be told the speaker didn't know. Tried not to be thinking of Johnny——

If the baby were his, he was the one who should have stood at this window, walked this corridor, agonized over Dr. Legge's absence. His hands, clammy, should have clamped and unclamped in his pockets.

I was two people, waiting there.

A dimpled and handsome nurse, after time had passed, came out to smile at the distraught young man. "Mr. Tevis, you've a fine seven-pound daughter, and your wife is fine too." The distraught young man, obviously so limp he was barely able to stand, lurched away with her. The complacent young man began frowning; he told me in an attempt at humorous complaint, "we got in here before *they* did." It was his turn to pace and light cigarettes he didn't smoke, complacency ebbing. After another while a tall thin man strode swiftly from the door across the hall, said in a clipped way, "Mr. Monahan, your wife is all right, but I'm afraid there's a little something——" That young man was led away too. I saw him just once later, stumbling past the door, his face white and stunned.

After that Johnny and I waited alone. For hours, in what came to be a cell. Until something after seven in the evening.

Dr. Grellman is well fleshed, but he can also look gaunt. He was looking gaunt when he emerged from the door across the hall, sleeves still rolled up, surgical cap covering the top of his head, mask under his chin.

He said, "She made it. God, it was a tussle, but she did it. Legge never did turn up; I guess he was in on a worse one. Nobody might think it, but when that girl comes to an end, she's got what it takes. No complications so far, either. You've a grandson, Gail——"

## CHAPTER EIGHT

IT MIGHT BE BETTER, he said, if she saw me an instant. Reassuring. So I saw her for the instant. She was feebly awake.

"You did awfully well." Bending close, I began on one of the things always said to new mothers. "Dr. Grellman says you did awfully well."

She smiled dimly. Someone—a nurse, it might have been—had washed her face. Or else in the valley she'd shed all her beauty aids, including the gummy substance ordinarily thickening her lashes. There on the high aseptic bed in the darkened hospital room, that ethereal hair loose on the pillow, features sharpened and cleansed, lashes a pale silky golden brown, she looked childish and ineffably innocent. I had a revolution of attitude so overwhelming that my interior seemed to rise, shake itself like an earthquake, and settle to a different pattern. In the reservations and doubts I'd been holding against her I was wrong, criminally and cruelly wrong, as wrong as Phil had been in asking, "She couldn't be putting on, could she?" Through the fortnight or so of my knowing her, I hadn't even been willing to think of her by her given name.

As an evidence of other surrenders, I got out a choked "Sherry Lee, you've a lovely son."

She smiled again and drifted off to sleep. Dr. Grellman conducted me out.

I saw the baby that same day too. As a counterirritant to the upheaval he saw I was in, as a relief from his own exhaustion, Dr. Grellman did what he usually does in such circumstances, attempt a pleasantry.

"Since you're here as a father"—as usual, too, the pleasantry was a little heavy-handed and obtuse—"I guess we extend you a father's courtesies." He went with me around to the curtained nursery window, rapped on the door beside it authoritatively, went in, and returned to stand beside me while, on the other side of the glass pane, one nurse, smiling, ran up the curtain on the room of little bundle-filled white canvas baskets and another nurse, also smiling, emerged from a side room after a short wait, to hold toward me the swathed infant in her arms.

Yield again, my emotions were begging me. Yield at once. You can't shut yourself off any more, you've decided that. This is Johnny's son you're seeing.

With a remnant of recalcitrance which it seemed unable to dislodge, my mind stubbornly shot back, "Maybe yes. Or maybe Roke Bradsher's son. A murderer's. A man who——"

"Five pounds, three ounces, I understand," Dr. Grellman was commenting. "Not bad for an eight months' child."

To him it may not have seemed bad; to my eyes the wizened little scrap in the blanket looked unfinished and raw. Reddish blue, thin—no, scrawny was the word. No other visible similarity to Roke Bradsher, but as thin as Roke Bradsher. Head no bigger than a baseball, soft and somehow mashed. Creases where the eyes should be, flat nose, barely perceptible lips. Bunchy cheeks. A neck so pipestem-thin you couldn't imagine it ever supporting anything.

Johnny was as bouncing as babies come. At birth he'd weighed almost nine pounds. He'd had hair, downy dark hair, and this baby was bald. There wasn't a feature to remind me of Johnny, not one. Nothing to make me think, "This is the way babies in our family look." The hands were so tiny, lying motionlessly up toward the cheeks, that the fingers might have been crumpled reddish twigs.

But then, just before she smiled more intensively, nodded and turned away, the nurse expertly shifted the child in her hands just a trifle, displaying the back of its head.

I don't think I was capable of another upheaval, not so soon after the last. But I went through something, in the midst of which my heart behaved as if it were a bouncing bubble.

You know how the backs of Dutch children's heads look, the ones in old paintings. Very full, especially next to the neck. Just above the neck there's almost a little overhang.

Johnny's head was shaped like that through all of his babyhood. So was this child's.

In the hospital lobby Phil was waiting. Sitting in one of the armchairs, overcoat folded aside in another chair, open magazine in lap. As soon as he saw me he was on his feet coming forward, the light of relieved expectation beginning on his face, only to be superseded by a more alarmed expectation as he came closer.

"Gail. Everything's all right, isn't it? There's no———"

"Everything's fine," I told him. I was able to guess how I looked; I'm not one of those people who can wade through a torrent of emotion unmarked. "The girl—Sherry Lee is all right and the baby's a boy. He's all right too."

He said awkwardly, "Oh. Well, I'm glad." Congratulation turned sober and reluctant, but he made it. "I suppose it's wonderful, whatever the circumstances. I suppose every birth successfully accomplished is wonderful. I ordered some flowers; I thought if no one else—— If you don't mind, I'll call Vince, he might like to know. Wait for me."

The last trailed in his wake as he made for a phone booth.

Left to stand, I felt myself being peeled, layer by layer, of all the isolating absorptions which had blanketed me since noon. Rawly chill, I was back in the restless disturbance, the endless questioning from which I'd been snatched away, and which made it impossible for me to reach any real peace, build any sound and lasting fellowship with Sherry Lee or anyone else, until some resolution was found.

"If you don't mind I'll call Vince——" While I waited abovestairs, while Phil, for a final hour or two anyway, waited down here, Lieutenant Winterung had been somewhere at the end of a wire, also waiting. A little perturbed, it might be, by what he'd precipitated, but bulldog-sure in his course. Roke Bradsher, who had been important enough to hunt as the described actor in a murder two years past, was now a killer who'd moved at what amounted to our feet. Who doubtless was all too ready to move again.

When Phil came back I was on tap with a query not actually rising as high as hope.

"I don't suppose——"

A headshake shattered possibility. "A little on Toomey. Nothing on Bradsher." He switched to an abrupt "You. When did you do any eating last?"

After my answer it wasn't until he had me across a table in a restaurant booth, with clam chowder making its way toward my interior, that he was willing to add to that.

Leonard Feasely, hauled in for a second questioning, had agreed that Ed Toomey was what Sherry Lee said he was. A roustabout who'd mostly helped tend a string of ponies. Feeding them, handling them in the riding ring, lifting children to their backs and down again. Sleeping anywhere he could find, which sometimes meant the pony trailer. No known antecedents, though he'd spoken of himself as a Westerner. No known criminal record. Not making much, but always having pocket coins. A shrewd poker hand. A crony of Roke Bradsher's, just as Toomey himself had said. If Bradsher could be said to have a crony. He'd also run errands for Bradsher, helped sometimes with his tent, hung about him a good deal. Yes, played poker with Bradsher, sometimes winning. Feasely had been in on games too. Bradsher had beat Toomey up a couple times, once knocked out a tooth. Toomey hadn't seemed to hold it against him. Bradsher was a guy for beating guys up.

Feasely hadn't been quite so talkative when it came to the knife. Yes, he had known Bradsher had one. Had seen it on him. Never had seen him use it, though. Oh, threaten, maybe, playful like. Not get serious.

"Vince is holding him, hoping he can shake out something more. Knowledge of the Alabama killing, maybe. He wouldn't be mad if he could get collusion. He doesn't really believe it, though. He says Feasely is fat, but outside that doesn't seem such a bad guy. What's got Vince's blood pressure boiling is what happened yesterday. There they were, they had Toomey in the workhouse. He was brought in with a busload, released at ten in the morning. Tailed. No scrummy tail either, Vince says. One of his best. Toomey shook this tail in the most unbelievable spot he could have picked, the newspaper reading room at the public library. The first thing he did at ten o'clock, the tail says, was start in at the Fifth Street end of Hennepin and buy a drink or two at most of the bars down to Ninth Street. There he went into the newspaper room, picked a paper from the rack, and settled himself among the other bums—you know how they use that room—snoozing behind the paper. The tail says he was three sheets to the wind, had to be, after the drinks he'd had. About once every two hours he'd shake himself to his feet and stagger to the rack for an exchange of papers. The librarians like to know, that way, that they don't have to be calling for a stretcher. Along about six o'clock he was up at the rack again; the tail was wondering how he could get a relief and some chow. All of a sudden the guy he had his eye on at the rack wasn't Toomey. One minute it was, the next it was a bum pretty much like Toomey, and Toomey was gone. The tail really rustled; he was in and out of that room like a whip, he says; he got janitors watching the doors. No use, the fellow was gone. They had a special detail all evening, around in the bars. Nothing until the Glenwood guy called his local station this morning."

I protested slowly, "There must be signs where it happened. A man as small as Ed Toomey, even—he was wiry and quick. He wouldn't simply have stood to be knifed."

"Oh, there are signs, all right." Phil's exasperation might have been a carbon of Winterung's. "I went out to Glenwood myself. They're just not signs that *point*. What Vince thinks happened is that Toomey did some thinking, those five days in the workhouse. Something that came up, maybe something he heard the girl say, maybe something about her having told of the Alabama killing—remember how flabbergasted he was by that?—made him guess where Bradsher could be reached. He deliberately set out to shake his tail, and the first thing he did, free, was get to Bradsher. Calling him, probably, making an appointment to see him there at Glenwood, back of the ski slide. The killing took place right there. Undoubtedly what Toomey wanted was money, just as he said. Only not for concealing the Alabama killing any longer, that was known. What he'd want pay for, then, was keeping quiet about Bradsher's whereabouts. Those whereabouts must be such that Bradsher doesn't want to give them up. Not having worked since May, he likely doesn't have too much money left. He pulled his knife instead. You can see the area where they threshed around. Not an awfully big area, roughly a circle, with the snow trampled and a little blood here and there. A few bush twigs torn off. It's far enough from people so if Toomey yelled no one might have heard it; chances are Bradsher got him by the neck first and he didn't have time to yell. Anyway the first couple of stabs got him, the rest were just vindictive. He——"

Pictures I didn't want to see, which brought back visions of the still figure in the locker drawer, which made the steak Phil had mistakenly ordered me something to shove aside.

I insisted faintly, "If twigs were broken off, then surely——"

"Okay, if Vince had the guy. There might be pine needles caught in his clothes. Threads snagged. Blood, even. But Vince doesn't have the guy. Doesn't know any more about where to look for him than he did before. Tracks from there lead toward the bus line. The bus drivers have hundreds of passengers in and out. None of them remembers anyone like the picture Vince's men are flashing. None of 'em so much as remembers Toomey, yet Toomey must have gotten there someway too. All we know is what didn't happen. Bradsher didn't leave his knife. Bradsher didn't drop any handkerchief. Bradsher didn't lose any buttons. Bradsher's overshoes in the snow made normal-size holes, and that's all you can say for them. He didn't leave any threads loose on bushes. None of the things killers conveniently leave in books. Just nothing. Except Ed Toomey."

I took in a breath, considering the exasperating ability the hot-eyed man had, not only to keep up the unlikely, which he'd done before, but also now effecting the impossible. Stealing out of his secure hiding, meeting Ed Toomey at an appointed spot, killing him, returning to the harbor of his hideaway without having cast off a single clue.

I said, "He can't get away with it. Not in Minneapolis. Not with Lieutenant Winterung after him. He's got to get food somehow. If Ed Toomey reached him so easily, he must have a telephone. There must be *people* who know where he is. With that description being broadcast, and the picture——"

Phil stayed bleak. "Oh sure, Vince will get him eventually. He's gone over the buildings at the fairgrounds. He's ransacking the flophouses. Only—well——"

He hadn't been eating much either; he'd ordered coffee and a sandwich. The coffee was gone, but the hand that should have maneuvered the sandwich had gone more often to let a forefinger run along the trail of the BB shot. His glance came to me, but then slid away. The lines around his mouth had bitten in another quarter inch.

Unable, as usual, to let time lag, I asked, "Well what?" and he let out his worst doubt.

"Toomey must have had time for talking to Bradsher; almost certainly the first thing Toomey would say was that the police now know about the Alabama killing, and who'd given the information. That's why the girl won't be allowed any visitors at the hospital, except you. Friends or no friends. Nobody. Vince has made that order flat. That's why I spent most of the day on apartments, and found one. That's why you won't be going back to your house tonight, you'll be staying at the Curtis."

I protested, as a matter of form. Seeing no motel room, now, but my own room swim up to me. My own wide bed under its creamy luxurious spread, the night table where the two decks of cards waited in case the dark hours proved empty of sleep, the light above set exactly right, the soft hooked rug on the floor, the habited path to the bathroom. For an instant, ridiculously and quixotically, I had a flash of what might have been fellow feeling for Roke Bradsher. There he was, he had somewhere a snug retreat too. And Ed Toomey, demanding the impossible, threatened to shut him away from it.

Naturally that flash didn't last long; in its stead came a pretty vivid realization of what it might be to wake in my house alone, suspecting that same Roke Bradsher was near in the night outside, not knowing that Sherry Lee, who had left him for Johnny and then transgressed a second time by making known his past crime, wasn't there but in a hospital.

For twenty years I'd thought of my house as being safer than churches.

Phil, that same evening, accompanied me to it, for picking up my night things. Together we secured it, checking the thermostat, the door locks, the faucets, the window catches. In the car, breaking into a rehashing of the killing and how it might have come about, he brought forth a fact which had nothing to do with the matter in hand and which it seemed to me he might better have kept to himself.

He said, "Incidentally, I suppose there's just a possibility you might see Evie. The room you'll be having is one I originally got for her; she wrote her case was coming up on November fifteenth, and to arrange a room for the twentieth. I haven't heard from her since; she must have had some delay. I wasn't able to get you anything else on short notice, and as long as there's this one empty——"

He was having the grace to be ill at ease; in fact while he was saying it he came so near running a stoplight I had to screech, "It's red!" and we shrieked to a stop four feet past the white line. He couldn't let it alone, either, but had to keep gnawing. "Not that I actually believe she'll turn up without letting me know; I'd expect her to wire me to meet her train. I just wouldn't want you to have any unexpected——"

That was just dandy too. That made it impossible for me to do anything but enjoy the night, waiting for a knock which would bring me face to face with Evie's skywriting brows. "Really, Gail, what are you——"

As it turned out, that wasn't one of the things that happened, either. Not that night nor any of the ten nights I spent high in the hushed and girded confines of Minneapolis' most impeccably irreproachable hostelry. All it did was add its small quota to my sense of being harried and pushed and shaken out of my orbit, with a goal ahead—Roke Bradsher's removal from activity—which stayed endlessly a necessity, endlessly not effected.

Except for a few divergences, what I did during those ten days came well under the heading of commonplace. Daytimes I went around to my house—even Phil didn't classify that as unallowable. I visited the hospital. I called people, fending off inquiry, alarm and astonishment. I bought a layette, crib, baby chifforobe and bathinette. By that time it caused me little surprise to find Sherry Lee hadn't laid in as much as a diaper. I picked up a few Christmas gifts. I went around to the apartment of which Phil spoke: trust him, it was right for the circumstances. An upstairs, being remodeled, in the home of a family of which the maternal member, coyly giggling through at least two hundred pounds of muscle, admitted she had done a little wrestling as a girl. The father was a truck driver and the two sons played high school football. The single entrance led up inside front stairs past this interested group. One drawback only: the place wouldn't be ready for another month.

I couldn't say Sherry Lee sounded elated over it— "You can go ahead and take it if you want" was her response to my description. But I did anyway a little, looking up sizes and makes of electrical equipment, lining up possible livingroom pieces. Try as I might, though, I wasn't able to keep my mind on such activities. Mornings I couldn't wait for the paper at my door, I'd snatch one in the Curtis lobby as soon as I was off the elevator. Poor Phil—I interrupted his working hours thrice daily. Men who answered phones at police headquarters got so they didn't ask my name. The eroding thing was that there appeared to be *no* progress.

"Can't understand it." It wasn't often I got to Winterung in person, but according to Phil that was getting to be one of his stock phrases. "In a case such as this they usually get floods of tips, people thinking So-and-so must be the wanted man. They're not even getting many of those. They've been checking over the summer houses in the Lake Minnetonka area———"

Unable to leave it, I did a constant checking of my own. Never a male salesclerk came up to me, never a bus driver gave me change, never a man passed on the sidewalk, but I tried to fit him to the picture. A good many men were dark, tall, thin. Many men had sharp jaws, prominent adam's apples and quick proud eyes; none was the man of the picture. All I got for my pains was more strain, more uncertainty, an invitation to dinner, and a tentatively proffered reflection that beautiful friendships had sprung from nothing more than two people waiting on the same street corner for the same bus.

Also I was pushed farther than that. Those were my divergences. Thanksgiving came on the Thursday which was the second day after the baby's birth; Phil and I, turning down outside invitations, planned to have dinner, just the two of us, but at the last minute Bunky came too. He phoned to ask how things were, lonesomely admitting he'd been scheduled to eat somewhere with his parents, but they'd gone out for a champagne breakfast at eleven—it was then almost seven in the evening—and weren't yet home. The three of us sat over plates of restaurant turkey, restaurant dressing, restaurant cranberry sauce, beautifully served in a setting of music and well-dressed people, but somehow not the same edibles as home turkey or home dressing or even home cranberry sauce. We tried talking about other matters—Phil that day had had a wire saying, "Happy thanksgiving writing soon Evie"—but before I knew it I'd fallen into a helpless "It mightn't have been Toomey who got to Bradsher, at all. Suppose it was Bradsher who got to Toomey. He could have read about the arrest, waited and tailed him, beckoned to him in that reading room——"

Phil contributed, "Vince must have considered that. He's not leaving out anything."

Bunky added, "What gets me is the girl. You wouldn't think she could be so bad. I ran into her on my way home from school one day and got in a talk with her. She seems just sort of—well, you take a girl like that——"

For the first time I had a vision of another thing I might be doing, bringing a girl such as Sherry Lee into my neighborhood. Into contact with boys such as Bunky. And Dorothy Albiguard's son Todd.

I was rigorous with Bunky. And, inconsequentially, it seemed to be this little incident which made the standstill more abrading to my nerves than ever. Somewhere there must be facts which Lieutenant Winterung and his cohorts were too dense to get.

Instead of going home from the hotel next morning, I drove up downtown Cedar Avenue, and I suspect from the way they ached afterward that my jaws were clamped. In the absence of accurate memory, I parked in the middle of a block, and set about methodically asking a question— "Is this where Miss Sherry Lee Givens was living last spring?"—until I came to one where a sour-visaged woman returned, "You mean where there's been all the fuss about? That ain't here, lady. That's four doors down toward the corner."

By then I knew what the neighborhood was. When I'd tramped along the sooted ice crusts of the sidewalk to the house four doors down, it was no surprise to find it well in the pattern of the Georgia rooming house. A tall rusty-green dwelling house pricked with soiled white, whose elaborate wood carvings and sidelit door spoke dimly of old claims to elegance, but whose yielding porch boards and splintered siding talked louder of later decay.

The woman who answered here, also, was pickle-faced. Demanding, "What do you want to know about her for? The cops been here plenty, ain't they?"

I told her what I was there for, trying to make it as mollifying as possible. Barricading the door with the gaunt bulk of her person, the woman wouldn't so much as let me in.

"I told you the cops been here. I had trouble enough now, all you snoopers." She was making it loud enough so anyone in the house, anyone on the street, for that matter, might audit her belligerence. "Who lives in my house is my business. What gets done in my house is my business."

I tried pleading, "All I'm hoping for is one little break. Someone you might remember who came to see Mr. Bradsher, it might be. Who'd know where he went from here. Some little fact which would help to identify him. Some——"

Instead of answering, she stood just as she was, looking more resistant rather than less. More resistant even when she began smiling, her lower lip loosening as she did so with an effect I can describe only as evilly contemptuous.

She said softly, slashing the words at me, "You wouldn't happen to be really looking for a room for yourself, would you, dearie, now? I get ladies like you, your age, looking for a room they wouldn't want their husbands should know about. Where they can come once in a while. If that's what you really want——"

I tried walking with dignity, leaving there. I knew what she was doing, she was cutting me to size. Just the same my face was so scorched my eyes kept watering even after I was back in my car. That should teach me to go sticking out my neck. That should show me what happened to amateurs. That should——

That answered one thing for me, anyway. It wasn't Johnny who'd picked that rooming house in Columbus for Sherry Lee's residence. She'd done that; it was her customed habitat. He'd left her in it. Maybe his feet hadn't rung on that sidewalk. Maybe he hadn't hastened there eagerly; maybe there never had been anything between them but the briefest of casual conquests, here in Minneapolis.

And the marriage. For which who was responsible? I. I who had taught Johnny never to cut and run, but to stand fast and take his deserts.

My descent on the Black Rose Club took place the next afternoon after I'd been to the hospital.

Between the Black Rose and the other bars along Hennepin there wasn't much to set it off as a supper club; merely a single poster, bearing a likeness of a handsome Negress in a low-cut sequined gown, and announcing, "Billee Dee, singing nightly." All last winter and last spring, that would be where Roke Bradsher's picture stood, saying he'd appear with his Hillbilly Sis. I entered under neon tubing which at that time of day was dark, coming into a long wide room split by a center bar and crowded by checkerclothed tables. When I asked a passing waitress for Mr. Golies she glanced at me indifferently, said, "That there door along on the right," and went about her business. There didn't seem to be any cinematic barriers surrounding Mr. Golies, no plug-uglies, no electrified doors. I walked along to the right, knocked on the indicated door, which said, Manager, and was accorded a peevish invitation, "Okay, okay. Come on in."

According to hearsay Mr. Golies was a survivor from prohibition bootlegging; he looked a harassed small business man. He looked, in fact, a beleaguered lower-class Milquetoast, not yet gone entirely gray. When he saw me he stood, limply, apologizing for the curtness.

"I didn't know it was a customer. Is there——"

He was even nearsighted; the small popeyes peered through thick lenses. I explained my errand, and he remained standing, leaning slightly forward to rest his knuckles on the desk top.

"Mrs. Kiskadden. That's the name you said, isn't it? I've given the police everything I know about Roke Bradsher. Roke Bradsher came here from the State Fair, where he'd appeared in one of the Midway shows, in the fall a year ago. He was an alcoholic, I'm afraid, and he could be surly, but he had a good act. He worked here until——"

Neat, precise, containing so many of the words Phil had used in relaying his testimony that it had the effect of a formula learned by rote. Yet I wasn't able to shake him from it, either.

"I employ forty people here. Entertainers come and go. I—well, Mrs. Kiskadden, I have ulcers. I go home early when I can. I don't see much of the entertainers. I'm not interested in their private lives." A slight increase in the look of harassment said he'd subjected his ulcers to quite enough additional badgering, and there wasn't much for it but to leave him with even less than I'd gotten from the rooming-house keeper, since I hadn't so much as a personal conclusion to draw.

You might have thought I'd had enough. There was yet one more thing I'd thought up to do, though, and I did that too. Making not for the Curtis, when I left the Black Rose, but for South Minnehaha.

# CHAPTER NINE

THE SIGN OVER THE DOOR said *Len's Diner*. The vapors emerging through the exhaust fan said the place specialized in fried onions, coffee and hamburger. The window held a fairly clean menu attached at reading height by scotch tape. The woman who wiped her way along the counter to ask what I'd have was reasonably clean too, even if the only locomotion left her was a duckly waddle.

Another woman, faster on her feet, was behind the partition; when I'd asked for coffee and a sandwich the order came right away. The coffee was passable too, even if the sandwich was a little dry. The only other customer, right then—it wasn't yet five—was a mailman with an empty leather pouch and a magenta face, gulping tea. When he left I had the heavy woman to myself.

And no trouble whatsoever. Not that it seemed, there at first, that she'd prove more helpful than the others, but what she had to give, she gave largely. When I asked if she might be Mrs. Feasely, she replied promptly, "That's me." When I told her I was Sherry Lee Kiskadden's mother-in-law, hoping against hope I might find something to end our tenterhooks, she swept me with a glance that took me in head to toe, said, "What do you know? Ain't it a caution what's been going on?" And within a minute sat balanced against a stool, launched into sisterly gossip.

Determination or no determination, I'd been having hard going with my resolutions about Sherry Lee. I'd not been taken by Joe Golies. I'd have hated to try putting into words my feelings toward the woman I'd come up against the day before at the Cedar Avenue rooming house.

107

But Edna Feasely, I thought, was a woman who, if I'd known her better, I might well have liked. It was relieving to find *someone* connected with Sherry Lee who was obviously an all-right human being. Edna Feasely showed herself as both warmhearted and life-loving. She wasn't an unshrewd woman, either. For her husband she indicated an honest respect—"You know about those cops holding onto Len? Len'll look out for himself, though. Always has."

On the killing, the gist of what she had to say was "You hear what they're telling about Roke Bradsher now? They're saying he killed Ed. Did you see him too, I mean Ed? All cut up. I can imagine Roke killing a stranger, like. That boy in Alabama, I guess he did that all right. I can't imagine him cutting up Ed, though. He always kind of looked out for Ed. Ed being such a little guy. Even when Roke got drunk and beat Ed up, he never beat him up as hard as he beat up some other guys. It's like Ed was one of Roke's people, like. Helping Roke put his tent up, back when Roke had a tent. Hammering his stage together, running his phonograph, helping with tickets when the girl wasn't around—it wasn't only the ponies Ed was handy about, he could be handy almost anywheres. Any time Ed wanted a job he could of got it right here with us. There was something about Roke, though. He always stuck to Roke."

Her voice was pleasant. Creamy, like a good tenor. As she continued talking I found myself being rocked a little. So far all I'd been told of Roke Bradsher had presented his surly side; she'd seen him at his more amenable moments, being a lord of the road, as it were, for Ed Toomey. I tried imagining the reversal which had led not only to the knifing but to its savagery. "The first two stabs must have got him," Phil said. "The rest were just vindictive."

Yet Bradsher must have been the one who killed Toomey. If he wasn't, who else was there?

Facing Edna Feasely across her counter, watching her three chins agitate as she spoke, I was caught back into the night thoughts I'd had once and dismissed. What were those? The shadows. Ed Toomey's, Roke Bradsher's. But behind Roke Bradsher another spreading shade.

No possible purpose was to be attained by going in that direction; all it did was make me feel dizzy from swinging out over such empty space. For no reason except that she now had apparently given everything she had to give on Ed Toomey, Mrs. Feasely was switching to comments on Sherry Lee.

"That girl's a trick, and no doubt of it. When she first come with the Shows she was pretty young—oh, I guess she'd been around a little bit before then, too. No, ma'am, I didn't know about her running off from any family. All she said to me was she was sixteen, and she'd been living with her folks somewheres, but she was sick of it and wanted to be away. We get 'em a lot like that. Kids. No more'n kids. I tried to keep her with me, like, and that went all right for a while, but then she met up with Roke——"

From there on the story was exactly the same as that given by the girl. Except that Mrs. Feasely hadn't known of the Alabama killing until Winterung had come around to question her husband. After the Shows had broken up a year and a half ago—"Television and all, it don't seem like carnivals get the business they used to get"—she hadn't seen much of Sherry Lee. Roke had come around, Sherry Lee hadn't. She'd heard the girl was selling tickets at one of the Hennepin Avenue movies, that was all. "I was glad she was going legitimate, like." Hadn't heard of her going with Johnny. Or with anyone except Roke.

"Roke sure didn't know it, her going out with your boy like she must of done. Roke was a real hillbilly, fetched out of Arkansas. Jealous as hell-get-out. She ain't lying when she says that."

With so willing a witness, I led her over what I wanted again and again. Had Bradsher lived anywhere else in Mineapolis except at the Cedar Avenue house? What other friends had he? Hadn't there been anyone of her acquaintance—someone from the Shows, it might be—

who'd spoken of seeing him? Who was there who might have harbored him?

She was obviously trying; at each answer her half-buried sloe eyes turned inward and her mouth pursed. "Let me think, now." Reluctantly, however, she was reduced at last almost exclusively to negatives. Except for Sherry Lee, Ed Toomey, and a little with Len, Roke Bradsher had been a man for sticking by himself. When the Shows closed he'd sold his tent and trailer, keeping only his car, his dolls and his phonograph. To her knowledge he'd had no other Minneapolis address. If he had other cronies she didn't know of them. Actually for the past year and a half she'd seen little of him. He'd come around late, after his show, about a year ago now, near Christmas. They'd put in the rest of the night playing poker, she, Len, Ed and Roke. He'd dropped around a couple of months later, just to talk to Ed. One afternoon. Then in May, both she and Len thought it was, he'd come around one Sunday, near dinnertime. The diner wasn't open on Sundays and his show wasn't on either. They'd played some more poker, lasting until around three o'clock in the morning. He hadn't been in any too good temper that night, but he'd said it was a good game and they'd see him around. He'd pulled on a sweater before driving off, taking Ed Toomey with him.

"He ain't been back yet. That's the last."

People, customers, had begun entering; she'd had to rise to attend them, bringing water, laying silverware, taking orders, shoving them through to the woman in the kitchen, returning to me to add a bit, rolling off to transfer plates from serving bar to counter. It was *impossible* she shouldn't know more. I had another of those flashes of knowing what it was to be someone else, this time Vince Winterung, beating against walls that forever stayed blank.

Business thickened, and still I stayed, piling question on question. Ridiculous questions, many of them, which wouldn't have led anywhere even if the poor woman had been able to answer them, which she wasn't. At the end I gave up; there wasn't anything else to do. Stood from my stool, reached for the coat which, in the small room's warmth, I'd long ago hung aside on a rack. Ignoring a customer impatiently tapping the counter with his menu, she lingered near, apologetic because she hadn't been able to be more satisfying.

In desperation I said, "There wouldn't be anywhere else in Minnesota he ever talked about either, I suppose. Somewhere not too far away. Somewhere he just mentioned in passing."

The partially buried eyes receded, the mouth above the hanging chins pursed. For another regret.

"I can't think of a thing. The only other place in Minnesota I ever heard him name, even, was Lake City. That last night he was here, he and Ed began having half an argument, like, about sand fleas. Ed said anyway, one thing about up here in Minnesota, they didn't have sand fleas. We had a window open. He said if we were a couple of other places, that time of year, we'd have sand fleas all over the place. Roke sort of snorted. He said anyone could say that, they'd never been in Lake City. That's all. That's the only——"

In the car, in the early winter dark, I was saying to myself, "This has got to be it, this has got to be it." I'd told Mrs. Feasely what I thought of her, thanking her with both hands. I must have been a menace, driving; there doesn't seem to be any recollectable space between my leaving the diner and the bump with which I backed into a curb at a parking spot near the courthouse. It was just turning six-thirty when I stood at the police information desk asking for Lieutenant Winterung.

Lieutenant Winterung wasn't there. Lieutenant Winterung wasn't busying himself elsewhere, either; he was off duty. The look on my face must have been expressive, because the uniformed man behind the desk informed me tolerantly, "Even police officers got to get time off." In the end I was passed on to an austere, gray-haired man who listened to me courteously but without comment, and then briefly nodded.

"I'll see that Lieutenant Winterung knows." A half rising from his chair said my audience was at an end. I went out churning.

In which, it turned out, I was somewhat in error. When I came upstairs at the Curtis, from having dinner with the Albiguards, my phone was ringing, and the voice on the wire was the creamy tenor to which I'd listened through the late afternoon. Now it was gratified.

"Mrs. Kiskadden, you know what? That Lieutenant Winterung, that cop you were talking about, he just went out of here. I think he thinks maybe we got something. He was real nice, anyway; he said likely Len would be getting home——"

Time off, for a police officer, obviously didn't mean time unbreakably off. The gray-haired man hadn't deigned to tell me what would be done about my little thread, but he must have got to Winterung immediately. Through dinner I'd been having a hard time not setting aside my fork to start for Lake City in person; maybe only my experience with Joe Golies and the rooming-house keeper, suggesting just how well I'd fare, going from house to house with no more than a newspaper print of Roke Bradsher's picture to accompany me, kept me at the Albiguard table. Trained men, working in pairs and with authority, methodically leaving no loopholes, were the people for undertakings of such a scope. Now I could know they were at it. Leaving me nothing to do but listen for yet other rings on the phone. Word from Winterung, it might be, direct. Lake City wasn't so big.

Lieutenant Winterung did get to me, but not direct. As usual, Phil mediated.

"Vince really appreciated that Lake City tip, I guess. He says he ought to be in his office this morning, and if you get around he'll grab time to see you." It wasn't that evening this response came, though, or the next day. It was Monday, December first. A time lag, I might add, causing my opinion of police efficiency to yaw severely once more. What I shot back at Phil was a testy "Would it be worth my while?" Let things go on this way, I'd been thinking, and I'd be mortgaging houses to hire private tracers. Another few days would have Sherry Lee out of the hospital. Hotels haven't place for the newly born. Friends' houses don't, either. With the apartment not ready, what loomed ahead was the house again, for both of us.

In that frame of mind, I was the one who spoke first when I got in to Winterung. I said, "You mean my lead to Lake City got you nowhere at all?" He'd stood up to meet me, and when I'd got in my query he laughed. The laugh and the toss of his thumb toward a chair said he was prepared to be largely indulgent.

"Oh, I wouldn't say that. As a matter of fact, it got us two places." Mixed with indulgence was a small trace of quizzicalness. "That wasn't a bad piece of work you did, dredging that little remark out of Mrs. Feasely. *Mr.* Feasely didn't remember Bradsher's having said any such thing. Maybe we're making a mistake around here. Maybe we ought to load our staffs with women. Only a woman would have held onto a comment so seemingly unimportant. I guess only another woman would have dug it out."

Now who, his voice and his shoulders said, could have opened a more magnificent sweep of liberality than that? I parted my lips but shut them again. There has to be some profit in having lived to be thirty-nine. I hewed to the straighter line.

"Those two places——"

"Right." When I'd lowered myself to the decorous edge of the indicated chair, he took up what apparently was his talking position, leaning against the desk, reaching toward a pocket for his keys. If keys wear out from being thumbed, his must have needed an annual replacement. He said, "We found a bar owner who isn't too sure, but he thinks Bradsher may have stopped in for drinks at his place last spring.

This bar is near the highway, where a good many casuals come in. The owner thinks Bradsher may have spoken to him—the weather, asking a direction, nothing memorable. That's our one and only pointer in Lake City toward Roke Bradsher personally. We've been over the town. He's not living there now."

The last two statements were both clipped and didactic. Against such cool certainty, the heat in which I'd arrived began cooling. He might not be as worked up as I about what was in hand, but when he said, "We've been over the town. He's not living there now," the words possessed a weight which opened a vision of an area in which not a filling station, not a hotel, not a motel, not a store, not a house, not a resident, had been left uncanvassed.

To me the situation was harrying, involving me personally. To him it was professional. But the disjunction was more one of attitude, it might be, than intensity. When next I prodded, it was a little more meekly.

"You said there were two places."

"Right again, Mrs. Kiskadden. Two places. One fact you come to accept, in my business, is that occasionally there are people who manage to escape you. Not often, and not forever, but for a while. Cars, though, almost never fade out. Car identifications are next door to holeproof. We've been hunting Bradsher's car as hard as we've hunted him, and thanks to you we've got it. At least we've got the car he registered here in Minnesota under his own name and for which he bought this year's plates. We found it right there in a Lake City junkyard. Wheels gone, cushions gone, radio gone, but no attempt made to file off the motor or serial numbers. Even the license plates we got; in fact we got those first. They were shingles on a shack some kids say they put up last summer; they showed us the yard where they'd got'em. Car wasn't jammed up, either. When we hauled it in and warmed it up it started; there was a fair amount of gas left in the tank. We———"

Forever, in what was going on, the few things we did find out made no sense. I said, and probably my mouth was open, "But why in heaven's name would he do a thing like that? Drive his car into a——"

My vis-à-vis halted what he'd been about to add, answering, "That we can't know. All we know is—there's the car. Something may have come up so he felt heat was on about the Alabama killing—Toomey may have been pushing him, or the girl or someone else. He must have felt he had to disappear—he did disappear. The car was bunged up enough so it looked right at home in the junkyard. We've taken all prints, of course. Dozens. Most of 'em kids'. That junkyard is a spot they haunt. Nothing that matches up with anything taken from Bradsher's room, but that's not funny, with three separate people having lived there since he did."

I said gropingly, "In other words, what you found out about Lake City was that he'd been there, left his car there. But not a single thing beyond that. No clue to what he was doing there. No indication of where he went from there. No——"

Winterung broke in urbanely, "His sole purpose there may well have been to junk the car; nothing would have kept him from grabbing a bus or a train back to the Cities. Or to anywhere else. At least, though, we no longer are looking for *that* car. If he's got one now it's another one, likely bought and registered under another name. He——"

"In other words," I summed, "I didn't add a lead, I took one away."

"If you insist," he agreed, "though I wouldn't put it that way. Give us enough leads like that, and sooner or later——"

I said, "The girl will be coming out of the hospital on Thursday. There isn't any reason she should stay even that long. Dr. Grellman is just——"

Nothing annoyed him. Not bothering so much as to remind me

of what I'm sure is the truth, that they were pushing every advantage, he grinned again.

"That's another thing I wanted to bring up. You know that Phil Sawyer of yours, he's quite a guy. He says you're in the Kenwood phone exchange, the only one in town that's still handled by girl operators. He's thought up a scheme for having a separate-line phone put into your bedroom, one you're not to use for any purpose whatever except emergency requiring help. The exchange will be notified to inform us immediately if you so much as lift the receiver on that phone. Or if there's any disturbance on it such as a cut wire. It's really a fancy plan; we may use it on other occasions. It should make you perfectly——"

Until then I don't believe I'd thought it actually would happen, that Sherry Lee and I would be together in the house again, not with Roke Bradsher still uncaught. Now, with this arrangement, adroit as it was, maybe foolproof as it was, I foresaw that the homecoming would actually take place. We'd be back where we'd been.

What I muttered was "I wouldn't call him my Phil Sawyer."

While he was ushering me out, Lieutenant Winterung had one more contribution to add. Friendly, but also once more quizzical.

"You're taking this big, Mrs. Kiskadden. Bigger than the girl is, in a way. I've had a couple more sessions with her, over Grellman's dead body. You'd think you were the one being threatened."

That too I disclaimed, indignantly, rather witlessly. "Of course that's not true. I feel responsible for the girl. She's in my care. Would you expect me to be easy?" But I was having a little interior shock.

Sherry Lee's the one threatened. I might say it again and again, but somewhere along the line it had quit bearing weight. Every logical faculty might insist I was merely a bystander. Instinct said I was more than that. Or else being a bystander——

We all know what happens to bystanders.

When it came to be Wednesday, the third, and there still wasn't more than that, I made my last abortive try. I'd avoided driving out to Glenwood to see where Ed Toomey had died; droves of curiosity seekers had been doing it for me. That day I did even that. Tramping about in overshoes to stare at the ski slide, which in a December thaw stood bare, yielding wisps of vapor to the sun. Police signs were gone, not a soul was around. In the area back of the slide I found nothing but bushes, trees, stretches of tufty and sodden grass, stubborn snow patches, other stretches of sodden and trampled mud.

I put in a full half day. Useless, knowing I was useless, whipping myself not with hope but with need—somewhere, somehow, on a twig, under a fall of grass, within the crevices of tree bark, must yet be found the thread, the button, which Phil said hadn't been found, and which if found wouldn't have done any good.

Nothing. Or, if there had been anything, it too was gone. I gave up in the thin wintry sunshine and went home.

Friday, Dr. Grellman said. He'd postponed the discharge one more day, but that would have to be the last. For half a week, now, he'd had Sherry Lee up, moving around. None of the complications he'd feared had come about; she was perfectly able to be out.

On Friday she and the baby came home, and the second doll awaited us.

# CHAPTER TEN

AS LIEUTENANT WINTERUNG had ordered, Sherry Lee's presence in the hospital hadn't been so much as entered on the receptionist's list. People who knew of her presence there had been warned not to mention it. No outsider had tried to get in to her. Phil wasn't allowed in. Friends had accepted my various explanations. At no time, though, had any bar been erected against me; I'd been in daily.

Of one thing there was no doubt: Sherry Lee luxuriated in that hospital stay. Apparently she felt at ease there entirely; through all of the ten days I didn't see one sign of the shrinking. In the lacy soft nightgowns and the flowered crepe bedjacket which had come in as gifts—some from me, one from Phil, one from Dorothy Albiguard—she lounged against her pillows exuding a kind of shine. Always her hair lay eternally sunny, always, after the first day, her lashes, when they lifted at all, lifted gummily.

It's not always easy for one woman to see in another the facets attracting men. I'd been so taken up by what she was I hadn't often asked if she was pretty. Even in the condition in which she'd been, just the same, there'd been indications that men found her noticeable. In restaurants. Janitors when we'd looked for apartments. Passers-by when we'd walked. Todd Albiguard, who happened to be home the afternoon we called on Dorothy. Men from the neighborhood. Bunky, if it came to that. With the birth past, though, the quality she emitted became obvious even to me.

Not that her eyes changed, unless their deep gleam intensified. Not that the hollows of her cheeks filled in, they didn't. Not that her coloring altered, except to become more transparent. It was just that she'd lost the bump; her figure, while still thickened, moved with a deliberate and schooled effort at lissomeness, while something inside her cried, "See, look at me. I'm a girl, I'm unknown, I'm a mystery all closed in. Why don't you see where you get?"

Taunting, never for a moment forgotten, ready to wake at no more than the passage of someone else's husband hurrying through the corridor. Every once in a while, when I entered, it was to break up a clot of interns and hospital staff men, who acted not unlike flies floundering on sticky paper. There were times when I left her with throat heavily aching, thinking, "Johnny, I got you whooping cough and diphtheria shots. Anti-tetanus shots. I guess there wasn't anything I could give you against her kind of girl."

In more ways than one she stayed inexplicable. Except for the brushing of her hair, she seemed to need no other pastimes. If I brought candy, flowers or magazines she passed the first to her admirers, prettily appreciated the second, and as far as I found out never opened one of the third. The only gift that appeared to move her was the layette. I brought that in to strew on her bed, unpacking all the soft little shirts, the shiny plastic-covered packets of diapers, the fleecy sleepers, the blankets, the socks and sweaters and booties, two tiny dresses, a blue bunting. More or less as she had fingered the ashtray in her room and, on occasion, the candy dish in my living room and the heirlooms from the diningroom bay, so now she took up the bits of wearing apparel, turning each piece this way and that, stroking the downy fabrics, caressing the satin of the bindings, stretching out the bunting's silk-lined hood.

"I never saw any bitty old coat like this before," she murmured softly. "I suppose kids need that kind of thing way up North here." Her glance toward me, too, was relaxed, grateful, accepting and including.

It was a moment which, I felt, should be preserved and solidified. I didn't know what to say, exactly, to bring about that result; what

I brought out, awkwardly but certainly softly, was "They're all yours and his now. I can put them in drawers here, to take when you go."

Maybe nothing would have strengthened that instant; certainly this didn't do so. She picked up one of the dresses for a second time, feeling over the sheer muslin and the embroidery. But the wall was up, and what she next offered had returned to being difficult, almost grudging.

"They're nice. They're real nice. You wouldn't have needed to get this much." By the time she'd laid down the dress, she seemed to have become indifferent.

As she was toward her son.

That was the big thing, the inescapable and important thing, which I found it hard to believe but against which I kept blundering.

"Look what Dr. Grellman okayed this morning." When I came into her room on the third day following the boy's birth, she wasn't alone. A sleeping basket had been set up at the left of the bedside within easy reach, and a nurse, over a high canvas table, was engaged in dusting talcum on the baby's bare red back and squeezed bottom. "It's a system we're trying out nowadays," the nurse pattered on fondly and brightly, "get mummy and son all well used to each other, so they'll be pals by the time they go home. Much better than the old way, we all think."

Dr. Grellman, a day or two later, was at once more succinct and more aggressive. "This boy is still losing. An ounce or two more and he'll be in an incubator. Now, you look here, young lady——"

The rest was for Sherry Lee exclusively, a scolding. She was to pick up the baby whether he cried or didn't cry. Nurse and fondle him. Keep him in her arms. Warm him with body warmth. She could start in right now.

Mildly Sherry Lee objected, "He's fast asleep." As directed, though, with the slight awkwardness she had for all manual actions, she reached for the bundle, carefully plucking it from its basket, settling it against her bared breast, pinching the cheeks—this also as directed—until the boy roused and began nuzzling. Then she glanced meekly and expectantly back at Dr. Grellman.

Not as if she asked timidly, "Am I doing all right?" More as if she requested, "See, you can go right on scolding me." As if she found satisfaction in being berated.

Not too odd that I, from what I had to go on, should continue finding it hard to give myself up to the baby entirely. A head shaped something like Johnny's, yes. But of all babies born, perhaps millions had heads like that. I managed to produce the expected cluckings and cooings, I stretched the truth—"He's a dear baby, Sherry Lee. Now that he's fading he's very nice-looking." Actually, each day, he looked more and more the minuscule, wizened, remote old man. Too much, all too much, like pictures of small Korean war refugees. His eyes, an inky purple, opened almost never. His hands didn't wave. He didn't seem to be reaching out from himself in any way. I remembered Johnny as poking about with his eyes and his fists practically within the first day. I may have been mistaken; after twenty years you can be good and mistaken. About Sherry Lee, though, it didn't seem possible I could be in error. *She* had no reason to doubt the child was hers, but she wasn't warm to him. As days went by and he continued losing weight she betrayed no anxiety. Whenever she touched him it was with that careful, objective lack of feeling.

Dr. Grellman, too, obviously saw the thing I saw. Often he dropped around to the room while I was there, to stand frowning and displeased at the foot of the bed, going over the charts.

"He's doing better on supplementary feedings," he announced curtly one day. "Barely holding his own, though. This keeps up, I'll take him off the breast altogether." It was another time when he'd ordered Sherry Lee to hold the child. Abruptly he turned to me.

"Gail, you take him."

I, too, did as ordered, trying, as so often before, to be adequate. Appreciating the softness and helplessness of the small wrapped bundle as I lifted it. Resting it cautiously against my shoulder, returning not to my straight chair but to the rocker which the room also afforded. As I sat down I made myself think, "The chances may be better than I think. Yesterday Dr. Grellman found out his blood type is an O, that's the same as Johnny's. No outside person could say for sure he isn't Johnny's."

In my arms the boy had a queer weightlessness, almost as if, lying against me, he yet held his own weight. He was sleeping, unmoving, the little bulges of his eyelids tight, nose pale under its fragmentary ridge, mouth crumpled. He didn't seem to be exuding nearly as much damp warmth as babies normally exude.

Dr. Grellman, as I shortly grew aware, was scowling at me with a baffled anger sterner than any he'd had for Sherry Lee. After a while he said bitterly, "You too, Gail," and stalked away, leaving me guilty but helpless. I offered the boy to Sherry Lee; she said, "You can just as well put him back in his bed, I guess."

Toward the search going on, also, the search which you'd have thought would have been omnipresent to every waking thought, she showed only the same unwilling, rather sullen interest which she'd shown before. I wasn't able to know, of course, how much information Lieutenant Winterung imparted during his sessions with her, or what she asked him, but with me her needs seemed to be satisfied by a single query which she made each day when I appeared. "They haven't found Roke, have they?" For that instant, before my reply was given, her attention seemed sharp, immediate, even demanding. After that, almost at once, even on days when I had events to relate, such attentiveness quickly ebbed.

"They won't ever find him." It might have been a faintly contemptuous reassurance she gave herself, over and over. Once in a while she veered to something else. "That Lieutenant Winterung—do you know is he married? If he wasn't so old he might be all right. For a cop." From her that was practically a freshet; our conversations were hard going. At another time she offered, "Poor old Ed. I guess they must of got him laid away by this time."

Maybe, I told myself, it was just that she had an unusual faculty for living in the moment. As time neared for her return to my home, certainly, she began evincing some mounting tension once more. If in nothing else, then in the jerkiness with which she lit a cigarette or stubbed one out, answered questions or set the boy aside. The shine grew less apparent; fewer interns hung about the room. One day, very curtly and out of a clear sky, she shot at me, "That Lieutenant Winterung, he wouldn't have Roke and not let on, would he?"

The idea had never occurred to me; all I was able to reply was that I didn't see why he should.

There was just one more thing I noticed about that hospital stay. The nurses, like Dr. Grellman, had gotten around to treating her with reserve. On the day she left, while the four of us—Sherry Lee, a nurse carrying the baby, and I—were crossing the downstairs lobby, an intern stopped in our path for a somewhat stammering farewell.

"I sure—sure hate to see you going out of here, Mrs. Kiskadden. Maybe you won't care if sometime I drop around."

Sherry Lee smoldered for him, raising and lowering the eyelash flags, shaking back the hair, letting him cling to her hand. No, she inferred, she wouldn't care. But the nurse, unpausing, clumped along dourly and silently, keeping her grip on the baby over the icy gravel of the parking lot, up to the very door of the car. She was the one who days earlier had gone through the formula about mummy and son getting used to each other; she was no longer ladling out any such sugar. At the car she handed the blanket-swathed bunting and its contents to Sherry Lee only after Sherry Lee was well settled in the front seat and I was behind the wheel. The good-by sentence was unsmiling, even grim.

"I hate to see *him* go out of here."

When I'd turned the car and came back past her she was stumping along toward the hospital steps, head slightly bent, not glancing our way. Not a young nurse who might be jealous, either. A woman gray-haired, thick-bodied, older than I.

I wasn't the one who first saw the second doll.

We were in the house, the boy was settled in his crib upstairs, Sherry Lee had rested and come down for dinner. While I transferred roast and vegetables to a platter, she stood in the diningroom bay, lifting down pieces from the shelves there, turning them in the light, almost fondling them before she returned them to their places. "One thing you have to give her," I was thinking, "she likes pretty things." In this case she might have been welcoming herself back to these bibelots. As I brought in the platter I began, "We can sit up, I believe," when I noticed her stance. It was rigid, the head thrown slightly back, shoulders flat, body frozen. From my position her face wasn't visible, but I was certain what would be on it.

Without speaking I deposited the platter somewhere and sped to stand beside her, glancing at her swiftly to confirm what was on her face, then looking as she looked, out through the unshaded windows to the winter darkness, broken by angled squares of reflected light on the side lawn and the cedars hemming it. Snow had melted here too, far enough so tawny grass patches were visible amid the remnants of drifts. No one moved in this area, nothing was visible except the white patches, the dark patches; my eyes flitted over them and toward the cedars, hunting mobility there. What caught me, instead, as it must have caught her, was an object light, colorful, not big enough to be human unless it was a child, hung somehow in the branches of a cedar facing the window. An object not identifiable, unless——

She drew in a breath that was audible passing her teeth, before she said tonelessly, "That's Roke's other Sis." She turned with a sudden movement as if she were about to run out to snatch it in. I wasn't in any too orderly a state of mind—the trouble with things such as this, they come up too fast and too unforeseen—but at least I had presence enough to grab her back.

"No, wait. You can't go out. That might be what he wants. We'll call Winterung." I flew not for the phone in the hall but for the one on the special wire which had been installed the day before in my room upstairs. As Lieutenant Winterung had said it would work, so it worked. The answering masculine voice in my ear seemed to come instantaneously; I told what we'd seen, the voice said, "Right." It was maybe a flat two minutes before the first car turned up.

In the meantime I'd pulled all the downstairs shades, an action certainly too tardy if there were any virtue in it at all. We ran up one in the dining room to watch the two uniformed men, revolvers drawn, whipping in and out of the cedars, vanishing to the rear of the house, returning more slowly, hands empty, to comb once again through the trees, perhaps more methodically. Within a few minutes their bulking shapes were joined by others, not now so fast-moving, mostly milling about, conferring and gesturing, pausing to examine the object unremoved from the tree, disappearing, returning. The chimes rang, announcing a uniformed man I'd not seen before, who politely removed his hat, asked, "Would you want to tell what you know about this, please?" and who then perched on two inches of hall chair, transferring our replies to a notebook.

While he still was at work, Lieutenant Winterung came in, nodding "Okay, Pete," toward the man, who stood as he entered. After Pete had departed, Lieutenant Winterung took us all over it again. No, Sherry Lee hadn't seen anyone moving in the side yard, the doll had just hung there, exactly as it hung now. No, I hadn't been in the yard this morning. I'd been busy in the house, getting it ready for occupancy. I didn't remember looking out toward the side yard. No, I hadn't dusted the china in the window today; I'd done that yesterday while the phone company men were putting in the line. It didn't seem possible the doll could have hung there since the night before without anyone noticing it, but I couldn't be sure.

"We put this block back on the alert schedule yesterday. There's been a patrol car down this street every half hour since. That Bradsher can't have been in and out of here. What would he have carried that dummy in? It wouldn't stuff into a coat pocket. He'd have needed a suitcase. There hasn't been anyone with a suitcase around here. He must have a car again. Even then, he'd have had to park the car somewhere to get from it to your yard. It's incredible, absolutely incredible, that he could have done so unseen."

Several of Lieutenant Winterung's official moods had been displayed for us heretofore. The courteous urbanity of our original meeting, the juggernaut phase following Ed Toomey's killing, urbane objectivity again when he'd granted me an audience after the discovery of the car. Now what seemed to hold him was the harsh chill of outrage. He broke off abruptly, "I'll be back," and returned to the side yard, from whence he came back moments later, bearing the dummy, which he wordlessly laid on the coffee table, shoving ashtrays and candy box aside to do so. Only when he'd stood back, frowning from the doll to Sherry Lee to me, did he again speak.

"There it is. Obviously like the other one you got. Obviously newer. You have anything to say about it at all?"

The last was to Sherry Lee, who tapped cigarette ashes into a tray held high against her breast. Returned to its more normal contours, her face yet was wooden, and her voice wasn't taking on much inflection either. Just as I had, she'd mostly watched through the window, saying little. Before answering Winterung, she gazed toward the doll soberly, lashes fallen almost to cheek level. On the table before her the doll lay limp. Winterung had let it drop with the head askew so that, unpleasantly, it gave an effect of being truly a remnant of hanging, its neck broken. From beneath the blue and white sunbonnet, fresher but otherwise identical to that of the other doll, extended the flaxen braids. The eyes gazed as woodenly, the plumped apple cheeks were reddened, glazed and also powder-marked, the latter, I guessed, from having been fingerprinted. The mouth pursed for the kiss or the whistle, the blue and white dress lay deflated and flat against the table, the legs were flung stiffly and lifelessly outward.

She said, "Why do I have to tell you? It's Roke's, all right. His good one. His other one."

"What I want you to tell me is why he brought it here."

"How'd I know?" The cigarette had gone quickly to her mouth; she withdrew it to throw out the words as, with a head toss, she blew out the smoke. "How should I know why he does anything? He's trying to scare me, that's all that he's doing."

"How many of these"—a finger pointed—"did he have when you knew him?"

"The two and that's all."

"That means he no longer has a dummy for his act."

It made her uneasy. Against cushions in a corner of the davenport, while the cigarette rose or descended, she had a look of being pinned. She was sullen when she answered.

"That's right, I guess."

"I can't imagine a professional ventriloquist giving up his last dummy. For any reason whatever. Without it he's no longer in business. He——"

The sullenness increased. "You got him running so fast, what use would it be if he did have one? He knows he can't put on his old act any more. He knows he can't work probably even with a brand-different dummy. What chance has he got?"

"No, you've got something there." Winterung's comment was as quick as her reply, but while he was making it, and afterward, in a little pause that fell, it was her voice, for all its tonelessness, that seemed to stay in the air.

I'd moved around to a chair at the end of the davenport; I saw his eyes asking a silent question. His lips, though, didn't inquire why she should be defensive on this point; they passed to something else.

"One thing it seems to me we can be sure about. There wasn't anything going on here around the house while you were in the hospital. Somehow that fellow knew you'd be home today. He's right here, in this neighborhood. It's the only explanation that works. Or else he's got a contact here. Somebody. Or in that hospital. Was there anyone there in the hospital who showed any curiosity——"

He went over the hospital. Rigorously. Staff physicians, interns, nurses, ward maid. Dr. Grellman. Dr. Legge. The pediatrician who'd been called in. Everyone to whom she or I could put a name. From there to the neighborhood. Grocers, butchers, drug stores, hardware store, banks she or I patronized. Men who came to the house—delivery boys, meter readers, postman, milkman, laundry man. Neighbors. Friends.

"What's his name? The Knowles kid. Horace Lorimer Knowles, Jr. He's the one already had one contact we know about with Bradsher. Phil. God, you wouldn't think I'd have to suspect Phil. Who else so much as knows the girl is here? No, everyone. All right, Mrs. George Albiguard, the Albiguard family——"

He too now had a notebook in his hands.

I'd gone around Minneapolis, watching for the one face. The hair, the sharp fox jaw, the proud eyes. Now there was scarcely anyone being left to me. Phil and Bunky—to them I clung; they couldn't be against anyone in any way allied to me. But I sat stripped and raw, faith in almost everyone else stealing away from me.

Winterung had the notebook back in his pocket; he was picking up the dummy in the train of one of his abrupt departures.

I wasn't to be so left. I said desperately, "Surely this time there must be *something* to be an indication. There's still snow out there. Footprints. Cord. How was she"—I pointed—"attached to that tree? Something caught in the branches, something dropped——" I thought he was going to stride off without answering, without tossing us anything by way of farewell at all. Toward the hall archway, though, he halted and turned, paused for reflection and then, more slowly, came back.

"The sunbonnet strings were what held the dummy there. Here"—he drew out a length of fabric crumpled and soiled—"you can see for yourself. I guess we don't get much out of that. Not a fingerprint; he must have his hands covered. Not that it would help us much to get a print, as long as we can't get hold of him. Jumbled footprints don't do us much good. Not on a terrain like that one, with everyone in town wearing rubbers or overshoes. This time there was one thing more, though. On the ground near the cedar tree, almost directly under the dummy. It doesn't look like anything that's going to get us anywhere, but of course we'll try. Here, you can look at it. Not your handwriting, is it?"

From another pocket, while he was saying this, he drew forth a small slip of paper, shoving the dummy carelessly into the crook of an elbow to do so. The slip came toward me.

In the mixture of anxiety and hope which seemed to be the natural emotions evoked, I took it. A torn strip of paper, once white, now stained and creased, as if it had been crumpled and then stepped on. The penciled words on it were: "Henry—binoculars, sports shirt. Mother—bedrest, slip. Lannie—Meccano set, Sorry, Mr. Potato Head. Gilda—Check or——(?)"

Unmistakable. I said, "It's someone's Christmas list."

"What I want to know, is it the right person's Christmas list?"

He was taking it back, not offering it to Sherry Lee, but turning his attention to her once more. "At the time you knew Bradsher, was he familiar with anyone named Henry, Lannie or Gilda?"

She moistened her lips but then shook her head.

"Not that I know about."

Something to add. "It's not a man's list," I pointed out. "It's a woman's."

He didn't grunt, exactly; he merely restrained his mouth from anything more than the motions of a grunt.

"That's what I'm afraid of," he said, and that time went.

## CHAPTER ELEVEN

MORE WAITING. More expectancy. More of that urgency which, whatever normal activities we also pursued, pressed almost all time and attention toward the one current. The morning newspaper carried no word of the dummy; the newspapers, in fact, had never connected us with Roke Bradsher at all. They'd noted the fact of Ed Toomey's being picked up for loitering, and his subsequent detention, in a collection of jottings from the police blotter. The story of his murder was accorded a fair play. Roke Bradsher had been described as being wanted for the Alabama killing, and later, of course, for Ed Toomey's. The original dummy, the whistling, the postcard, Sherry Lee's connection with Toomey and Bradsher—these were all cards Winterung and his men were playing close to their chests. I hadn't let them out either, not to anyone.

What the papers did carry on the next morning was a photograph of the Christmas list, with a request that whoever it had belonged to come forward. Results on that, as I found from Phil, came almost immediately.

Before then, though, there were other chances to see just how rigorous and far-reaching was Winterung's latest hunt. Bunky dropped in toward noon. His young flesh is so solid it takes something to deplete or dent it, but he was both depleted and dented that noon.

What he first announced was a dampened "One thing I know for sure, I'm never in my life again going to be carrying around any briefcases. I've been getting so much paper to haul I borrowed one of Mother's old legal bags. Now Lieutenant Winterung thinks maybe I had the dummy in there. He took the case away, he took all my books so I can't do any studying. With finals right on top of me. They're going over them for fingerprints. They're going over them to see can they find any signs I had that dummy in the case. They think I've been meeting Roke Bradsher somewhere, getting money for helping him and for telling him about you or Sherry Lee or the baby. They want to know how much allowance I get and how much I've been spending."

Suspicion, so suddenly dumped over him, had overwhelmed him to such an extent that, while words spilled, he might otherwise have been partially paralyzed. Not until I began soothingly, "Sit down, Bunky; no one really believes any of this; no one actually thinks you're helping Roke Bradsher; look, I'll make cocoa to warm you up," did he so much as get off his feet. Even then, fallen into the depths of the living room's largest chair, jacket still zipped, stubbled head low and light-lashed eyes dazed, he presented as bleak a picture as any you'd be apt to see. One so miserably bleak, in fact, that I might have been tempted to laugh.

Phil too met his questioning. One not as directly challenging as Bunky's, but still letting him know he wasn't being left out.

"Look, Phil," he quoted Winterung as asking, "you sure there couldn't be any leaks through you? How about your office help? How about George Albiguard? How about your friends? Suppose Bradsher has picked up your office girl, gotten to be her boy friend. Suppose he's a gardener, chauffeur, anything, for one of your friends."

"I told him Mrs. Minty was fifty-eight. I told him my friends didn't come into the gardener or chauffeur class. God knows I've racked my brains——"

Comparatively light as the imputations against him had been, he too was shaken, sitting late that afternoon in the armchair occupied a few hours earlier by Bunky. The finger tips of his right hand brushed along the cheek scar so continuously it had the effect of a tic.

It was after he'd repeated the details of his own questioning that he told what else Winterung had imparted.

Results from fingerprinting—including that of Bunky's briefcase, if we'd had any doubts on that score—had been nil. Work with footprints in my side yard hadn't yielded anything likely to be useful either. The two telephone men who had put in my special phone had run their line only a few yards south of the cedars in question; they'd recalled nothing whatever of any dummy.

"Vince thinks that means the dummy couldn't possibly have been there while they were working. It means Bradsher or someone acting for him must have come around late in the afternoon, quite shortly before the doll was discovered. He's done the hospital. He's got men out now doing a house-to-house canvass around here; there won't be as much as a stray roomer or visiting cousin left unquestioned. He'll be going over every person who enters this yard, even for picking up garbage. None of them will be Bradsher, he's pretty sure of that; what he's looking for now is the contact."

Worst of all was the result on the Christmas list. No later than midmorning, a woman named Louise Villeroy, wife of Henry Villeroy, a milling company executive, mother of Lannie Villeroy and possessing a sister named Gilda, had phoned to say she recognized the list as hers. She couldn't recall exactly, but she believed that, after a shopping trip, she'd crumpled the list and let it drop to the sidewalk, somewhere downtown.

"Vince drove out to see her, himself. She lives in a good house on the Parkway. She's positive she hasn't and never has had any knowledge of anyone named Bradsher. Certainly not with the man whose picture Vince showed her. All she could offer was that for some inexplicable reason someone had picked up her castaway list and conveyed it to your yard. Vince is checking, of course, but he believes she is telling the truth. He thinks Bradsher is teasing him, carefully dropping that list under the dummy as if he were thumbing his nose. Vince doesn't like it much."

Only Phil, likely, would drop a conclusion as much an under statement as that last.

I had reason to know the neighborhood search went on as Winterung said it would go on, and also how it was being taken. Previously, when they'd been questioned, my neighbors had been taken aback but also intrigued. My phone had rung. This time it rang much less, and when I went out no gossiper neared a back fence, no hand hailed me from porch or window. Typical of what I got from my friends was Dorothy Albiguard's response——

"You must really have something going on there, Gail. It turns out Todd met that daughter-in-law of yours one day near the drugstore, while she still was pregnant; he didn't do more than say hello. You'd think it was a capital crime. We've had detectives here twice so far, questioning him, questioning George and me, questioning even Nancy. I think you might drop them a hint or two. If anyone you know has any connection with that Bradsher, it isn't us."

There was to be a slightly stronger complaint along that line, as well. One which, to my oppression, I couldn't decry any more than I decried the others.

Back near the first of November, when the Reverend Mr. Raeburn had asked if I'd handle the Christmas pageant, I'd begged off. "Please, no. Not this year. Pat Evers is doing well at dramatics at the U; let her try. It's time, anyway, you had someone new." He'd demurred, but accepted it. During Sherry Lee's stay in the hospital, though, he'd hunted me out at the Curtis.

The Reverend Mr. Raeburn is eighty, now, well loved and frail. Human enough to know about the well-loved part, and depend on it. On one of the sofas in the Curtis alley, refusing refreshment, he leaned toward me wistfully, transparent hands laced over a knee. "I wouldn't want you to think I'm making complaints," he said. Something like ten years ago, when he'd been more vigorous, he'd once snapped at me that complaints were a thing a man of the gospel learned never to make, but that didn't mean he never felt like any. This, obviously, was forgotten now. "No complaints at all. Miss Evers is doing an acceptable job with the pageant, I'm sure. When Christmas comes, I'm sure the congregation will find it passes muster. It's merely—well, Miss Evers hasn't yet a practiced hand at discipline. At my age I find it disconcerting to have St. Joseph threatening to jump from the balcony. He'd certainly break a leg. If you could see your way to do nothing but drop in at rehearsals——"

During the whole affair of Roke Bradsher, there always were these choices. Choices between cowering, under cover and near people, or of maintaining a more normal routine. Sometimes I gave in, cowering, but there also were occasions when I resisted. If I did nothing but cower, then I'd be giving Roke Bradsher a victory which pride wouldn't let him have.

So I saw my way about the rehearsals. They came on Saturdays or in late afternoons, there at first; getting to them was no worse than getting from hotel to hospital. By December tenth, though, with less than a fortnight before the performance, the hour was pushed up to seven, for working with lights. Since by then I was back at home with Sherry Lee, and the church only three blocks distant, I walked. Scurrying, but reminding myself I was in no personal danger, and how well the area was policed. A police car, in fact, came up from behind me and trundled alongside for several feet, obviously taking a look. When Phil found out what I'd done, though, he went through the Sawyer roof. Patrolled area or not, he and Bunky were taking over. One staying with Sherry Lee, the other escorting me any time I went out after nightfall.

I can't say I disparaged this forcefully. I'd been a little worried leaving the girl alone, even if she'd promised to open no doors. I couldn't help noticing that, when Bunky was around, the girl lingered near him. I saw to it Phil was the one who stayed with her, Bunky the one who accompanied me. But there too a situation called for repercussion, and one promptly came.

There've been times in my life when I've wished the neglect Bunky's parents went in for might have been of the gross kind, so they'd have been brought to book. That's somewhat past, now; it doesn't seem as important for a mother to bake a birthday cake for a son of twenty as for one of ten. Or for a father to give him something else, once in a while, than a check too ridiculously big. At the Knowles house there's been hired help, always, to keep the doors open and food on the table. Bunky's had a luxurious room, too many toys, too much sporting equipment. The best clothes. Never, though, a mother who was anything but Pamela Knowles, brilliant legal researcher for Knowles and Knowles. Or a father who belabored his conscience to be anything useful except a handsome courtroom showpiece for that same firm. Oh, Pamela Knowles laid down rules. Rigid ones. She was the rigid type. Horace Knowles laughed or ignored it when Bunky broke the rules. I'd had set-tos with Pamela before, so it wasn't anything new in my experience when I came home one night with Bunky to find her in the living room instead of Phil.

Coolly, as soon as we were inside the door, she said, "I sent Phil on home. He wasn't feeling any too well. Anyway, you don't need more than one guardian here. You can go on home too, Bunky. Not anywhere else. Home."

Of all commands apt to make a young man of twenty see red, that, I'd have said, was some kind of a model. Bunky's feet instantaneously went wide, his head lowered and his shoulders hunched, while he shot back, "Who's making me?" He as well as I, though, knew no real purpose would be served by mutiny; when I'd agreed quietly, "You can just as well go, Bunky," he turned to snatch the door open, said, "All right, I suppose you don't want any fuss," and left as bidden, slamming his way out.

Leading me on toward the living room, Pamela Knowles stepped neatly, mink coat loosened but not removed, handbag over wrist, gloves in hand. Once, a few years back, she'd gone in for effects— one winter she'd had pale green hair. She wasn't being that bizarre any longer; if I was thirty-nine, she was more. Her hair now was platinum, closely sleeked, combining with a mink-rimmed halo hat to throw her classically chisled features into sharp relief. It's from Horace that Bunky gets the red hair and the bulkiness.

When she'd wheeled to face me, in the exact center of the living room, I invited her to sit. She made no move to do so, which meant I stood too. Once this little imposition was clear she said sweetly, "I hope you won't mind, Gail. I've had a little talk with your daughter-in-law. It's no secret, you know, that you've got her here. Or what she is. I've sent her upstairs; I'm sure she understands my position. You may as well get it clearly too. It's not hard to see what you're up to, Gail. You're thinking of foisting that girl on me. You've had Bunky coming here, you've got him so embroiled the police force is after him constantly. He's falling off in his studies—how can he keep them up? Not sleeping well, losing weight—you've set yourself up as a friend of his. Even you can't pretend you're a friend to him now. Without Johnny's bad influence I've hoped he'd straighten out to be what he's supposed to be; in fact I'm afraid I shall see that he does so. He's to have no more encounters with that girl. If you knew what the neighborhood thinks of you, bringing that trollop here, embroiling us all in some kind of mysterious mess——"

With what I hope was dignity, I told her the idea of foisting Sherry Lee on Bunky had never come to my mind. I might have added that I was as helpless as Bunky when it came to police investigations. My conscience hurt me enough, though, so I mainly was silent; I'd been uneasy over the girl's juxtaposition to Bunky too. I said Sherry Lee would be moving within a few weeks, and that until then I'd deny Bunky the house, even if he wanted to come against his mother's wishes. I wasn't able to keep from appending, "You don't trust Bunky far," to which she riposted an inevitable "You trusted *your* son."

She didn't actually say Bunky wasn't to see me again; maybe she had an idea how far she'd get. When she left it was as imperiously as she'd borne herself throughout.

There were other things, too, which took place in this current division of our strained, waiting lulls, the last such, incidentally, which there was to be. Things which, at the time, seemed unrelated to Winterung's unavailing search and our anxiety, but which turned out not so.

For one thing, there was Sherry Lee's continuing apathy about her son. True, she took on much of his care. Not going as far as laundry; we signed up with a diaper service and I did the rest. But she bathed and dressed him, learned to mix his formula and to boil it the necessary number of minutes without having it billow all over the stove. Under her ministrations the infant couldn't be said to thrive, exactly; Dr. Grellman, forever dissatisfied, dropped in at least twice a week. The weights on the baby scale did creep up: six pounds, two ounces, three ounces, four, but never as they should be rising. When I managed to arrange a furniture-hunting expedition—a matter on which the girl also stayed peculiarly inert—I was more apt to be the one who carried the boy than she. She took it for granted I'd take over when she went out for afternoon walks. Yet she held him too, and I couldn't say it was infrequently. Passing her half-open door in the late afternoons, I'd glimpse her sitting in the old lullaby rocker, the one I'd had for Johnny and kept in the attic all these years. She'd be giving the child his bottle, and as she looked down at him a kind of mournfulness seemed to lie around her mouth and the lowered lashes.

Seeing her there, one day, I had a flash of recalling an incident otherwise long forgotten and past. When I was six, maybe, or seven, I'd gone once with my mother to call on a neighbor who'd had what was called a blue baby. During the space of our visit the young mother had sat in her living room, very quiet, and with a similar look of mournful detachment. The child at her breast lay with the same motionlessness this child had. Very gently, while she talked with us, the mother tapped the child's hand against her neck, imparting to it an activity it didn't have of its own accord.

"Poor soul," my mother said of this neighbor on our way home. I could recall her tone, her words, the damp freshness of the spring day, the way I was hop-skipping, avoiding the sidewalk cracks. "Poor thing, she knows her child isn't long for this world."

Sherry Lee had no reason to believe her child wouldn't survive. That was one of the things Dr. Grellman said with most anger. "He's a perfectly well child. Bones soft, but we're taking care of that with the Percomorph oil. I've gone over him again and again. Not a reason in the world why he shouldn't take more of his feedings. Not a reason in the world why he shouldn't be making good gains. Pick him up more. You too, Gail. All right, you are picking him up. Pick him up more than that."

Apathy toward her son wasn't the only facet of the girl's personality that I found trouble excusing, either. With time and familiarity, she began evincing an intolerance toward years and authority which isn't too uncommon at her age, but which she seemed to possess in unusual degrees. "That old gink." When Dr. Grellman made a departure, her comments grew more and more contemptuous. If I reminded her that Dr. Grellman had done and was doing a good deal for her, the reply was a sullen "Why not? He's getting paid for it." So far her manner toward me hadn't been bad; here and there, though, there began being indications she was finding me hard to bear too. "That kind of thing's all right for you," was her reply to almost any suggested diversion. When I heard Phil was housebound with flu—that was what he'd had coming on the night Pamela Knowles sent him home—Sherry Lee's comment on my worry was a tossed "What difference does it make, his age?" I blew up on that one, telling myself I was ridiculous, and that I couldn't pay attention to a chit not yet dry behind her ears, but furious just the same. There might, I hinted, be reason for living even after one passed the sere and yellow year of forty. On this she made clear her philosophy— "Not for me, there won't be. I'm not getting old. When I quit being young, then I'm getting out. I'm not sticking around to get gray-haired and ugly. I'm getting my life and my fun while I'm young."

Enough perspective stayed with me so I was mild in return to this, biting back a retort that, as far as I could see, she was handling her youth in a way which meant she wasn't getting much fun from that either.

The twin ideas, first of her being wrong with the boy, second of her resistance to anything like discipline or precedent, were so firmly impressed on me that when, during this second week of the final lull, she made an abrupt announcement, late one morning, "That preacher was right, here the other day. We ought to be having a baptizing," I had another opportunity to be nonplussed.

The preacher of whom she spoke, naturally, was our Reverend Mr. Raeburn, come for his new-baby call. The time when the Reverend Mr. Raeburn plunged deeply into parishioners' troubles is pretty well past; gingerly, from one of my straighter chairs, he indicated that I had met difficulty, new difficulty, but he hoped it wouldn't prove pervasive or too harrowing. I didn't burden him with how pervasive or how harrowing that difficulty had come to be, or how, at that moment, the fact that Lieutenant Winterung as before had got nowhere, and that I couldn't so much as think up anything I could do either, was so excoriating to my nerves I was scarcely able to bear the idea of another such day adding itself to the ones we'd already had.

Sherry Lee, as requested, came down, bringing the boy dressed for viewing. The Reverend Mr. Raeburn produced all the proper observances, including the one about a christening.

"Since the child seems a bit—delicate," he'd offered, "I'll be glad to come over. Home christenings are quite as much in order as church ceremonies. In fact I'm not sure they're not preferable. I must say they lessen competition at sermon time."

Sitting then on the davenport, the sleeping infant in her lap, Sherry Lee left it to me to answer. Which I did, before her silence or disdain should grow noticeable. We hadn't yet decided on a name, I said. The boy wasn't yet four weeks old.

When she so suddenly plumped for the christening I probably looked as astonished as I felt. I bit myself from saying, "I wouldn't think you'd bother about any such observance." Just because she sometimes was unpleasant toward me didn't mean I should be unpleasant with her. What I did proffer, lamely, as an excuse for my surprise, was, "I thought you might want to wait until you were in your own place. You'll be there in a couple weeks."

No muscle moved in her straight poker face.

She was in the kitchen when she'd brought up the subject, sterilizing bottles. Tongs in hand, she reached for a bottle from the bubbling kettle, nipped it up and transferred it to the rack.

"I've been thinking it's about time I began calling the baby something," she said. "I've been wondering if it's all right he should be called Johnny."

What rose in response to that was a good deal stronger than astonishment. I replied shortly, "No one in this house is going to be called Johnny ever again." The very idea had veins, which bled.

At any other time, over an answer as repulsing as this one, she'd have edged away, leaving me to do any bridging over. These last days there'd been several such breaks to bridge. In this instance, though, she merely said, "Maybe Jeffry, then. Jeffry is a nice enough name. Jeffry Kiskadden. It sounds nice."

Soreness might remain from the original suggestion, but the second, I was forced to admit, was a better name than any I'd have expected her to choose.

"You may think of something you like better. Right now before Christmas the Reverend Mr. Raeburn will probably have a hard time squeezing out time to come." My mind was still for temporizing, but she wasn't having any.

"I could ask. Today's only December sixteenth—we could maybe have it this week. The minister lives in that house right against the church, doesn't he? I could stop by there."

All that enterprise. More, so much more, than she'd displayed about anything else. No hint that, if Dr. Grellman was elderly, the Reverend Mr. Raeburn was tottering. If it hadn't been unreasonable, I'd have said there was a quality of obstinacy in her determination. Leaving the baby with me, that same afternoon, she went out. Returning some two hours later, she was in a mood of such satisfaction that her eyes were almost three quarters of the way open and her cheekbones were touched with pink. In her hand, too, she held a department store box.

"I got him," she said. "Your Reverend Mr. Raeburn. He was perfectly sweet to me. He said he had a free hour this Friday afternoon and he could drop over, well as not. I thought maybe Mr. Sawyer would want to come. I guess—well, I guess Bunky Knowles can't come; his mother said he couldn't." This was a single reference, so far, to the laws Pamela Knowles had laid down, and was spoken with no evidence of abashment. "If you wanted, though, you could ask Mrs. Albiguard, and I thought maybe I'd ask Don Knight. You remember Dr. Knight, don't you? He's that intern, the one I got to know at the hospital. He's called me two times now."

Not just pink and satisfied. Not just all of a sudden chummy.

Newly nervous. Avoiding my eyes. "What's she up to?" I asked myself. "What can she think she's putting across?" Was the answer of the simplest—that by having the ceremony now she'd evade carrying it through at her own place? Reply to that was simple too. If she'd shown herself as wanting help, I'd gladly have given it, at her domicile as much as at my own. Or was she just arranging an occasion to get on with the intern?

The box held a christening dress, for which she'd taken a bus all the way downtown and back.

I'd paid her one installment of the suggested allowance before we left Georgia. She'd had another just after her return from the hospital. In the meantime she'd also had a pension check. Just the same, she'd let me pay the hospital bill and the deposit on her first month's rent. I suspected I'd be paying Dr. Grellman. She'd not offered to furnish her apartment. What she was doing with her money, except keep it, I wouldn't know. Except for one new dress, a ginger-brown shantung, this christening garment was her single voluntary purchase. Proudly she held it up—an elaborate production, I was ready to agree. Made not only of lace and embroidery, but of organdy, which would scratch.

As arranged, we had that christening. On Friday, December nineteenth. Certainly it fulfilled no function of bringing the intern into the family circle; he was on duty and couldn't come. Dorothy Albiguard refused too, at first, but thought better of it; she and Phil stood as sponsors. Bunky sent a silver spoon. Only six of us present, the five who were adults shoving aside other preoccupations for the tender and smiling sobriety which goes with such occasions. Old Reverend Mr. Raeburn, back to the livingroom windows, facing us, water at his side on a table in the bead-edged silver bowl which had held water for Johnny's christening and, I understand, mine as well. At the last moment I'd weakened enough to get it down from its shelf. Sherry Lee carrying her boy herself. In her arms he lay quiet even in the scratchy dress, but, as so seldom happened, his eyes were open. Eyes, still unseeing, of a faded purple-blue, like washed crystals of grape sugar.

I was the audience, alone.

When the Reverend Mr. Raeburn asked the baby's name, there was a barely perceptible pause before Sherry Lee answered. She said, "Jeffry John."

Dorothy and Phil, flanking her, were so carried away they were fatuous, I'd have said. The Reverend Mr. Raeburn's thin ascetic features betrayed no lift of brow either; all was proceeding in an expected pattern for him. Dipping his hand to the bowl, he lifted it, letting a few drops trickle over the pink, still bald little head being held close to him. Twice more he repeated this, speaking the familiar, beneficent words.

"Jeffry John, I baptize thee in the name of the Father—and of the Son—and of the Holy Ghost."

The little moment was past.

## CHAPTER TWELVE

IT WAS AN UNIDENTIFIED member of the police force who called, letting us know of the event which meant the end was nearing. Only neither he nor I, then, was aware of there being an end, or how close it was, or what its horrors would be.

When the ring came I'd been asleep. Fast asleep, exhaustedly asleep, almost naturally asleep. The evening was that of Sunday, December twenty-first. There hadn't, on that Sunday, been any overt manifestation from Roke Bradsher since the second doll was left, sixteen days previously. Jumpy we might remain; it was impossible to be less. But the tide of everyday living had also swept up, to wash partially over the jumpiness. Christmas would be the next Thursday. With Monday and Tuesday earmarked for baking, Wednesday for last-minute activities and the pageant, I'd taken the day for setting up the tree, trimming it and the house, stringing the outside lights on the cedars.

In one of her more affable moods, Sherry Lee helped a little, or at least stood about watching, once in a while hanging a colored ball or handing tacks. She'd had a date with her hospital intern the night before, making up for his absence from the christening; maybe that helped. Yet I couldn't say the spirit came to be lightheartedly festive, not when, for me, Johnny moved in with the tree. Every once in a while the dragging sore weight in my breast sent me off to my room. That, though, wasn't all of the trouble; there was also another impression from which I began ailing, especially when Sherry Lee was at hand. "Here we are." The actual words formed themselves in my mind.

# MABEL SEELEY

"Here we are, getting ready for Christmas, when we know it won't really come." This second incursion I also fought—what was the sense of it? Christmas had always come. Wanted or not, cruelly grief-stirring or not, it would be with us this year as other years.

Sense or nonsense, though, the feeling stayed with me. While I wrapped gifts through the evening. While I fell asleep, rather early. For an hour or two ensuing, when I struggled with a dream. In which the phone's ringing came to be one of the forces I opposed. It was only after I'd begun rising to a level where distinctions were possible that I recognized the ring as real, and as coming, not from the familiar instrument downstairs, but from the new one on my bed table. Even then, groggy, I was in robe and slippers, halfway toward the door, before realization connected with action well enough to turn me about.

"Mrs. Kiskadden?" The voice on the wire sounded as if it came from a man in a swing. It rose and ebbed. "Sorry to bother you if you're abed. Lieutenant Winterung asked me to check. There hasn't been any disturbance around you this evening, has there? No? That's good. Yes, I'll wait—— Thank you. Fine. Yes, there is. Someone saying he was Roke Bradsher attacked a girl an hour or so ago in Wayzata; we don't know for sure if he actually was Bradsher, but whoever he was we'll soon have him. This time we're sure of it. Just keep your doors locked and that phone handy; we're maintaining the strong patrol——"

No more than the ring, waking me, had been enough to start up my heart's heavy thudding; I'd been wakened at night to hear about Johnny too. To the question about a disturbance I was able to return only a choked "Not that I know about." The caller's promise to wait followed when I offered to go around to the other occupied bedroom to see if all was well there. It was in response to the results of this—my stumbled journey down the hall having produced nothing, by the aid of the hall night light, but a glimpse of Sherry Lee peacefully asleep in her big bed and the baby equally at rest in his crib—that the questioner said, "Thank you," and "Fine." His "Yes, there is" marked the point at which I began guessing something new must be up.

When he left his phone I didn't leave mine. Not for at least a minute. The receiver, fallen with my hand to the bed edge, sent up the faint twang of a line gone dead. Someone saying he was Roke Bradsher had attacked a girl in Wayzata. Lieutenant Winterung wasn't sure he actually was Bradsher, but whoever he was——

Winterung had been sure of Bradsher's early capture at other times too.

"Keep your doors locked and that phone handy. We're maintaining the strong patrol——"

I'd had occasion, before then, to think of my house walls as thinning. Thick wood siding, doors, plaster, locks, hooked storm windows and sash catches—for long years they'd held me secure. I couldn't feel them as enfolding me any longer. Or, if they did so, then only with the fragile transparency of a glass bubble. I, sitting on the bed which had been so warm, Sherry Lee and the baby, asleep—inside our lighted casing the three of us saw only darkness, while the prowler outside, peering in, had us well in sight.

Was it imagination? For the barest of seconds, I might have been hearing a whistle. No more than three notes, sharply halted. "Oh, I wish——" As if cruelly, sneeringly, hovering just beyond me with eyes pressed to my shell, Roke Bradsher saw even my thoughts, and stood ready to confirm them. I groped for the telephone, found it still off the hook. Pressed the button to get a live line, listened again for the whistle, heard nothing. Hesitated over the phone, but instead of taking it up ran to the south window, the east one, ran downstairs and listened there too.

Should I call back? Shouldn't I? Wayzata is less than twenty miles west. Anyone could commit a crime there, easily be in Minneapolis in much less than an hour. Anyone could also whistle—from a passing car, say—and be twenty blocks away within five minutes.

If there was a chance of success for the police in Wayzata, I shouldn't deflect them. I didn't call. Didn't go back to bed, either, but sat in the living room with the unlit Christmas tree for company, one lamp giving me sight for solitaire. After a while what I might have expected happened—I can't say I was startled by it. The chimes softly tinkled. The face I saw through the peephole wasn't Roke Bradsher's, and the uniform wouldn't have been his either, but I didn't open the door.

"All right, aren't you, Mrs. Kiskadden? Your lights on this time of night——"

"We're all right. You know what's happened——"

"We heard. Don't you worry though. You go on back to bed, ma'am."

Since they'd approached me, things were different.

"I thought I heard the whistling. Not much, I couldn't be sure. But——"

"When was that?"

"After I was called. Almost immediately afterward."

"There hasn't been anyone around we haven't checked, ma'am." His voice, like mine, was being held to a low and unresonant level, but he also managed to express patience.

I said, "Thank you. I'll turn out the light."

He said, "You do that. Then if they go on we'll come running."

A very nice man. Outside my glass wall, guardianship was so thorough no one could possibly get through. Or whistle.

I sat up the rest of the night in the dark. Going so far as to think of myself as an inner defense for the two upstairs. Toward morning dozing a little on the davenport.

Phil said, "The man's out of his mind. Must be out of his mind. I suppose he thinks he has wrongs enough and is being hunted enough to make him that way. Only a man out of his mind deliberately invites capture and punishment by giving his name. Or else——"

The *Morning Tribune* had the facts. "Wayzata Waitress Knifed En Route Home," was what it supplied, adding in the subhead that, while critically cut, the victim was expected to recover. Her name, also as given, was Mara Hillstrom. At ten or a few minutes later, she'd told police, she'd left the café where she worked, together with a girl friend who'd dropped in to walk home with her. Something less than two blocks from the Hillstrom residence, the friend had turned in at her own place, Mara had gone on alone. At a vacant lot the attacker had slipped up behind her, presumably from a lilac thicket, and gotten an arm over her windpipe. He'd muttered something like "Let's you and me go places." She'd struggled and the man had struggled too. Laughing.

"She was almost more worked up over his laughing than she was about anything else." Having gotten to one of Winterung's men, Phil was able to elaborate. "The words she used were that it was awful, terrible, a greasy kind of laugh. She was in shock of course when Vince got to her, and the doctor called by the local police had her under a good deal of sedation. But she seemed to be giving a perfectly coherent account. She's no flyweight; she'd thought she could get the man's arm from her throat so she could scream, but she hadn't been able to do so. It seemed to her the struggle continued for quite some time, and her clothes were torn enough to give credence to a fair amount of battle. She lives rather far out, where houses are widely spaced. The man quit laughing after a while; that was when he said, 'You better quit fighting me, you've been hearing about me, I'm Roke Bradsher.' The next thing she knew were the stabs into her back, under the shoulder blade. She didn't lose consciousness; she was aware of lights nearing, and then of his dropping her and running. She was able to weave out to the approaching car. It held an elderly couple, and there was so much confusion, getting the girl home, waking her people, that it wasn't until the

Wayzata police came that any search was begun for the man. By then of course he was clear. Winterung believes the locale is significant, though; he went over that area before, checking the lake cottages; he's fine-combing them now. The man's certainly there. Close enough to get in touch with whoever is his contact. Close enough to come for groceries to big markets where he won't be spotted. Keeping himself in some out-of-the-way cul-de-sac——"

Sherry Lee was on hand to get the account too; I'd told her of the event when, toward six in the morning, the baby's early whimpers had put an end to my dozing, and I'd warmed his bottle and taken it up. Sometimes, at six, if I wasn't up, she herself got that bottle, returning to bed after she'd done so. This morning she sat amid the tumbled blankets while the news was relayed, not going through the whole of the shrinking routine but emerging as pinched and pale. So much so that, for several minutes, she didn't even begin smoothing her hair.

What she said, lamely, was, "That could be Roke, all right. All shut up by himself somewhere—he could go crazy like."

She'd stayed just as she was, hunched forward against the blankets, while I changed Jeffry, stripped his bed, remade it, and settled him dry and warm with the bottle. The only other comment she vouchsafed was, "I suppose there'll be stuff going on now, all day."

I didn't think she lay down again. I went on to my room to snatch a little daylit sleep of my own; through it I seemed aware of movement in the house, and when I got downstairs once more, at noon just before Phil came, she was in the kitchen, lethargically stacking the kettles she'd used for a new batch of formula. Washing a dish or a kettle was a low to which she never fell under any circumstances.

Comment she produced for Phil was as listless as that conveyed to me. "I wouldn't want to live out a lonesome place like that. It's not safe." And "I wouldn't think Roke would cut up a strange girl, not unless he knew her first. He didn't ever do anything like that before."

"That's a possibility Vince is checking too, of course." Phil was able to cover this ground, as well. "The girl says absolutely not, though, and there doesn't seem much reason why she'd lie on such a point. She looked at the picture good and hard. No one else in her restaurant remembers any such man around, either. No, Bradsher is a stranger to the girl, all right. She didn't get so much as a glimpse of him, unfortunately; he was behind her, and likely masked. The left arm stayed over her windpipe; it was the right that wielded the knife. A five-inch blade, the doctor thinks, probably a push-button knife of the kind used on Ed Toomey. I can't see why such weapons aren't outlawed. The way it is, any punk can buy one at almost any hardware store. You'd think commerce favored criminals, instead of the rank and file keeping the law."

The last was morose, an expression, I knew, of oppression rather than settled belief. Phil is a businessman.

Just the same, facing our helplessness anew, I felt what he meant. So far, against the inflictions being visited by this man who killed and taunted, we'd made no headway whatever, while he'd worked at will.

When Phil left I began on a cooky batch—this was Christmas Baking Monday. In front of the oven I stood in my frustrated and frustrating millrace. "*Other* criminals get caught. They're seen, or someone informs on them. Why isn't there anyone to inform on Roke Bradsher? Sherry Lee, if she wanted to, might tell where he is. That's what Winterung believed for a while. Or there should be fingerprints. Or a dropped clue leading somewhere——"

The smell of burning would hit my nose, and I'd jerk open the oven door on a sheet of blackened rounds. I gave up.

Sherry Lee stayed away from me. When Phil had gone she went up to her room, emerging from it only for Jeffry's bottles, her own dinner, and a phone call from the intern. Comments she supplied went no farther than those earlier evoked, the most telling one being "All we can do is wait, I guess." By then—it was dinnertime—impulse said I might scream, "We have waited." I managed to utter the words tightly, instead. More and more, as the day progressed, it began being apparent that a different quality had entered our waiting, one of imminence.

"Only a feeling you've got," I tried telling myself. "You're imagining things. Again. Maybe that's how this thing will end. We'll be pushed so far we'll go over the edge. All of us. I haven't the nervous system to bear up under endlessness. Maybe that's what Roke Bradsher wants. Maybe he never intends getting closer to us, maybe he intends teasing us from the fringe forever."

As soon as I'd thought that, an antiphonal response came back. "That's not true. He's worked on the fringe, he'll be moving in closer. Any minute now while Winterung and his men are busy at Wayzata. Maybe that's what the attack on the waitress was for, a withdrawing action to get Winterung and his men away——"

Even by daylight the patrol car came past every half hour; the phone in my room awaited any demand I made on it. We were perfectly safe. The baby, with the new name to which I must accustom myself. Jeffry. Sherry Lee. I. All of us, in our glass bubble.

A man as adroit as Roke Bradsher could handle the police patrol. Perhaps even the phone.

Tension tightened with every swing of the pendulum, winding me up.

Since he was the one not interdicted, Phil stayed with Sherry Lee that evening while Bunky walked me to church.

Bunky was quiet that evening. "At least they can't think I was mixed up in what happened last night," he offered as we walked. "There weren't two people in that attack, only one."

Pat Evers, getting out of her convertible at the side door of the church, said that she'd see me home, but Bunky's finals were over so he offered to stay, holding scripts, herding choruses and hammering tighter the back stable wall. Until six years ago he'd been in that pageant, with Johnny; that was what we reminisced about on the way home. Outside the house he waited for Phil; the two went off together.

Sherry Lee was already abovestairs when I got in; the baby was fretting a little, that night. In the davenport corner with my table on my lap, warmed by the incongruous fire of the tree lights, I sat for a while listening, hearing all the familiar, reassuring sounds—the swish of tires in soft snow outside, the distant rumble of the bus on Twenty-fourth, an equally distant car horn. From upstairs came the sound that was new— Jeffry's thin, querulous, somehow inexpectant wail, the slide and tap of Sherry Lee's feet in the blue satin mules.

All afternoon there'd been no later word from Winterung; the evening papers had rehashed the earlier account, adding only a depiction of the current hunt, house to house, cottage to cottage, store to barn to boathouse, in the whole Lake Minnetonka area. In thought I also pursued that hunt, slogging along with three men or four, rapping at doors, searching houses, asking for keys, peering through windows. Eyes quick for the one detail wrong—footprints over an expanse of snow which should have been unmarked, swept paths on a porch which should have drifted smooth, smoke from a chimney which should have stood unwarmed, litter on a table which should be clear, rumpled blankets on a mattress which should be winter-stowed among rafters. It would have been easier, my mind said, if I could have joined that hunt, spending my tension in action.

No, it wouldn't, my body answered wearily. After little rest the night before, I was so tired no danger was as important as getting to bed.

I went to bed. Before ten, I think; I didn't look to see. Jeffry was still fussing when I fell asleep. When I woke it was before dawn, and Sherry Lee's hand was on my shoulder.

"Wake up. Oh, wake up," she was whispering, gasping. "Mrs. Kiskadden, the baby's gone. I woke for his six o'clock bottle, but he wasn't there. Ma'am, he isn't there——"

I was all the way alert, all at once. No staring at her groggily, no groping around for circumstance. "That's impossible. He must be there." Speech didn't come from my throat, it echoed from the dark outer edges of the room. "He was fussing last night. He must be in your bed. He's there somewhere. He can't have——"

Maybe I wasn't as awake as I felt. She turned in the dark, moving away from me. At her heels I went too, snatching my bathrobe but not pausing for slippers or to turn on the light, dimly aware of detail, such as the prickle of the hall rug under my feet. Blinking at the light of her room as I came to it, though she had on only the two small vanity lights. Passing her, I got to the crib.

She was right. In the crib was nothing but the smooth undersheet covering the mattress. No huddled rolled bundle, no fleecy pink and blue blankets.

I whirled to the bigger bed, ripping back the blankets there, separating them. Expecting that somewhere within them would be the tiny figure, more motionless, more rigidly motionless, than it had been in life. Thinking, in an instant's flash like lightning striking in jagged streaks across my mind, "She planned this. It was Johnny's baby. She didn't want Johnny's baby. That was why she looked at him so mournfully; she knew he'd never survive. She had to be free to go back to Roke Bradsher. That was what those dolls meant too. The whistling. The card. 'Lo, I am with you alway'—he wanted her to remember what she was to do. Get rid of the baby as soon as it was born, and come back to him, to her life and her fun that she wants while she's young. Only she needn't have done it this way; she could have given Jeffry to me. If she'd done that, if I'd had him without her between us——"

The mind can cover aeons in an instant's time. There was no baby in the bed, though, living or not living. No baby on the hooked and flowered rug under the bed. No baby in the dresser drawers, the closet——

I must have looked a madwoman, running to jerk open drawers and doors, overturning chairs. When I wheeled on her she was where I'd passed her, cringing against the wall beside the door, face narrowed to a white streak, eyes all the way open, fear-struck. So different from their usual schooled drowsiness that she mightn't have been the person to whom I'd partially grown accustomed. Hands in back of her against the wall, body bent, arcing.

I accused, menacing, knowing I sounded menacing, quite willing it should be so. This wasn't just threat, suspicion, danger. Not any longer.

"You knew you'd be doing this. You've been waiting——"

She didn't pretend not understanding. The whispering gasps with which she answered were more hoarse than those with which she'd wakened me.

"It's not me, ma'am. Don't you see, ma'am? It's Roke. That's who's got him. He'd know I'd want the baby back; this is the worst hurt he can do to me. It's the way he can make me feel terrible. He's going to ask for money. That's why I've been saving it. Only—only I thought maybe he wouldn't dare. Not with the police out there. Not with the new phone in your room. I could—I could as well have known. After Ed went that way, after the girl out there—I guess I did know. He got in here someway. He's got him now——"

No more of the peculiar hardihood. No more, even, of the rigidity, the shrinking. She wasn't standing against the wall, she was collapsed against it, remaining partially upright only because of its support, swept away into a state where she was part way at least out of control, babbling, "I said Roke could go anywhere. I said Roke could do anything. I said he could be dead, even, and come back alive again——"

Against her hysteria what possessed me was hardness and coldness. More hardness and coldness the more her hysteria increased. I'd gone to stand near her, understanding her extremity, but—in spite of all there had been to prepare me—still finding this development beyond belief.

I argued, "You were right here in this bed. Bradsher would have had to walk in here. You'd have waked. Why didn't you wake?" Thought once more pounced. "Unless you were helping him. Knowing he'd be here. Giving him the baby so that he——"

She emitted a low, straining cry, trying to pull herself straighter by her hands along the wall, failing, falling more into herself.

"I wouldn't do that. I wouldn't let Roke in with me. Why would I? Roke wouldn't even need me to do it, he can slide in and slide out like a snake. Why would he care if I waked up? He'd have his knife. Or if you waked up, either one? He'd know he could get away."

I was backing away from her. Sensing, suddenly, that the cold harshness was about to break and that my knees wouldn't hold me up. Breath was vanishing too. I got to the bared bed, sinking to it.

I said again, "It's not—possible. The baby's so little yet. No man could take care of a baby that little: he'd know we'd know it. I can't believe——" Harshness might be breaking, but not incredulity, which wasn't a thing to think, but an uprushing, outspreading resistance which kept jetting in my breast like a fountain.

Empty crib. Empty bed. Empty room. Dresser drawers holding nothing but innocent small piles of folded lingerie, folded diapers, folded sheets, folded blankets, towels, sleepers. Dresses. Socks. Nothing else.

I took a second look from where I was, the bed. And for some reason then began believing it. At least part way. I began rising.

"I'll get in to the phone." My voice was echoing this time too. "It won't be seconds before we have the——"

I was on my feet, but no more than that. Through all of the foregoing—in experience long, but in time occupying probably no more than two minutes—the girl had stayed near the door. No sooner had I said the word "phone," though, than she'd hurled herself forward, snatching at my wrists with a strength I'd never have guessed she owned. Glaring at me, shaking me, her mouth gone horror-struck.

"No. No. No. No. Don't you see you can't do that? Roke's got him. Got Jeffry. He'll kill him. He wouldn't have to cut him, even. Just a hand over his face. Ma'am, not this time. You can't get those police here. Roke'll get to us somehow, he'll let us know what he wants. Whatever it is he wants, he's got to get it, ma'am. I'll watch you, ma'am. This time, ma'am, I've got to see you don't get the cops in here, can't you see I can't let you do that? We've got to do this the way he wants, ma'am, we've got to, we've got to——"

The idea of mothers being savage when their children are threatened isn't new to me; there'd been times in Johnny's life when I was savage too. While she was pouring out her plea I slipped out of time and place enough so I had a fleeting moment of being almost objective— "This in a way must be funny, her being so desperate, yet calling me ma'am." Yet I couldn't be there, in the grip of her hands, looking on at the contortions of her white features under the smooth niagara of hair, and not sense her exigency. I stood my ground, not giving way. In this matter it wasn't just my mind that spoke, and not just instinct. The two joined.

"You have only one chance of getting Jeffry back. No one can get away with kidnapping. It's not local crime, it's federal crime. There'll be federal men on it. We're wasting time——"

She wanted to hit me. The hunger to hit lay in eyes lit from behind like tiger's eyes. One hand lifted, to claw. She began babbling again, always with that ridiculous formal address, which I suppose came to her tongue because she hadn't accustomed herself to any other.

"Ma'am, you don't know Roke. You don't know the kind of thing he can do. You don't know what he'd do to me if anything goes wrong with any plan he makes."

In a way she was out of bounds, yet also she was exercising superhuman control, restraining herself from physical attack. So desperate was her rage that, in spite of myself, I found myself once more weakening. When she began on a new plea—"Wait a little bit, anyway. Wait until we hear from Roke. There might be a note from him somewheres right this minute if we find it"—I knew I was giving way.

I repeated, "It can't be anything but wrong." Earlier disbelief returning, I said, "Suppose you walked in your sleep. You could have taken Jeffry down, dreaming you went for his bottle——"

She seized that. "Let's look, then. I'd be glad—don't you think I'd be glad?—if we found him. Only don't go near any telephone."

That was the compromise on which we moved. Collecting enough sense from somewhere to look over the rest of the upstairs first. My room, bathroom, Johnny's closed room where his pictures, his pennants, his *Esquire* pin-ups, his books, his bed with the pineapple spread, sprang to harsh temporary existence when I flicked up the light switch, vanished as quickly into winter darkness when I flicked it down. We looked in at clothes closets, linen closets—a sleepwalker can do anything, and looking is so sane, so hopeful a thing to be doing. A patrol car, passing, wouldn't be alerted by lights after six o'clock.

Downstairs there were so few places to look. Davenport, chairs, Christmas tree, hall closet, dining room, half bath, kitchen.

No baby. But, finally, something else. Something making me accept that Jeffry indeed was gone. Icy air flowed across the kitchen floor; I felt it running over my feet as soon as I rounded the diningroom arch. That air came from across the kitchen, from around the door opening on the three steps down to the side entrance.

I flew toward there, snatching open the inside door. Over the landing below me, the outside entrance door—one I never went to bed without locking—swung idly inward.

"Someone opened that door from this side." Once more I was accusing. "There's only the one key; I never take it from the keyhole. It couldn't have been pushed in——"

But then I saw the door to the milk chute, just to the right of the entrance door. It also ajar. Two milk bottles on the milkchute ledge, awaiting the dairyman's round. Between them, protruding, a buff rectangle, with the door key set neatly on top.

I bent to the card.

"Ye shall find the babe wrapped in swaddling clothes, lying in a manger." So read the Bible verse, pasted, exactly as the other verse had been pasted, in the lower right-hand corner of the card.

Only there hadn't been verses, not Bible verses, to cover all the contingencies. Above the verse ran additional typewritten lines.

```
    Didn't know how easy it is to reach
in through a milk chute and turn a key, did
you? Now you can go around to your church
again, midnight. I'll trade the kid for
three thousand in small unmarked bills. Ask
Sherry Lee what will happen if you don't
do this right.
```

# CHAPTER THIRTEEN

"DIDN'T KNOW HOW EASY it is to reach in through a milk chute and turn a key."

One thing I'd been sure of was my locking up. Here in front of me was the simple and wily means of evading my guardianship. A milk chute forced, leaving space for an arm to reach inward and upward to a key in a lock not eighteen inches away.

Just as Sherry Lee had put it. "I said Roke could go anywhere. I said Roke could do anything. He can slide in and slide out like a snake." He'd slid in for extortion. "Ye shall find the babe wrapped in swaddling clothes, lying in a manger." Melodramatic, again a thing that might happen to someone else, but not to me or anyone connected with me.

Through the evening before I'd begun seeing a plan, one directed and scheduled. Not hard, any longer, to see the clearer outlines of such designing. Not so hard, now, to begin guessing at the puppet's part I'd played, and at the skillful hand somewhere that had managed the strings.

It wasn't from Sherry Lee, who had little, that this killer asked tribute, it was from me, who had more. Here, as the close of my puppet's dance, I was to take three thousand in bills, a rolled bundle. Go to the church which at midnight would be dark, awaiting the morrow's pageant. Exchange my inanimate bundle for the other, which was supposed to be breathing, lying in the strawfilled manger in the straw-strewn stable at the altar side. Would Roke Bradsher in his insanity, his hunger for vengeance, be able to restrain himself from the one cut more?

"These are orders you can't possibly carry out." Revolt at continuing in my puppethood had risen, and flaringly, but I struggled to thrust it down. What we must act on wasn't emotion, it was common sense. "Where do you think Jeffry is now? Being fed? Being bathed and changed and cared for? Or shoved aside somewhere, maybe in a car trunk, where he'll be dead inside minutes of cold? It's eighteen hours from now until midnight. You must see we can't chance it; the child's only hope is our call for help. Phil will be phoning, or we can call him. He can handle everything from his house. Bradsher need never know——"

While I talked, she'd snatched the card. As soon as she'd read it she was shaking me as she had upstairs.

"No. No. No. Don't you see? It don't matter what Roke don't know. If things don't work out, then he'll have to kill Jeffry. He'll have to. It's the way he is. He'll kill me. Not fast. That's what he means when he says ask me what will happen if you don't do this right. I know, ma'am. I do know. If you don't have that much money, just take what there is. You can talk to him, anyway; just so he knows you're believing him, trying to do what he says. I'll be along. You don't know Roke; it's like he goes wild when people won't do what he says. Ma'am, you've got to——"

In anger and desperation I was ready to do a little shaking of my own. "He won't be able to do any of the things he threatens. He's no part of a gang; you know that. He's alone. If he tries for the money he'll be at the church, and that will be Winterung's chance. You can't actually think he'd risk taking the baby there. What do you think the patrol would do at midnight, glimpsing a strange man with a bundle? He can't——"

She shrieked, "I said you don't know him; you don't understand at all." She began on the phrases so familiar they were a refrain. "Roke could do anything, Roke could go anywhere——"

About truly intense, truly frantic, truly unalloyed emotion, there's a power almost nothing else has. With every bone of my body I was certain—or thought I was—that I was wrong in once more yielding. Certain that in so doing I was throwing the baby, throwing myself, throwing Sherry Lee, to a wanton destruction and terror. Yet against the strength of her vehemence I wasn't able to take contrary action, either.

We moved up, after a while, from the freezing entry to the kitchen. Fallen, by then, into sporadic bursts, on my side, of continuing resistance and on hers of denial. The phone rang. It was Phil. "You all okay this morning?—No, I guess not yet. There's a posse now, local Wayzata men. Stayed out most of the night."

Deliverance was so near. I stood with mouthpiece at lip, receiver at ear, nothing barring me but the fury at my side, the hand outstretched to strike the phone from me if I began on the one wrong syllable.

She was younger than I. Not so much bigger, but more heavily boned. Just the same, I was no weakling; not long ago I was holding out pretty well on hikes with Johnny and Bunky, even at climbing hills. One scream would bring Phil. I could get that much in.

Yet I put in neither scream nor word.

After a time has gone by, it's not easy to bring back the impulses and responses, the myriad convergings, which bring you to act as you act. It might be that, so far out of my usual orbit, I just passed to a kind of lost limbo. Maybe I caught the emotion beside me as a sort of infection. Maybe I was taken by a kind of fatalism. Six weeks before, in Georgia, I'd invited Sherry Lee home with me. What was going on now had ensued from that.

What I did was continue protesting, but also letting myself be herded.

Herded. Yes, that's the word. In midmorning a call came from no one less than Lieutenant Winterung. "You've been keeping in touch, of course." His voice over the wire said he was rackingly tired. "I thought I might give you my personal assurance that everything possible is being done. We've got to consider, of course, that the assailant may never have been Bradsher at all, but some localite grabbing the Bradsher publicity."

"No, not so," I might have told him. "It was Bradsher, all right. But this is the center, here. It's here he's playing his drama out. Come back." The fatalism, though, or the indecision, or the feeling of its being somehow unavoidable, of Sherry Lee so closely hovering, once more operated to hold me. I again hung up having said nothing.

Banks close at three. I was at mine well before noon.

"You want three thousand in small bills?" From the other side of his grill, Fred Tischler repeated my request. Fred Tischler has stood behind that grill for some twenty-odd years.

"Yes," I said, Sherry Lee at my elbow, "I'm making some unusual Christmas gifts. Tens, if you have enough. Some twenties."

Fred's slightly protruding eyes peered at me, narrowing. Surely he must guess, I thought. This is the request for which bank cashiers everywhere are taught to watch. But he turned and, methodical, businesslike, moistening forefinger and thumb on a handy sponge in a small glass saucer, began counting out, stacking up bills.

Not long ago there'd been a little over five thousand in my checking account. The trip to Georgia, the hospital bill, later purchases had depleted it. As of that morning there'd been thirty-two hundred and sixty-nine dollars. A sum, I thought, so near the amount demanded it was almost as if the bank, too, were a glass bubble, or as if Bradsher saw through stone and steel. Three thousand. Not an amount for which I'd have to go to other people, thereby rousing attention. A modest and moderate sum. For a kidnapper.

"Glad there's someone along with you." Finished with his counting, Fred began shoving the stacks under the grill.

"Wouldn't like to see you walking out of here with that much all alone." He grinned, expecting repartee, and when there wasn't any looked dampened. But let us walk away.

We drove back to the vigil.

"Jeffry. He's so little. If we could hope——" Once and again, but only once and again, because there was so little response, I tried waking Sherry Lee to what I thought she should be wakened; she quickly got to a place where she didn't even reply. Except for the new and different alertness, the harsh readiness to pounce, she'd reverted to the woodenness she'd displayed at times of stress earlier. The brilliant hair surrounded a face permanently shrunken, so much so that almost all of its underlying bone structure now showed.

More and more, as the day wore on, it was the infant on whom my thoughts fixed. Where was he by that time, poor small mite of humanity? He who'd existed so quiescently through his few days, as if, in some measure, he had known what was coming, and so stayed inexpectant of living. I'd thought I wouldn't be capable of another grief, not for long years yet. I'd thought I hadn't attached myself to the baby. Now I found a dead slow weight dragging at my breast once more, and it wasn't for Johnny. Into my hands, unobtrusively, had grown the way Jeffry felt—his weightlessness, his softness. The way he looked— that small round head, the inky purple of his eyes, the barely perceptible beginnings of down over his head, his very solemnity—these had grown into my mind. Into my ears had grown his single communication, the thin querulous wailing.

I got up to walk, clenching my hands. Back and forth in front of the Christmas tree.

We hadn't had breakfast; I wanted none. At noon Sherry Lee made herself a sandwich and got milk from the refrigerator; her pallid rigor said the sandwich was sawdust, the milk rancid. I didn't join her.

Just after four o'clock Phil followed up his earlier phone call by dropping in.

# THE WHISTLING SHADOW

"What's wrong now?" He no sooner saw me than he jumped to my tension. The dark glance shot from me to Sherry Lee and back again. "There's nothing new up, is there? Winterung hasn't——"

Sherry Lee at my elbow, I said, "No, nothing new." The words inched forward over a sandpaper tongue.

He said, "Whew. The way you look, both of you——"

The glance leaped again, and I saw the surmise he made. He believed me at odds with the girl. As I was. The reasons supplied by his rational mind, though, were the rational reasons. The next glance he sent me was intended to soothe, to say, "Now, Gail, she won't be in your house too much longer. That apartment is pretty near done."

Unaware of the absence of welcome, he threw overcoat and hat aside over a chair and settled into the davenport. He talked over latest reports from Wayzata—in my state it barely was possible to listen. He talked of plans for attending the pageant, next evening; no reason, he said, why Sherry Lee and the baby shouldn't go too; he'd take us all. After that it was obvious he expected Sherry Lee, as usual, to take herself off so he could talk with me privately. I wasn't offering much, Sherry Lee wasn't offering much, we had pauses in which he didn't say much either; I wished only that he'd go. Instead, after one of the longer pauses, and after running a finger tip up along his cheek scar, he brought from an inside jacket pocket a yellow telegraph form which he rose awkwardly to hand to me.

"I know you won't be too much interested in this," he apologized, "but since it's bound to come up, you may as well see it now."

I took the message being offered me. "Wish me joy," it read, in the hilly pasted-on capitals of all Western Union typing. "Have met wonderful man here on same sad errand as mine wearing new solitaire could use fifteen hundred love Evie."

"I'd begun thinking it was a little odd I didn't hear anything more at all." Again it was difficult to make the jump to the fact that, in

165

addition to his communion in our lives, Phil still had affairs of his own. While I looked at the wire, in a dim, unconnected way, I was able to make the reflections and get echoes of responses I'd have had if I hadn't been so strung. How like Evie, not so much as letting him know another liaison was in progress, keeping him and his hotel reservation dangling, expecting money, and as a final extravagance sending her news not by dayletter or nightletter, but by straight wire.

I tried dredging up adequacy, but from the heaviness holding me it wasn't possible to squeeze any real warmth. He knew it and was hurt.

"I shouldn't have brought it up," he excused himself. And then, at last about to go, turned in forced jocoseness to Sherry Lee.

"Where's that godson? He can just as well begin getting used to me, now I'm supposed to have a hand in bringing him up."

If I'd been awaiting this, half hoping, half fearing it, so must she. What I thought, with a little spurt which in anyone else I'd have called vicious, was, "Yes, let's see how you'll handle that." I needn't have wondered.

She answered coolly, "I had a bad time getting him to sleep this afternoon, Mr. Sawyer. He didn't sleep well last night. Maybe he's got just a little bit colic. I guess most babies get colic. It's nothing to worry about."

Not even a clash. Phil acceded, "We'll do it another time," and left. In slow motion. Hours, agonizing, never-to-be-regained hours passing while he slid into his overcoat, stood with hat in hand thinking he was staying us against the exasperations of the Minnetonka hunt, proffering one lame reassurance after the other. Taking new hours to get through the door. But disappearing at last, striding down the front walk, getting into his car, driving off.

Taking with him my last hope.

I hadn't faced to it earlier; through the morning I'd kept the dark thought at bay. But now, with a real dusk descending, standing at the window watching the taillight of Phil's car vanish into the gray mist toward the lake, I considered not only Jeffry's chances but my own, and saw them as few as his. Since Roke Bradsher had spoken to Bunky at the Palladium parking lot, no one had viewed his face. Except likely Ed Toomey, who hadn't lived to tell of it. "I'll be along," Sherry Lee said, but she wasn't the one picked for a go-between. I was expendable. Of me, except as a source of money, Bradsher knew little and cared less.

From Phil's departure onward, I don't think I sat. It was dinnertime, with no dinner to help the hour pass. My stomach had shriveled to the size and substance of a peach pit; when I moved I had pains, because the muscles holding that peach pit were too tightly stretched. Something, I told myself, must yet happen. Phil, away from me, thinking over what had been said, thinking over my reception of his news from Evie, must decide I'd been too unnatural for any quarrel with Sherry Lee to be a cause. He'd return, this time demandingly. Sometime, any moment now, I'd reach a final rebellion. I'd go to the phone which had been installed for just such a purpose. Or someone somewhere, seeing a man with hot vengeful eyes, carrying a baby where no baby should be—that someone would leap to conjecture. The phone would ring one important time more. It would be Winterung, jubilant. "You might like to know, Mrs. Kiskadden. We've got him. The baby too——"

In that case there'd be no trip through the chill and deserted night. No empty church waiting. No manger.

I counted hours. Thirteen, already thirteen, since Sherry Lee waked me. Five more, then four more, to go.

Long before the four hours were over, I'd already in imagination begun making my way. To the tall vaulted interior where on nights previous to this there'd been light, noise and color, skittering children in the aisles and the pews, marshaled children on the platform, Pat Evers harassed with script in hand, "Now look, Michael——" While in back of the stable, with the Reverend Mr. Raeburn fluttering and advising, Bunky had hammered nails.

No children in the church tonight. Not Pat Evers, not the Reverend Mr. Raeburn, not Bunky. And no lights. Nothing but darkness, space, the altar, a stage setting, the pews. Until a footfall came, and then, if we were lucky, the smothered thin querulous cry. The settling of a blanket-wrapped bundle into the manger where on the morrow the carved and dressed image of another Child was to lie. Then the stealthy drawing back, the waiting for me to come.

Risking my life, to such an extent over, wasn't too much to pit against the chance of Jeffry's life, barely begun.

Only that wasn't all that began moving me, either. Not everything that by midevening made me impatient, striding the floor to make the hours pass. All of this time we'd been teased so much. All this time, keeping himself tantalizingly aloof, Roke Bradsher had avoided the hands and eyes seeking him, refusing any appointment with capture. Ahead was one appointment he wasn't so apt to miss. I might die for it, but I'd see what manner of man he was. Whistling, killing, leaving tokens, stealing a newborn child.

I was possessed by a terrible urgency. One sweeping up, rocking me, fearful and arrogant, shaken and sure.

No one else had got at Roke Bradsher. I would.

That must have been ridiculous too. That mood in which, weaponless, I went out to pit myself against the man Roke Bradsher was known to be.

I decided to take the car. Sherry Lee didn't like it. Somehow in her mind there seemed to have been an idea that we'd walk, but when I insisted she didn't demur too much. She merely saw to it I was never left alone for an instant before we left. Not for getting so much as a paring knife, not for lifting the receiver from my special upstairs phone. In the car, while I drove the short distance, she sat huddled and small, hair loose on her coat collar, hands thrust into pockets, but a coiled spring for all that. In a night slightly misty, chill rather than icy, the houses we passed stood out dimly amid their shadows. At half past eleven most of those houses slept, lit if at all by the blue, red and green of exterior Christmas lights, enclosing people intent on laying in backlogs of sleep for the full days ahead. In each block, though, there were bright-windowed homes where mothers and fathers were still at work, painting small wooden boats, doweling the corners of dollhouses, tying packages in a litter of patterned papers and ribbon. None of those fathers and mothers, so absorbed, hearing my car's low hum, would know on what errand I went, and rush to prevent me. Cars met us, headlights gleaming up in the haze ahead like amber animal eyes, swallowed past in a rush of sound. Other cars came up from behind us too—one a patrol car which trundled past, movement in the head and shoulders of the figure to the right saying he glanced toward us. Two gals, he'd say to his partner. Why should he stop? He was hunting a man.

Against my right hip, in my coat pocket, lay two hard lumps. The bank notes, held by rubber bands. Not much for a kidnapper, but a wad too big to go into my handbag.

Three and a half blocks from my house to the church, three and a half long, too short blocks. No word had been said of a door being open, but one, I could guess, would be open. Not the big double doors at the front. The grade door at the side, the one by which we'd entered for rehearsals, leading down toward the Sunday school rooms and the kitchen, under the church. I drew up alongside that grade door, bending to my wrist watch under the faint light of the dash. Twenty minutes to twelve.

Was I afraid? Yes, I was. So much so I scarcely felt the fear any more, I was too much pushed by the need for getting there, for meeting Roke Bradsher at last face to face. "Maybe this is the way men feel in a war," I thought. "Afraid, but knowing they'll go ahead." It was as if, in the hours while I'd waited to get where I was, I'd moved from my body a little way. As if I were still secured to it, but not attached as I once was, not combined with it. Yet my awareness of that physical shell was more acute than at other times; I felt toward it a sad farewell fondness. It had been so mobile a housing for me, so compact, had compassed me so soundly, obeyed me so well. "The car keys," I told my fingers, and two of them plucked those keys from the ignition lock, dropping them into the coat pocket that didn't hold the money. "Come with me," I said to my body, and it did so, though a numbness pervaded it. It wasn't asking much of me any longer, not even that I keep it safe.

Sherry Lee must have got out, though I hadn't noticed. The door was open on her side; I slid after her, asking, low, "Are you coming in?"

She said, "I'll come with you up to the door." At that door she might have been the one who, finally, faltered. More uncertain than she'd been at any other time during the day, with more breaks in her speech, she said, "I've been thinking. He didn't say anything at all about me. I could wait out here. In the car. I could hide like, so he wouldn't see me. Then if you aren't out in ten minutes—— I've been thinking I could do this. I'll follow the time on my watch. If ten minutes go by, I'll go get the police. I'll promise, ma'am. I've been thinking, all the way, I could promise that. You can tell him. If you don't get back out——"

Dimly I compassed the thought that it was nice of her to be so concerned for my welfare. We stood together on the stone step before the church door, and she was so near me her breath was warm on my cheek. Yet her voice might have come from a quarter block away. I'd already gone on, leaving her. Not only my body had drawn slightly away from me now, but my mind as well.

I put my hand to the heavy dark knob of the door with the carved fleur-de-lis on its paneling. The knob turned and the door came outward.

# THE WHISTLING SHADOW

One glance I cast back, the same glance, it might be, that Lot's wife cast. At Sherry Lee, still bent toward me in her anguish of necessity. Face a white streak of desperation, as it had been all day. Eyes hidden under the low lashes. Hair smooth, oh, so faultlessly smooth, waved into the one deep faultless indentation that curved slightly outward at the right temple. I saw the mist behind her, the foot-trampled snow of the walk, the loom of my car at the curb, and beyond it the distant bulk of houses which extended to be all Minneapolis.

"That's what you're leaving," my mind said, but like my body it too was obedient, facing about to the darkness ahead. Behind me, when I'd taken the important steps downward, the door stayed open a moment and then gently sighed to a close.

For some twenty-two years I'd been a working supporter of the edifice which now enclosed me. I'd been there so many times for rehearsals, so many times for church dinners, so many times for Sunday-school services. Even in darkness, I knew where I was. This door by which I stood opened into the big downstairs hall which doubled for so many purposes. Along one wall stood the long table tops which could be unfolded on trestles for serving. In the center stood the Sunday-school chairs, set up by classes, little chairs at the front, big ones at the back. The superintendent's desk occupied the platform to my left. Beyond it were doors giving on the lavatory hall and the kitchens. To my right, under my hand on the wall, was the light switch.

Finger on switch, I paused. Roke Bradsher would never chance lights, I was sure of it. He had been here, no doubt of that either. Neither the Reverend Mr. Raeburn nor the janitor would ever have left a door unlocked. A deft man, Roke Bradsher, as Sherry Lee said. How, for instance, had he gotten a key? Not that it mattered, but a question to ask. Why had he picked the church as the site for his——

I flicked up the switch. As expected, no lights came on. So easy to manage—merely a bar pulled at the fuse box. Suppose I went there first. Suppose, instead of pattering dutifully upstairs, to the manger in the stable setting, I went to the fuse box. Suppose, at this hour, lights flashed on and stayed on. Would that wake aged Raeburn husband or aged Raeburn wife in the house next door? Stir up the janitor, two blocks down? Halt a patrol car——

Lights in the church could mean nothing, to the patrol car, but Christmas preparations in need of last-minute completion. Roke Bradsher, besides, had probably taken the fuses out.

And if it came to that, darkness might be on my side. The other being in this building couldn't possibly know it as well as I.

Misty as it was outdoors, there still were glimmerings of visibility from windows and streetlights. Once my eyes were oriented, I didn't have to guess at the placing of the Sunday-school chairs. The switch made a click, a loud one, but that seemed a single sound. I stood quietly, waiting for other sounds, expecting, in a way, that I needn't go farther. From somewhere beside me a figure—masked, likely, as it must have been for the girl in Wayzata, gloved as well—would materialize.

"That'll be far enough, Mrs. Kiskadden," the voice would say softly. "The kid's upstairs. You can hand me that money now."

He'd want his minutes for getting away. Getting the money while I still had to run upstairs for Jeffry—that would give him his minutes.

I wondered if, as she'd promised, Sherry Lee waited in the car, watching the minute hand of her watch.

No sound from outdoors came through to me; for the sake of attentions all too easily distracted, the church had been built to shut out sound. Not from inside, either. Nothing for any sense, from inside, but the faint smell. Musty, rubbery. No. After a while, when my ears were fined, there was one sound, a lingering drip from a faucet. Nothing else but thick silence which in its empty way also was audible. Especially when, as now, it pulsated with my heart's thudding, the running of blood in my arteries. Or simply from another heart's waiting.

Along the wall, slowly, I inched a way. There wasn't, I suppose, any reason why I should be stealthy, but stealthy I stayed. It seemed important to hug the wall. I moved a few feet, stopped, listened once more for the faucet drip and the audible quiet, moved another few feet, stopped again, hearing now the echo of my shoes' slow brushing in galoshes. Galoshes, it came to me, were heavy and hampering; at the foot of the stairway near the front corner I stooped to slip them off, setting them neatly along the wall below the bottom step. If ever I came that way again I might find them there.

The church offered three means of ascent. One, from the back lavatory hall, led up to the sacristy, which likely was locked. The two at the front were a pair, two long, steep flights leading up to the vestibule. It was to the right-hand one of this pair that I'd come, but after taking off my galoshes I didn't mount by it. Surely, I was thinking by then, Roke Bradsher must have preceded me; if he'd heard me he'd be waiting directly above. I crossed to the left. Not that it made any difference, merely that it seemed important not to act as he expected. I found the first step, easing my weight to it. Just the same, it creaked. Not loudly—rather a whispered complaint than a creak, from the settling of the board against its supports. Yet audible, to let Roke Bradsher again know I was on my way.

Above and ahead of me, as I well knew, at the curve of the flight, stood a ledge, a triangular niche, where for festivals and weddings we banked flowers. Anyone, a tall man, even, could poise there, ready to drop on whoever came up from below. I shrank to the opposite wall as I neared that ledge, expectant and, in my defenselessness, armored. A gun, I thought. How a gun would have helped if I'd had one. In the glove compartment of my car, outside, lay a flashlight; if in sliding past it I'd managed to get that compartment open, the flashlight into my pocket, would Sherry Lee have been quick to that too? No matter, the time was past.

Stairway and vestibule were unwindowed: any light from behind, as I neared the curve, was as swallowed as the faucet drip; space appeared a black pit. Yet when my head came level with the ledge nothing leaped at me; I drew past it and still nothing leaped at me; it was with a sensation of dull surprise that I found myself on the vestibule carpet. With, a few feet to the left, the two outside front doors, and, only an arm's reach to the right, the swinging doors giving on the church proper.

Palms flat against the varnished oak of those inner doors, I once more paused. Certainly, on those tall stairs by which I'd mounted, I'd been at my most vulnerable. Yet nothing had happened there; I was up on a level; on the other side of these doors there'd be light again, more than in the basement because the windows were taller. If I'd got this far, could it be that arrangements would go as described? That when I got to the manger I'd actually find in it——

I pushed one door inward. Not far. An inch. Enough to tell me that, as foreseen, space lay lighter. Enough to show, vaguely, the sweep of the central aisle, the range of pews flanking it, the two farther side aisles, the pews beyond them. Ahead, far and dark, bulked the altar, the pulpit, the ceiling-high Christmas tree, the mass of the stage setting.

There've been times in my life, such as Johnny's confirmation, when, sitting in one of the pews now in front of me, I'd felt a Presence not too far off, one I've reached for and hoped for, which I've thought I might touch if I were tuned as I should be tuned. More often I'd been aware only of more human beneficences—the nearness of pleasant well-dressed people, Sunday well-being and decorum, words being spoken that might stir uncomfortably but that on the whole were solacing. Bouts of spring and fall church-cleaning had tempered even this much with matter-of-factness. Now I reached out for anything—

Presence, social warmth, matter-of-factness—all were equally gone. Why shouldn't they be? Only two or three gathered in His name brought the Presence. Social warmth didn't coincide with emptiness, or with oil furnaces turned low. Matter-of-factness couldn't co-exist with the waiting, the pulsing, stronger here than downstairs, though nothing before me moved.

No cry from the manger, no thin querulous wail. But I had to find out.

So far I'd done nothing but move softly and slowly. The way to the manger, though, was so far and so open. Here too it might have been possible to slink along the far wall, but the other pull, the urgency, was stronger. I thrust both doors firmly, splitting them wide, and ran. Feeling as I did so the bouncing of the bill wads against one hip. Ran not for the center aisle but the one to the right, leading directly to the stable setting. Before I reached it the straw smell hit me sharply, and then the crushed slipperiness was smooth underfoot. I brushed aside, toppled aside, the three-legged milk stool on which the Virgin Mary was to sit, and got my hands into the manger.

Nothing there. Nothing there, of course. Nothing but straw, sliding silkily, scratchily. Nothing that squirmed, that fitted its blanketed softness to my hands, nothing to send up a beginning thin wail.

Instead and immediately there was a creak beside me. I whirled.

Not Roke Bradsher who stood by me, bulking in the dusky dimness. No one looming, vengeful, poised, waiting knife in hand. No one to menace me.

Someone to rescue me. Every aspect as familiar, as relieving, as home showing when you've been lost. Comforting stockiness, comforting breadth of leather jacket, comforting freckled face. Comforting bullethead.

Bunky.

In the weakness of letdown I wasn't able to throw myself at

him; I fell toward him. Clutching him, gasping for absent breath and almost equally absent words.

"Bunky. How did you know? All day—did you know all day? Did Sherry Lee get to you? Oh, Bunky, it was something I had to do, but I was so frightened. I didn't know until now. I've been frightened so desperately——"

He laughed gently, stroking me, holding me, patting my shoulder blades. He said, just as comfortingly, "Remember one time, Gail? That time Johnny and I got pulled in for the way we were handling that motorboat on Minnetonka? Johnny was over to the right of the driver's seat; he had his left hand out so it wouldn't show, steering. I was humped down below, where I didn't show either, working the controls. That's the way it's been this time too. I had Roke Bradsher up in the driver's seat. Only he wasn't there. There isn't any Roke Bradsher, Gail, not any more; he's been dead half a year. I was the one, Gail. All the time. Down below, where it wouldn't show, I had all the controls."

# CHAPTER FOURTEEN

THE CHURCH BEGAN leaving me. Drawing away its dimness, its pews, its altar, the tree and the stable, swaying them as it did so. Pulling its windows back. Tilting its floor. I wasn't anywhere. I was in a stillness and emptiness such as I'd never before in my life met. Yet in the empty opacity, the sightless, soundless and senseless stillness, my voice somewhere beat.

"Bunky, you don't know what you're saying. Bunky, that's not possibly true. You couldn't have——"

The other voice beat back. "Surprised, aren't you? I've really got you shocked. Roke Bradsher didn't come up to me out at that Palladium parking lot—didn't it ever hit you it was funny that was the only time anyone saw him after last May? You didn't so much as check. You didn't ask who else I was out there with. That was all made up—I had to make it up because Sherry Lee's a chicken. She stuck there in Georgia and wouldn't come up here to start on you. I had to wind my clock someway, and that was the way I picked. Worked, didn't it? Like to know where Roke Bradsher really is? In the bottom of Pepin, with stones at his head and feet; I'm the one ought to know, I'm the one sank him there. You kind of had us going there for a day or two, Gail, when you dug up that he'd been snooping around Lake City; he followed Sherry Lee and me there to some cabins I knew about. That was the first guy I ever killed; I was stronger than he was when he pulled a knife. You never would guess, Gail, how easy killing is. Knife in, knife out, and that's all."

I was trying to back away from the hold he maintained. A hold no longer comforting. A hold too familiar, one hand on my shoulder, the other at my back. Not much strength was left me, but I began exerting what there was, shrinking away, shriveling away from the horror my mind wasn't yet able to compass. What I continued to babble was likely more disbelief; my own words weren't registering. Against them, somewhere along, breaking into his easy unloading, he laughed once more. A sound coming to my ears as entirely alien.

With a different kind of numbness, perhaps one in which paralysis was easing enough so I was aware of the numbness, I thought, "That's Bunky laughing. I haven't heard him laugh, not really laugh, for long months. I haven't heard him laugh, not too much, for years. He wasn't like Johnny that way; he never laughed much. This is what he's held in." The waitress at Wayzata had said it was a terrible laugh. Greasy. I knew now what she meant; the sound was a satisfied chuckling, fatly happy with itself.

Once more, in the hands so inexorably gripping, I tugged and strained, without affecting either the grip or its possessor; he merely laughed again, clamping closer, talking on now as if this was his long-awaited moment for venting and vaunting and waving a cleverness.

"*Johnny* was always the one, wasn't he? The one did all the planning, the one in the lead. What he wanted for me was to scrabble at his heels. Any time I wouldn't play by his rules, he kicked me out. Ever notice how much of the time I began to be out? Oh, Johnny didn't tattle on me—maybe that was a mistake you made, teaching Johnny not to tattle. Johnny could have told you some tales. Johnny was used to me, Johnny could take me when I held myself down, but Johnny got so he didn't like me, not really. Though I got away with some things even he didn't know. You think that was accident, that time I knocked Pat Evers off that grandstand? Pat liked Johnny best too. You think it was accident, that BB shot getting Phil under the eye? Any luck I'd have had the eye. It's been fun, seeing what I could get, without being pinned down. Sherry Lee—you think Johnny had her all to himself? You think Johnny hooked onto her by himself? I got them together too. That kid you've got at home—you think that's Johnny's kid? Just as easy it could be mine. That kid's set now, though, he's all christened and named, in your house. Once she got going, Sherry Lee did all right by me——"

So much, when darkness wouldn't lift. I groped and strained, out of this last catching at the errand which had brought me where I was.

"Jeffry. The baby. He's not at home. Someone took him away from there——"

The laugh again, the oiled, indulging laugh.

"Look, Gail, I can't let anything happen to that kid. Not yet for a little while. That kid's not out of your house. Sherry Lee's got him back in his bed by now, feeding him. She doped him a little, that's all, in his morning bottle. Wrapped him up good and stuck him in your attic. I'll bet she's been on pins all day, scared he'd wake up somehow. Scared you'd hunt too hard. She's the worst scaredy cat anyone ever saw. Look, Gail, the malarky that goes around—malarky like Johnny believed in, malarky you go for, malarky my mother hands out—you think I've fallen for that? You think I'm going to take living the hard way, sweating it out in an office? My father knows better; he never did a day's work in his life. I'm taking mine easy too. Yours, Gail. That kid—Johnny's kid or my kid—he'll be inheriting. Nobody's going to have any suspicions of me. Me? Bunky Knowles? Nobody's going to cry harder at your funeral, right here by this altar, than I will. Why, I've been right next door to a son for you. Roke Bradsher, that's who'll have killed you, just the way he did all the rest. Sherry Lee can't be taken up on it either; she's fixing herself a good out. Sherry Lee handles what you've got, for the kid. I get it from Sherry Lee. Not half trying, I get it from Sherry Lee. Gail, I'm ashamed of you. It's so simple you ought to have seen through it. Before we get any farther, let's have that dough. I can use that to go on from here——"

The one hand, steel palm and steel fingers affixed to a steelbar arm, stayed at my back. The other groped in my coat pockets, finding the two wads within an instant, transferring them to other pockets. "There, that's fine. You're a good girl, Gail, acting just the way I knew you'd act, every inch. There's not too much left now——"

The last was still cheerful, but a little more lingering, a little regretful, even, as if now he was come to successful completion of his long stratagem he was sorry to have his play be ending. In that little interim, dimly still, vaguely still, I stumbled sickly toward some comprehension. That other boy, I thought. In Chicago. The one who murdered the little girl. There must have been people who'd loved him, too, from his babyhood. People who believed him to be what he'd seemed to be. Who'd been stupefied, unbelieving, when they found what he was. That other boy as well, the one in Detroit who killed his young playmate. Surely, surely, the chubby four-year-old who'd lifted his funny light owl's eyes, who'd said so gravely, "You're not such a cross mother as my mother"—he had been innocent. But sometime after that, in the unregarded years, the soul owned by that four-year-old had grown ill and been eaten away by another soul, cancerous. The Bunky who stood with me occupied Bunky's shell, but inside it the spirit was one of malignancy, spread now until it had devoured the other entirely.

Against that discernment, nothing else counted much. Not the way he had used me, or his goals, not that he quietly intended killing me. All I could do, in that discerning, was break in tears. Not struggling against him any longer, moving forward to hold what was left of him.

"You can't ask this of me; I can't lose Johnny, and now you too. Don't ask me, Bunky, please; say it's a thing I've dreamed; you still can go back; if you did kill Bradsher that must have been self defense. You can be what you ought to be——"

He said, "Hey! This isn't a way you're supposed to act! You can't cry, not for me." For an instant, that last instant, his arm wasn't forcing me. Within his stocky body there might have been a wavering, as if in a far corner some last remnant of another personality struggled to assert itself, and in a tremendous upheaval unseat the incubus. But it was the incubus that had the power. After no more than that instant the wavering died; surprise faded away. He said in indignant injury, "You can't do me like this; come on, now, we'll have some fun. I didn't get any fun, hardly, out of those other two. Roke Bradsher—we were fighting and I got the knife and pushed it in, that was all. Ed Toomey—you know that little skunk? He knew Sherry Lee wouldn't ever tell about Roke Bradsher killing that Bement guy, not while Bradsher lived. He'd snooped so much he'd seen me, and he figured it out. Any way he figured too much out. He got to me and wanted dough. I didn't have fun with him either; I was too afraid he'd yell. That girl in Wayzata—I couldn't go any way at all there; I wanted her alive for pulling the cops away. Those cops! They've sure been all over the place. Not too much for me, though. You can yell all you want, Gail; no one will hear you in this tight block. Come on, fight me back. Run. Look, I'm not holding you. Look, you're as free as air."

Actually he was loosing me. Shaking away my hold, dropping his own hold, stepping back. Eyes moved in the dimness, lips stretched in a cajoling smile. I hadn't seen him produce anything, hadn't seen any motion of a hand toward a pocket, but in his right hand, now, extending toward me, was a blunt-headed short shaft which, even as I watched and his finger pressed, shot forward a thin sharp blade.

He meant it. Meant to kill me. I accepted the fact, but it no longer had power to move me; nothing lessened my grief. I wasn't any more conscious of forming an answer than I was of how the knife had come to his hand, but what issued from my mouth was steady.

"I won't fight you, Bunky. Won't run from you. If you're going to kill me I'll stand to be killed."

The note of cajolery merely grew stronger.

"You've never been a spoilsport, Gail; come on, don't be one now. Look, I'll give you a running start. I'll back off a ways. See. Three good feet. Look, I'll give you some other odds. That door downstairs is locked again. I had to do that—I didn't want to be interrupted. But the key's down there, one I got years ago. Stuck up on the edge of one of those trestle tables. I was afraid I might lose it if you put up fight enough. But suppose you fouled me up somehow and got to it. You could unlock the door and be clean away. There's a chance, isn't it? Worth a try."

I said, "I won't run, Bunky."

He said, "Oh, you won't, won't you?" For the first time good humor broke; he shot forward the few feet by which he'd divided us. Yes, run, one surging instinct said, but another voice, perhaps that of pride, held me fast. All the time I'd been wearing my coat; he ripped it away from me, letting it fall, ripped at the neckline of my dress until the buttons flew; the hand with the knife lifted toward my left shoulder while the other again held me tight. I was unable to keep from flinching and reaching hands halfway upward, but made no other struggle; along my one shoulder there ran a queer quicksilver stinging, an echoing trickle and smart. Not much of a cut, a bare opening of the skin, but promising what deeper cuts would be.

He said savagely, "See? See how easy that is? It's like cutting cold butter. There'll be more than that. I'm telling you one last time. Fight or run."

I didn't move. "If I'm to die"—this, I think, was what my mind commanded—"then at least it's not to be as a game for him." He stepped back once more, and the cajolery on his mouth and in his light-lashed eyes was fading for something uglier.

He said abruptly, "All right, you won't run. You think you're so strong you'll stand up to me. Let's see what you do when you know one thing more. I wasn't going to tell you until right when you died, but I'll tell you now. You think it was fair, Johnny should have you for a mother, when what I had was mine? You think I liked it, all those years, your being sorry for me? *You think it was fair Johnny always had everything— Phil liked him best, the kids at school liked him best, everybody liked Johnny best? I got even with Johnny. You think it was accident, Johnny died. You think he got drunk and crashed into that pole. That was no accident. I went up to Johnny in the Palladium parking lot, like I said Roke Bradsher came up to me. He wasn't being too pally to me, Johnny wasn't— — Oh, he didn't guess I was the one took care of Sherry Lee, after Roke Bradsher died, by sending her down to marry the big GI; she didn't give me away; she knows better than that. He just didn't like me so well any more. But when I gave him the bottle and said for old time's sake, he took one little drink. One small drink, and that's all. Maybe to prove he could take a drink. That was enough, though, I'd seen to that. You didn't so much as have that bottle analyzed. Any time anybody our age gets killed in a car crash, nobody thinks a thing. It's always those crazy kids, drinking and getting killed. So all right, you know better now.*"

I was standing too near a white fire. I was crisped and blacked. A husk, to waver and fall. But then from somewhere a different wind lifted me. *Johnny was murdered too.* Not dying from wildness, not from carelessness, not from recklessness. Not filling himself with illegally bought whiskey—he'd been sent to that telephone pole with deadly intent, from a single small drink as he started his car.

"Johnny." I don't know if my lips spoke his name, or not. "Johnny." And then suddenly I knew I'd be running. Dignity or no dignity, pride or no pride. I had to live to get out of this. Not just to let people know about Johnny, not just to let Phil know, but to savor for myself that he'd been more what I thought he was. I didn't announce my intention, I merely twisted, with a movement which astonished me by its swiftness and celerity as much as it must have astonished him; I was up on the edge of the platform, speeding its length; my mind didn't seem to have to think up things for my muscles to do. On a table back of the Christmas tree stood the case of spurious gold, the jar of frankincense and the bottle of myrrh, awaiting the morrow's wisemen; behind me Bunky—the thing Bunky had become—uttered an inarticulate cry and was immediately after me. The thudding of his feet was audible, and when I turned, pausing just long enough to aim, he was already so near I could see the satisfaction on the mouth grown so unholy.

"That got you, didn't it?" He was taunting again. "I expected that would get you." He wasn't expecting the gold casket, though; it caught him on the forehead, hard enough to halt him temporarily, make him shake his head. He shouted, "Why, you—!" while I was fleeting farther in back of the Christmas tree, snatching a turn at the knob of the sacristy door, finding it immobile as I'd guessed it would be. I ran on and around the tree; when he doubled I doubled too; his breathing came so loudly it made me aware of the turn. Back and forth for long minutes, but he caught me at last, panting then, striking harshly in toward me, saying, "Okay, here's one for that." I jerked my arm up so the slash glanced from my upper arm instead of getting me in the breast, which was what he'd aimed for, twisting again in a grasp grown damp so I was once more away and free, running now for the front of the church through the other side aisle, snatching up a hymnbook, hurling it. He faltered enough to catch the hymnbook and hurl it back, catching me in the small of the back. I got to the double doors, ran for the long stairs and the basement, hurtling myself forward, brushing across the top edge of a stacked table as I sped through the lower room. If he'd told the truth of the key's whereabouts, I must at least try for it. The try slowed me enough so he was on me again. This time the knife really cut in, striking a rib. I bent forward, thinking I'd faint. He held me up, laughing victoriously.

"Already, you've had enough? With your spunk I'd have guessed you'd last better than this."

From where the strength came, I don't know; maybe he deliberately once more loosed me. I was away again, running for the entrance door. Locked, as he'd said it would be. I got to the kitchen, threw a pitcher, for a second time missing. Ran again——

"This can't ever leave me. If I live, if I sleep, it'll be only to run again." At some time during my flight there was space to think it. Time mixed to a blur in which I didn't know what I did when, or why. I was upstairs again, in one aisle, another aisle. Once I had a hymnbook again in my hands, thinking, "Suppose I threw this through a window. If someone were passing, then someone would come. Would know of my need in here."

"Break a church window?" my training asked, appalled. "I could replace the window," my more judging mind answered, but I tossed the book at my pursuer instead, for another time missing. Not long afterward, though, I got in my second blow. Holding one of the swinging doors as I passed until he was right there, then shoving it, hard. It hit him, must really have slammed him. He'd been in the midst of some vainglorious bleat to which I no longer listened; he yelled a curse and came on with no more humor in the chase. "If you think——"

All the way down to the basement. Around to the other stairs. Up the tall flight and behind the Christmas tree once more. He charged through the lower branches, ruthlessly toppling the tree, which fell halfway, supported by its guy wires and light strings, tangling him enough so I got to the basement for another brush along the table edges. Nothing. In the kitchen I snatched a second pitcher; that one, I think, clipped his ear. Back upstairs.

If Sherry Lee had done as she said she would, the police would have been with me long before this. But Sherry Lee wouldn't be doing what she'd said she would. That had been merely a final push, to get me here at Bunky's mercy.

Maybe an absence of hope makes one furious and stronger. I

couldn't keep running as I was running. Not with my dress ripped and more ripped, not with new little slashes every time my pursuer came within arm's reach. I throbbed, I ached, I bled. Yet I also knew a satisfaction of my own. I'd been asked for struggle, and I was putting up one that told. Bunky might laugh, savagery increasing, but he was heavier than I; for all his youth he also was feeling the effort, especially the climbing of those stair flights, growing lengthier with each ascent. He was running more heavily, panting more heavily. Cursing more, snarling more. Taunting less.

I managed another hymnbook. He'd grown chary of the doors.

Up. Down. But not forever, as I began to know. Fury was being spent. I couldn't breathe deep enough, couldn't gasp loudly enough. Distances I managed to establish were shortening; I no longer tried for the key. Any moment my pursuer would have me, and by this time he was ready for his kill.

It was somewhere along there, at the last ebb of my strength, that, having struggled for yet another time up the stairs, I thrust in the vestibule at the two outside doors, to see if by miraculous chance they might be unfastened. They weren't. I was so spent I went off balance, caroming against a wall. And against one of the window poles, the long thin wood poles with a metal hook at one end, which ushers use for opening and closing the high windows.

A weapon. One unthought of, offered me by nothing but chance. Feeble, easily snapped. But a weapon, one for me. I snatched it, turning to confront the figure which even now was beginning the plowing climb I'd just finished.

I didn't confront it, though. Didn't stand. Didn't think anything out. I was beyond, or below, planning. I ran on. Not into the church, this time, but to the companion stairs ahead of me. When I was level with the niche, at the turn, I set the pole into it. Not having enough time, knowing it might topple, hearing Bunky already in the vestibule, knowing he might hear and suspect what I did, and so stop to find out what I'd left on the ledge. But running on through the rest of the descent, not hiding my progress in any way. Calling up a last reserve of strength to get me from the foot of those stairs to the stairs in the other corner. The climb by now seemed interminable, but I made it. Got across the vestibule. Then, having gained the ledge with the pole once more, hoisted myself up to it.

When I did so, Bunky was rounding the curve of the other stair.

What I had was one last little moment. One single, small moment. Not long enough for prayer. Long enough only for despair, for knowing I hadn't moved quietly now either; I had neither strength nor breath for quiet. Breath in my mouth was stertorous, my body shook, the pole shimmered in my hand.

The assailant, though, was beyond quiet too. Moving then in what had come to be murderous frenzy. Half stumbling to a fall at the head of the other stairs, lunging across the vestibule, hurtling himself forward for the steep downward flight. Yelling, "This time I get you, you——"

It came to me that he still was Bunky. This was Bunky at whom I was poised to strike. Strange, evil, but Bunky.

I wasn't able to do it. The pole slipped from my hands. Slipped just before his foot fell to the step against which it struck.

I think the pole caught him between the legs. There was a snap, and then a queer moment of hesitance; perhaps one in which he snatched for balance. But then went forward. Headlong. Shrilling and thrashing and crashing all the rest of the way to the basement floor.

To be quiet where he fell.

I waited for him on the ledge. To pick himself up, to come back. Where he'd know, then, that I'd be, because I had no strength for moving on from the ledge, where I'd sunk.

Waiting, I huddled and crouched. The whole church was grown quiet, unbelievably quiet. Only the beating of my heart in it, the beating of a heart swollen so hugely it crowded my chest walls. Only the pull of my breath in it, breath for which my lungs cried even when they too swelled to bursting. Only the throbbing, hot and sore, of the nicks and slashes I'd suffered.

I crouched, but he didn't come. Waited, but he wasn't picking himself up from the basement floor. "He can't be that quiet," I thought after a while. "He can't have knocked himself out just by falling downstairs, even if it is a long flight. He's waiting there. Waiting as I wait up here. He knows I can't get out. Not really. Not without finding the key, without reaching the door."

But then, after what was perhaps a long while, I moved again. Slid stiffly from the ledge. Of the top of my dress, nothing remained but tatters, stiffened and wet with blood. "You ought to cover yourself decently," some part of my mind said, and what vestigial part do you think that could have been? "Your coat's up there by the manger. The car keys may still be in the pocket." Perhaps I slipped, perhaps I crept up the aisle to the manger. In the straw of the stable, by the overturned stool, lay the puddle of my coat. I got it on; in one pocket my hand closed on the metal ring of my keys.

Unable to stop being expectant, yet by now inexpectant too, I got back down the aisle to the swinging doors. Descended by the stairs on which I hadn't dropped the pole.

Across the basement, at the foot of those opposite stairs, lay a shapeless, dark mass. Unmoving. But then, even as I halted, moving. Struggling about itself. Beginning a sound, a guttural snarling.

I was at the stacked tables, my hand running edge after edge. It was there, just as he'd said it was. Fifth table in, at the farther end.

The key turned in the lock.

When I had the door open he was halfway across the floor.

Dragging himself toward me. Conscious, by that time, not snarling any more. Crying. With loud, unimpeded, gulping sobs, the way a small child cries.

"Gail, don't go away. Gail, you can't go away. Can't you see that I'm hurt, Gail? My leg's broken, I can't get up. You can't leave me. Gail, help me. Gail——"

# CHAPTER FIFTEEN

IN A WAY, I suppose, this is a story with three endings. That was the first ending, there, when I turned the key with my strength that was like the burned ash on a cigarette, holding shape but ready to be blown away at a puff. Dragging myself across the doorstep. Tottering to the car.

"I can't drive." Probably I said it aloud, out there in the deep of the clear cold night, with no cars going anywhere, no lights anywhere except the impersonal street lights. Parents weren't waking any longer, for toymaking or gift wrapping, not at something like two in the morning. Probably it was then I began sobbing, from the impossibility of the one little thing remaining to be done. The two men in the patrol car said that, when I'd slewed my car directly in their path only a block from my house, I was so wrenched by crying it took them at least fifteen minutes to get any idea of what I was trying to convey.

The second ending began nearer morning, when Lieutenant Winterung walked into a room off the hospital surgery, where I was resting on a cot after having my cuts taped.

"Did you hear about Johnny? My Johnny?" As soon as the large figure turned up in the doorway I began on the thing which, I suspect, I'd told the two patrolmen before anything else, and also the doctor. The thing which, no matter how many times I said it, still crowded my tongue, needing utterance. "Johnny didn't kill himself. He was killed too. Like the others. He——"

Lieutenant Winterung nodded. "So I understand." The voice with which he said it was hard, unpleased, a little flat; when he got to where my eyes could focus on him he appeared unpleased and flat also.

Broad face paler than usual, nose creased at the bridge, mouth drained. The keys were in his hands as if, somewhere, he'd been resting against something, questioning and listening. This wasn't a finish he'd like for a hunt; if there was fighting at a finish he'd want to be in on it. "I don't suppose it can actually make you feel better, but I guess you have a right to know your son's killer is here in this hospital, signed, sealed, delivered, confessed and guarded. He was still wallowing around on that basement floor, crying for help, when the boys got to him. Hip broken, collarbone broken—nothing that time and what he's got coming won't cure. How you worked that business with the pole—what's happening to you here? Are you staying?"

A house doctor walked in from the surgery. Yes, I'd be staying, he said. He was booking a room for me. In cases such as this there was shock to consider.

"No," I said. "I'll be going home. I haven't seen about Jeffry yet. If he's really safe. Someone must have gone there, but I've got to see for myself."

I'd been given a hypo; I possessed my own flatness, a floating kind, in which details didn't strike sharply, but in which what was important stayed important. The house doctor couldn't have put up too much of an argument; not long afterward I was outdoors once more with Lieutenant Winterung, breathing in deep gulps for lungs which at last weren't straining for such gulps. Inside the satin lining of my coat, swathed by thick bandaging, the upper part of my body told me occasionally that it was stiff and sore; otherwise it was once more removed from me. My dress had survived as little more than a skirt, neatly barbered by hospital shears.

Lieutenant Winterung had been in bed asleep, so he began telling me, when the desk sergeant got to him.

"I'd driven in from Wayzata around eleven. I knew then the Wayzata lead was petering out like the rest. I was so fed up—— Here, you're in no shape to drive, Mrs. Kiskadden, you get in with me."

The last was command, which I meekly obeyed, especially since I didn't so much as remember where my car was. It was a police car that had brought me to the hospital. In the back seat of this second car, while someone else drove, Winterung kept talking of Bunky.

"What's funny—you'd never have suspected him, he was a friend of yours. But I had him in mind more than once. His briefcase—actually that was how he'd transported the dummies. After he killed Bradsher, away back last May, he seems to have got the girl to clear out Bradsher's room. She could do it easily; she lived in the same house. Most of the stuff she pawned. He'd driven the car into the junkyard himself, right after he'd killed Bradsher and sunk the body in the lake. The dummies, though, were a problem. Not pawnable—not with Toomey snooping. Not to be stuffed in a trash basket anywhere—someone would have picked them out. The rooming house had an oil burner and the Knowles house is heated by gas. He was going to burn them in the fireplace, but while he was waiting a chance when the housekeeper was out, he stored them away among boxes in his family garage. Parking them on you served three purposes—got rid of them, reminded the girl of the part she was due for, and made us believe Roke Bradsher was current. All that whistling—it's easy now to see what that was for, too. One thing he was afraid of throughout was that the girl would soften and refuse to go through with his plan. He wanted her reminded he was right at hand, ready to get even if she faltered. The same with that first postal card. The list he dropped under the second dummy was left for exactly the reason I figured—to be distracting. I got awfully close to guessing Bradsher might be out of the picture when that second dummy turned up—remember? I said it put Bradsher out of business, and the girl got the wind up. I should have seen through the whole thing right there."

"What's one of the hardest things for me to understand"—I

also had a dull wonder to contribute—"is how the whole plan came about. He couldn't have laid out all the rest, just from having killed Bradsher. That the girl should marry Johnny, that Johnny should be killed and then I. That——"

That wasn't one of Winterung's wonders. "It couldn't have been planned all at once. Bradsher's killing, or so he says, was almost an accident. If the two of them had been willing to leave it at that, if Knowles had pleaded self-defense, he'd have gotten off not too badly. No, they had to hide it. The marriage seems to have been a result mainly of effort to get the girl taken care of during her pregnancy—Knowles wasn't able to do it on his allowance. It was after that marriage that the rest of the scheme must have been hatched, maybe almost on the spur of the moment, when your son came home on his furlough. Death from a doped drink wasn't any certainty. But when it worked so well—the rest, then, must have looked a clear road to that perverted mind. What's hardest for me to take, is how close they came to succeeding. The acting they went in for—remember the two of them in my office, Knowles telling about Bradsher's approach to him in the Palladium parking lot, and then the girl stumbling along so unwillingly about the Bement killing—every word of that must have been laid out beforehand. Recall how she kept looking toward the kid for backing? Only to us it looked different. Well, they'll be finding out now where their acting gets."

I shivered. Dulled I might be, but there were things of which it wasn't bearable to think. Not of what was being said or thought or felt in a guarded room behind us at the hospital. Not of what would be done or said or felt at the expensive house four doors north of mine, where two people who never had had time to waste on a son might now find themselves able to spare him some. Not of what the future must hold for all three.

Winterung was going on. "I wonder what would have happened, in Lake City, if we'd asked about a blonde girl and a redheaded boy, instead of about Roke Bradsher. Someone in those lake cabins they went to should have remembered them. There must have been marks of a fight; I suppose owners who rent to young overnight couples expect disarray in their cabins, but even then—— Pepin will be the devil to dredge, one of the deepest lakes in the state. It may be we never do get Bradsher. No matter now. We won't need him, especially."

Increasingly it wasn't Bunky who filled my mind, not any longer. Not Johnny entirely, either, though he was with me, so much more closely than he'd been for months. Not even entirely Jeffry.

"Sherry Lee," I asked, shrinking. "The girl. What will——"

Winterung had still talked on about Bunky. At my words, though, he switched.

"Nothing's been done to her so far; all I had time for was to send a couple men over to hold her down until I get there. I wasn't sure, at first, just how deep she was in."

The hypo maybe was wearing off a little; I was getting back my feeling of being the burned ash on a cigarette.

"You don't suppose there's any chance——"

He shook his head vigorously. "You can't kid yourself, not on that. She was in it to her neck. She assisted in disposing of Bradsher's body, and in disposing of his effects. She met Knowles out on her walks, getting orders from him, called him when she was alone in the house. Don't forget she must have carried through that fake kidnapping, right down to leaving the card on the milk-chute ledge. She must have suspected about your son's death, even if she didn't know that for sure. She got you to that church, and don't think she didn't know what you were there for."

I sat silent, thinking over the day back of me, the day when I'd waited and she'd hovered. Oh yes, she'd known all right. Known, cringing, the day she first saw me. I was right, feeling that room as a lair. She'd been reminded when we heard the whistling, when we found the dummies. Bloomed happily in the hospital, because she was having a respite, but dutifully returned to her task.

That morning, when she waked me, her hair was smooth. After stowing the boy in the attic, she'd taken time to brush out her beloved hair.

As I sat silent, piling detail on recurring detail, Winterung abruptly opened on something else.

"You a Gilbert and Sullivan fan, Mrs. Kiskadden? 'A policeman's lot is not a happy one.' Would you like to know, Mrs. Kiskadden, what I sometimes dread? I'm afraid, sometime, I'll run across a criminal I'm sorry for. No matter how black his crime may have been, I think, I'll see why he did it, and sympathize. Ridiculous, isn't it? It won't ever happen. Just the same, you want to know one thing I'm feeling now? It's relief. You know, and I know now, what the Knowles kid is, he's a psychopath. The girl—she's as conscienceless as they come. They didn't either one of them have a single motive, behind what they were doing, except wanting money to blow on what they'd think of as high living, without having to work for it."

A new light on Winterung. I'd never have thought he had fears. Wouldn't have thought of him as suffering this dread. He was a man like other men. May have had children, like other men, including a son Johnny's age.

I didn't add, "No other motive except a need to strike back at circumstance which left them both, boy and girl alike, orphaned of love."

So I came to my house. Thinking of Jeffry again, but not so anxious, once I was there, to move from the car. Asking, "Would she like it better if I stay here until she's gone?" But then answering, "She must see me. She can't go off thinking Jeffry is alone in the house."

I went with Winterung up my front walk. It was then, I think, shortly before five in the morning. Lights were on in the living room; through the nylon ruffles winked Christmas ornaments on a tree unlit but glowing from the table lamps. Winterung punched the doorbell and the chimes sounded inside. Not often, I thought, that I'd rung for admission to my own house. The keys were in my pocket, but things were different this morning; Lieutenant Winterung's men held the living room. The house had come close to passing from my ownership.

One of Winterung's men answered the door.

"Yes, sir." Two short words, carrying a mountain of relief.

"Okay, Kirby," Winterung said, and walked in, leaving me, leaving Kirby, to follow as we would.

A second patrolman was there in the living room also, standing, looking faintly harassed and uneasy. As well as a young man in gray tweed whom at first it took effort to place, since I'd seen him only once, and then very briefly, in anything except a white coat. He was Dr. Don Knight, the young hospital intern. He too looked harassed and taut, nose so shiny it might have been trying to vie with the tree ornaments. As we entered he rose.

"Sir, can you tell me what's going on?" he asked Winterung. "I came to stay with Mrs. Kiskadden; she was frightened here alone. Her mother-in-law had gone out somewhere. Then these men here have kept me——"

Sherry Lee was there too. She also beginning to rise when the intern rose, looking toward Winterung. Behind him she must have seen me. She sank back. But then slowly, almost with a kind of dignity, got all the way to her feet.

I thought, "Actually, she hasn't known until now. Through this whole night, she's had nothing but surmise. The two patrolmen had orders to tell her nothing. Seeing Lieutenant Winterung, even, she may have thought he came to tell her I was dead, found in the church. But as soon as she saw me, she had to know."

She said, "It didn't come out, then. It just never come out." No concealment. No effort at concealment. Her face wasn't shrinking, but a different movement was going over it, a kind of rippling.

I stepped toward her. "Sherry Lee——" but Winterung blocked me. Loudly, imperiously, the humanity of the latter part of our drive once more hidden by the mask of official sternness, "You admit you knew Mrs. Kiskadden went from here to be killed?"

She mightn't have heard him. She had a question of her own, too upsurgent to allow anything else.

"He—did you catch anyone?"

Winterung repeated his own question, and that time she heard, though apparently it still seemed only secondary to her. She answered almost carelessly, "Oh, I guess I knew. He—did he get away?"

Winterung answered when she had. "We have young Knowles under sure restraint. We know everything. What happened to Roke Bradsher, what happened to Ed Toomey, why that waitress in Wayzata was attacked, that John Kiskadden was murdered—everything. I'm afraid I must ask you to come with me."

Again she might barely have heard. She stood perfectly quiet, murmuring, "He'll blame it on me, the way it didn't work."

Lieutenant Winterung turned to give Kirby an order. Hands clasped at waist height, the head with the golden fall of hair drooping, she continued to stand in her quiet, but now the eyes under the barely lifted lashes were staring at me, angry and cold.

"You. What's your life, that it's so much?" those eyes might have been asking, contemptuously. "Couldn't you see it was time you got out of the way? Couldn't you see it was our time to live? We're the ones who're young. You're gone. Next year you'll be forty. Bunky wanted so badly to kill you. We needed so badly the things that you had. Your house and your money, the dishes in your window. I've never had pretty things, you've had so much. Couldn't you have let him kill you, just that one little death more?"

I made what, as far as she was concerned, was one final,

convulsive effort, to reach from my person to hers. To be, not myself, but a girl of nineteen, born Givens, abandoned, raised by people named Slade, favored perhaps by an easygoing tolerance, but forever an outsider. Coming in adolescence to be used by any man who picked her up. Conditioned from infancy to please, because that was how she came by her crumbs. Looking in always from the outside at people who to her must have seemed another order of beings, owning their own comfortable houses, not subject to the savage whims of men such as those who held her in possession. Hadn't she in any way discerned that the people who lived in such separating comfort were also the toys of despair and grief, that their husbands and sons died, that they were capable of terror and pity and compassion, that there might have been someone to succor her? In me she'd have had that chance; toward me she had had mostly one fear—that she wouldn't be able to carry through her part in the plan.

There'd been times when I'd felt for her both understanding and compassion. At the morgue, when she must have feared it would be Roke Bradsher's body she'd see, with the whole scheme uncovered. At the hospital, when she'd borne her child. Other times. But I wasn't able to reach acceptance now. Pity, yes, not the other. She wasn't even sick in the way Bunky was sick. She was clear and cold. Even for people unhappily circumstanced, there is choice. She had made hers, wanting her life while she was young, without earning it.

With no more than that one cold long look, she dismissed me. I was as much in the past, for her, as her parents, whoever they had been, or the Slades, whoever they had been, or Edna Feasely, who had also befriended her. Her glance was back with Winterung.

"How long could I get?" Not childish, though the words may look childish, put down. Just direct and bold.

Winterung swung back to her austerely. "I'm no judging arm of the law, merely a part of its gathering arm." But then feeling broke through in him too, and when it came it was brutal. He told her harshly, "You'll be lucky you get twenty years. Now come on, we're not taking all day. You can get your coat——"

She said, "I'd be old, then. I'd be older than her." For just an instant the glance dredged me from her past, over a mouth fixed in a grimace more wooden than that of the dolls. She'd stayed planted, resisting the command of Kirby's hand at her elbow, but after she'd spoken the last she began a slow stilted advance toward the hall and the stairs.

Winterung said, "Stick with her, Kirby."

Guilty she might be, but I wasn't able to see her go that way, either, surrounded by such harshness. I started forward.

"We'll—Phil and I, we'll do what we can for you. Find a lawyer——"

She said, "I suppose I don't take the kid." Addressing not me, not especially Lieutenant Winterung, just any power that might answer.

Lieutenant Winterung did the replying. "Right. Mrs. Kiskadden, I imagine you can carry on there. I'll call Phil right now, so you won't be here alone. Probably you should get Grellman. He'll be mad as hops if you don't. I'll get at that right now."

He too moved for the hall, while Sherry Lee and Kirby began mounting the stairs. Jeffry—I'd been caught aside from running up to him, but he must be upstairs. I'd have to wait now until his mother was out of the room.

The young intern had guessed, by then, what his part had been; behind me he was sputtering, "You mean, you mean all this time—she's been planning to get somebody killed—— She said she'd been threatened by a man who used to be her boy friend. She said——"

"She's fixing it so she won't be suspected," was what Bunky had told me. And so she had.

I was just formulating some sort of condolence to proffer the young man, when the shot came.

So there was a second ending. An hour or so later, toward six in the morning, when Dr. Grellman stood back beside the young intern, to brush a dispirited arm upward over his face.

"No use. It never was any use. She's gone."

Before then, several times, Lieutenant Winterung had said, "She didn't give any sign of being about to do any such thing. I hadn't an idea on earth she might try anything of the kind. Mrs. Kiskadden, you gave me no indication whatever that she might have a gun. There hasn't been any gun in this case first to last. Not the slightest——"

Kirby, several times, had said, "In the baby's bedclothes. That's where she had it. Someplace in the baby's bed. She said, 'I'll just tell the baby good-by.' She walked over to the crib. I turned my head away a little. She couldn't have stopped any, to think. She must of just snatched it from under a blanket and fired. She didn't say good-by to the kid, either. She just——"

He might be an experienced officer of the law. He might, sometimes, be detached and unfeeling. He wasn't detached and unfeeling then. Neither was Lieutenant Winterung. They stood about, the two of them. Just as the rest of us stood about, after the first rush of the little there was to be done. I was remembering the way she had inched her fingers over her tooled leather handbag in Winterung's office. The way she had clutched the shoulder strap of that same bag when we went to see what she feared might be Bradsher, at the morgue. I wondered if the gun had been ready then too.

I stood clasping the bundle I'd run for, I stood holding her son, safe. I said, "She told me she'd never stick around to be old. She told me she'd never be gray-haired and ugly. She wanted her life while she was young."

But then there was a third ending, as well.

Lieutenant Winterung gone, Kirby gone, the second patrolman gone, the young intern gone. The other men who'd been called in, they too gone. Sherry Lee carried away from the house she had thought to own, and not to the apartment in which, understandably now, she had never been interested. Away from the child who, for her and for Bunky, had been a pawn. Away from the shell-handle candy box on the coffee table, away from the heirlooms of china and glass in the diningroom bay. If I kept feeling as I did now, those heirlooms would be packed away. Someone later on might value them; it didn't seem to me I could.

Dr. Grellman was the last to go.

"I can wait until Phil comes," he'd offered me. "Winterung didn't get him that first time; he hung up on the shot. But he got him before he left; the bell should be ringing any minute. You're in no shape to be left alone. Do you hear what I'm saying, Gail? I've another sedative here for you—this yellow pill. You'll take it with this glass of water. I'll lift your head——"

"No," I said. I was lying on my bed by then. Not undressed, still in my coat. On my back. Someone—maybe that had been Dr. Grellman too—had at some time, rather lately, taken Jeffry from me and brought me to it, urging me to rest. I shoved aside the pill and the glass, shoved aside the other hand offering to support me. "There's something I can't do while anyone else is here. Something I need to do all alone. Before Phil gets here. I—I'll take the pill. I promise. After Phil comes. After I have a minute for that something else, first."

He stood looking down at me. Not frowning, but not encouraging with any false, out-of-place smile. Just quiet. He placed the pill and the glass on the bed table, nodding.

"Very well. I gather you wish me to go too."

He went in the same quiet toward the door, where he paused. Not turning back, just pausing.

"This isn't an especially good time for you to be making decisions," he reminded. "You may very well leave anything of that kind for later. Before you do make up your mind, you'll want to be certain. I'll want to know you're certain. For both your sakes."

Quiet but firm, almost stern.

I agreed, "I know," and he went on. His footsteps sounding on the stairs, in the hall below. Halting while he got into his overcoat, picked up his hat. Sounding again as he walked toward the door below. That door didn't open, though; instead the trail of his footsteps grew louder once more until he was back in my doorway, and then at my bedside, where he once more looked down at me. A tired old man in an overcoat, hat so neglectfully placed that again a long strand of gray hair edged from under the brim.

"Maybe I was wrong," he said. "Maybe this is a time for you to be making decisions. When're you coming to your senses about Phil? I'm very fond of Phil. When was Evie a wife of his? Hasn't it struck you you're doing Phil no favor, leaving him around for Evie to take over again if she feels like it? The next time she divorces a husband, he shouldn't be loose. I don't know what's been holding you back; if it's scruple, you might remind yourself it's just as possible to have too many as too few."

He didn't want a reply from me, or argument, or explanation or discussion. He just shot at me, testily, what he had to say, and then wheeled sharply to leave once more. This time really going. The front door opened, sighed toward a close, clicked as the latch caught. Maybe, on the porch below, he tried it to be sure it locked. When it wasn't necessary, not any longer, to make certain of locks. The phone that couldn't take care of all contingencies might be taken from my room, the patrol from the street. My walls, that had been so thin and transparent, were back at being thick again.

Dr. Grellman's car outside started up and its tires swished it away.

From where I lay it was little more than an arm's reach to Jeffry, asleep in his crib. In my arms he'd cried awhile, waving his arms in complaint, contracting his minuscule face, expressing dislike for a world in which noises exploded. But not really surprised. Already, a little, expecting a failure of comfort in a world where, not long since, he'd been thrust aside in an attic, to sleep drugged, wet and unfed through a day.

Men had carried his crib in here; the intern and Dr. Grellman had seen to him. He hadn't, they both said, suffered serious physical effects from the long drugged day; probably what he'd been given was laudanum, the same drug which, not too many generations ago, the infants of perfectly respectable households were given, to keep them from fretting the adult ear.

He slept calmed, forgetful of anything back of him, unknowing of what, for good or ill, he'd been bereaved.

Not waiting, because Phil was coming, I pulled myself from the bed as soon as I heard the departing car. The hypo had worn off entirely; beneath the bandaging my arms and shoulders were being eaten away by slow fires. I reached down, though, and got Jeffry up again, the small warm bundle of him from under the blanket. His softness and weightlessness answering the unsatisfied need of my hands, his tiny hands, the creases concealing his eyes, meeting the hunger that stayed in my mind. He didn't wake as I took him, though he stirred a little, protesting more disturbance. I returned him to my shoulder, settling his head to the curve of the unbandaged part of my neck, supporting his back.

Johnny's son. Roke Bradsher's son. Or, as Bunky had said, maybe his son. Suppose, in the days ahead, Bunky pushed that claim.

Suppose, though I couldn't imagine it, Pamela and Horace Knowles pushed it. Inside twenty years he might be another Bunky.

"He's in your house," Bunky himself had said. "Established as your grandchild. Christened——"

No, they never could do it. Whatever the paternity of this small human morsel, he was legally mine.

How much did I believe in heredity? How much, that I held, was innate and not to be changed? How much could I nurture, so that when I'd done what I could, he would really be Johnny's son? I hadn't been entirely wrong, bringing Johnny up——

That last was a flame that had flamed before, one to vie with my hurts in its triumph. With triumph a goal might have appeared, too, a determination formed, but I threw them aside. It wasn't to be anyone's son, it wasn't to be anyone's grandson, that a child was born. A child was born for himself.

Against neck and shoulder I held the small living bundle more closely. Not trying for anything any more, not reaching for any thing, doing nothing but wait. Giving up that this should be Johnny's son. Accepting only that he was a child. Any child.

Love isn't anything inanimate. Love was a seed that had been closed in my breast and my heart and my hands. Love could sprout everywhere, curling out, spreading its green, pushing until all of my person was possessed.

I stood feeling the love and warmth growing; stood feeling it flow. Against my shoulder Jeffry gave what sounded like a little sigh. He seemed to collapse slightly, nestling closer. I'd swear he got heavier. I know he was suddenly more damp. He hadn't waked before, but now he began doing so. One of his hands struck out, his face brushed back and forth hungrily on my neck; he pulled back his head to emit several loud squawks.

Not in the least querulous. Not in the least inexpectant.

Demanding and imperious. Knowing what he wanted. Insisting he get it.

Not especially the way Johnny cried. Just the way any baby cries. Any loved, secure baby.

The chimes struck, they too imperiously. That meant Phil was on the porch. Phil, who wouldn't have been told about Johnny, yet. Phil, who——

I clutched Jeffry closer, and the two of us started downstairs.

I didn't go straight to the door, though. I had a silly, irrational impulse, and detoured. To the desk in the living room where I'd last left my solitaire cards. They made a white, black and red shower, falling into a wastebasket; I scarcely paused to see.

HURON PUBLIC LIBRARY
333 WILLIAMS STREET
HURON, OHIO 44839